Infamy

Also by Tom Milton

All the Flowers
The Admiral's Daughter
No Way to Peace

Infamy

Tom Milton

NEPPERHAN PRESS, LLC
YONKERS, NY

Published by Nepperhan Press, LLC
P.O. Box 1448, Yonkers, NY 10702
nepperhan@optonline.net
nepperhan.com

PUBLISHER'S NOTE
This is a work of fiction. Names, characters, places, and incidents
are the product of the author's imagination or are used fictitiously,
and any resemblance to actual persons, living or dead, events, or
locales is entirely coincidental.

Printed in the United States of America

Library of Congress Control Number: 2009908860

ISBN 978-0-9794579-5-1

Cover art was licensed from Corbis.

For Marie

"Yesterday, December 7, 1941—a date which will live in
infamy—the United States of America was suddenly and
deliberately attacked by naval and air forces of the
Empire of Japan."

Franklin Delano Roosevelt

Madrid, 2007

ONE

AS FENLY GOT out of the taxi on Calle de las Tres Cruces he spotted a person who could be the colleague they had sent to meet him. Near the entrance of the building where he would live while on assignment in Madrid, a young woman was leaning against the wall with her arms folded and one foot crossed over the leg that bore her weight. Her shoes, her pants, her top, and her open leather jacket were all black, and the only decorative element in her whole outfit that caught his eye was a silver buckle on her black belt.

Wheeling his suitcase, he strolled to the building and stopped at its entrance and faced the street as if he were unaware of the woman. For a while he just stood there in silence, and then in Dominican Spanish he said: "I hate traveling."

"I do too," the woman said in Castilian Spanish. "I'd rather stay at home and listen to music."

"What kind of music?"

"I like rock."

That was the exchange they were supposed to have in order to identify each other.

"I'm Fenly," he said, turning toward her and getting his first close look at her. She had straight dark hair that was pulled back from her face and passionate dark eyes. She had a strong chin, a generous mouth, and an aquiline nose that an American girl with the wherewithal for cosmetic surgery might have had fixed. A silver cross hung from her neck on a silver chain.

"I'm Raquel," she said, appraising him.

They shook hands professionally.

Then, stepping to the door with keys in her hand, she said: "Come on."

It was an old building, but the door was new and made of heavy glass, so that you could see who might be on the other side before going in or out.

He followed her into a vestibule where there were mailboxes and then through another glass door, which she unlocked with another key, and into a well-lit lobby. Behind her, he couldn't help noticing how tightly she filled the back of her pants.

There were two elevators, and one of their doors opened immediately after she pressed the up-button as if it had been programmed for them.

Inside, she pressed the button for the third floor.

When the door of the elevator had closed she said: "We really didn't need those stupid code phrases. I could tell by your accent that you're Dominican."

"I'm American," he said, correcting her.

"I meant that you speak Spanish like a Dominican."

"Are there a lot of Dominicans here?"

"Oh, yes. So you won't stand out."

They rode in silence the rest of the way.

When they got out of the elevator he followed her down a long hallway. She stopped at the door of an apartment where she unlocked a deadbolt lock and then another lock.

"Do you have a lot of crime here?"

"We have more than before."

"You mean before the Dominicans came here?"

She glanced back at him over her shoulder. "I mean before the immigrants came here, including the Dominicans."

"Where else do they come from?"

"They come from other parts of Latin America, but also from countries that recently joined the European Union, and of course from North Africa."

She opened the door of the apartment, and he followed her in. "So you don't like the immigrants?"

"I didn't say that. I only said that we have more crime than we had before they came here."

"What kind of crime are we talking about?"

"Crime that's mostly related to drugs." She must have been speaking from experience since she had been an investigator with the Madrid police force. They had told him that, but they hadn't told him much else about her.

He followed her around the apartment, which like the rest of the building's interior had been remodeled. The bedroom and the bathroom were connected to a large living and dining room by a long hallway, with the kitchen next to the bathroom. The heating unit was in the kitchen along with a stove, refrigerator, and washing machine. Raquel explained how to use these appliances as if she didn't expect him to use them.

"Well, you must be tired," she said after completing the tour. "I'll leave you now, but I'll meet you later for dinner."

"Okay." He knew from the guide that the Spanish ate dinner late. "What time?"

"Around nine. We can meet at a place on Calle de la Montera. It's called Arizona. It has tables outside, where we can sit." She explained how to get there.

"That sounds good."

She was at the door, with her hand on the knob, when she turned and said: "I should warn you about the prostitutes. You'll see them standing in front of the buildings across the street from the place where we're meeting."

"They're allowed to stand there?"

"Prostitution is allowed in this country."

The guide for travelers that he had downloaded and read in preparation for this assignment hadn't included that information. "You mean it's legal?"

"It's legal for women to offer their services, but it's not legal to pimp for them, and it's not legal to traffic in them."

"That sounds contradictory."

"Our legal system hasn't resolved the conflict between our traditional values and our modern values."

"Which side are you on?"

"I'm on the side of the girls. When I see how young they are under their makeup," Raquel said with a surge of compassion in her dark eyes, "I want to help them."

"So you'd like to get them off the street."

"I'd like to get them into another line of work. But in the meantime I'd rather have them on the street where we can see them and protect them. Also, they can be useful to us."

"They can? How?"

"Their clients are mostly foreigners, including people we have under surveillance, so we can get information from them."

"You mean on how their clients perform?"

Raquel didn't smile. "The girls don't talk about that. They don't have any interest in sex."

"I wouldn't either if I did it for money."

"You don't have any interest in things you do for money?"

"No. I don't," Fenly said. "But I'm not doing this assignment for money."

"I'm not either," Raquel said, looking directly into his eyes. "So maybe we have something in common."

When she had gone he wheeled his suitcase down the hallway and into the bedroom. He went to the window and raised the *persiana* and looked out into an airshaft, which now was getting its daily dose of sunlight. Across from him a woman's underwear in various colors was hanging out to dry on a line strung outside the window. There were lines outside all the windows, but only that one had clothes on it.

He lifted his suitcase onto the bed and unzipped it. He unpacked his suits, shirts, and ties, which he hung on one side of the closet, and then his underwear and socks, which he put into the drawers on the other side. He stashed his shoes on the floor of the closet and stored the empty suitcase in the space below his hanging clothes. On an upper shelf he found sheets and a blanket, and he spent the next ten minutes making up the bed, which was bigger than he needed. Finally, he took his bag of toiletries into the bathroom and left it there unopened.

By then he was overcome by fatigue, not having slept on the overnight plane from New York, so he lowered the *persiana*, stripped to his briefs and tee-shirt, set the alarm on his cell phone, and rolled into bed.

For a while he lay there, too tired to sleep and eager to begin his new assignment, but his mind finally shut down.

Whatever peace he may have found in sleep was shattered by a nightmare in which he was helplessly staring at the twin towers engulfed in flames, spewing smoke and shooting particles into the air, which he suddenly realized were people jumping out of the buildings, choosing that form of death over being burned alive in the conflagration.

He awoke feeling sick as he always did after this nightmare, and he got up and went into the bathroom, where he stood for a long time with his head over the toilet, retching and ridding his cramped stomach of airline food.

After flushing the toilet he went into the kitchen, where he found a glass in a cabinet to the right of the heating unit, and he drank some water. What he really needed now was a jolt of caffeine. He didn't find any coffee in the cabinets, though he did see a percolator of the type used by Dominicans, which made him feel a bit less like a stranger here.

He had to go out and buy some things, beginning with coffee, so he went down the hallway to the living room and found the carrying case for his computer, which he had left on the dining table. He took out a notebook and a pen and sat down at the table and made a shopping list. Then he went back to the bedroom and got dressed, putting on jeans and a sweatshirt.

Down in the lobby he met the *portero*, a jovial man with fair hair and lively blue eyes, who welcomed him and showed him where to dump his garbage.

"Is there a food store around here?" Fenly asked him.

"Oh, yes," the man said. "There's one on this block. Just walk toward Gran Vía."

The store was only a few doors away, and it had everything, including a counter where you could buy a variety of cured meats. With a basket in hand, Fenly roamed around the store, collecting coffee, cream, orange juice, a fresh-baked roll, butter, and jam, and then examining the shelves of wine, brandy, and liqueurs before deciding on a Torres brandy, which a Spanish colleague had introduced him to. Miguel was one of the hundred and nine colleagues who had died in the attack.

A man in a blue smock checked him out and helped him find the right bills among the euros that he had gotten from a cash machine at the airport.

Outside, he decided to walk the rest of the way to Gran Vía, which he knew from his reading was a major thoroughfare. At the corner was a large restaurant where people were sitting at a bar and at tables and in booths, relaxing and drinking and eating. It looked like a good place to have a coffee, so Fenly decided to go back there after taking a walk. It was only a few minutes after seven, so he had almost two hours to kill before he was supposed to meet his colleague.

He headed to the right on Gran Vía, where the traffic was dominated by taxis and buses, moving faster than they would have in New York—maybe because the drivers seemed to know what they were doing. The sidewalks were crowded with people of various nationalities. In fact, while walking only a block he heard people speaking English, German, Italian, and a language that he identified as Arabic. At the corner, where there was a busy McDonald's, he saw that he had come to Calle de la Montera. Across a plaza he saw the Gran Vía metro station, with people climbing out of it. There were police cars parked on the plaza and as many as twenty police officers in bright green vests standing around, giving the impression that a crime had just been committed there.

Not wanting to get involved, he headed back toward Calle Tres Cruces. In the window of a large bookstore he saw a book on terrorism that had recently been published. He had read a review of the book in *El Mundo*, which a flight attendant had offered to him, evidently figuring that he spoke Spanish, and he decided that if he had time tomorrow he would go into the store and see if the book was worth buying.

When he came to the restaurant that he had noticed—it was

called Zahara—he went in and headed for the bar. He found a place next to a woman who was gazing blissfully into space, with a cup of coffee in one hand and a cigarette in the other.

He hung his bag of groceries on a helpful hook under the bar and ordered an espresso. Within a minute he was sipping the coffee and gazing into space but not blissfully.

The tooth had started to bother him over the weekend, but he had tried to ignore the pain, taking aspirin and hoping it would go away. By Monday at lunch it was so bad that he couldn't eat or drink anything hot or cold, and sitting across the table from him, looking concerned, Camila said: "You should go and have that tooth examined by a dentist."

"What can a dentist do?" he said, resisting her advice.

"He can give you an antibiotic," she said, drawing on one of her reservoirs of knowledge.

"An antibiotic? How would that help?"

"It would kill the infection."

"Maybe it would. But he'd probably want to pull the tooth, and I don't want to lose it."

"There are worse things than losing a tooth."

"But this is a molar, a major tooth."

"Oh, stop being such a baby," she said, but not the way other people might have said it. There was humor in her eyes and love in her voice.

"All right," he said, his resistance finally overcome. "I'll go to a dentist. Do you know one?"

"Yeah." Camila got out her cell phone and found a number, which she gave him along with the dentist's name.

"I'll call him as soon as I get back to my office," he promised her. "Maybe I can see him tomorrow."

He was able to get an appointment first thing in the morning, so he could see the dentist before going to work on Tuesday. The dentist's office was in midtown, and Fenly arrived there at quarter after eight. He was sitting in the dentist's chair by eight-thirty and within a few minutes he was relieved to hear that the tooth wouldn't have to be pulled.

The dentist had just given him an injection when the hygienist rushed into the office, saying: "I heard on the radio that a plane crashed into the World Trade Center."

"What?" the dentist said in shock. "What kind of plane?"

"A big plane. It hit one of the twin towers."

Fenly sat up, feeling as if he had been kicked in the stomach. Camila worked in the south tower. "Which tower?"

"I don't know," the hygienist said.

"I have a television set in my office," the dentist said.

They rushed to his office and got the news in time to see a plane crash into the south tower.

"Oh, my God," Fenly said, ripping off the bib and running out.

The fastest way to get there was the subway, but they made everyone get out at Canal Street. From there he ran over to Broadway, where looking downtown he could see the ugly smoke rising from the towers. He ran down Broadway as far as they would let him.

"You can't go there," a cop told him when he tried to break through the barrier.

"I have to," he cried. "My fiancée works in the south tower."

"Most of the people got out, so she's probably all right."

"I have to go there."

"I'm sorry. You can't."

When he tried again to break through another cop held him back, saying: "Hey, man, just do what we say. It's for your own safety."

"I don't care about my safety."

"Well, we do. And even if we let you through, there's nothing you could do to help."

"All you can do," the first cop said, "is hope and pray."

So he stood there and watched while the buildings collapsed, first the south tower and then the north tower, filling the streets with smoke and debris. It was as if a volcano were erupting, driving a river of lava toward them and darkening the sky.

He paid for his coffee and got his bag of groceries and left the restaurant and went back to his apartment, where he killed time exploring the different channels on television and finally watching the news on CNN.

The top story in America was about a student at Virginia Tech who had gone on a rampage and killed thirty-two people with semi-automatic handguns before taking his own life.

Fenly imagined the grief of those who had lost loved ones in the attack, and he empathized with them. He felt anger against the attacker, just as he still felt anger against the men who had hijacked the planes and flown them into the twin towers. It was an anger that would never go away since he could never forgive them for what they had done.

He left the building at ten minutes before nine, believing that he should arrive at the restaurant before Raquel so she wouldn't have to wait for him.

Across the street older people were lining up for a show at the Teatro Principe, and younger people were sitting at the tables in front of Doner Kebap. A man with a sandwich board that said "Compro Oro" was standing at the corner in front of Zahara, and a young man with pink hair and a poodle on a leash was crossing Gran Vía.

As he approached Calle Montera he saw that the police were still there in about the same number. Rounding the corner, he encountered a girl with bleached hair, wearing a very short skirt and boots. Her face was made up as if for the stage, and her ears, nose, and eyebrows were pierced.

"I can give you a really great blow job," she said in heavily accented English.

"No, thanks," he said, moving past her.

Looking ahead, he saw a line of girls waiting to accost him, so he left the sidewalk and crossed the street to the plaza, where a tall, robed black man with a white kufi was being questioned by two police officers. Evidently, there was a problem with the man's papers.

Fenly found a table on the sidewalk in front of the restaurant that Raquel had indicated, and he sat down and ordered a *caña*, which in Spain meant a small glass of beer. He had learned a number of words and phrases used in Spain, not so he could pass for a Spaniard but so he could be understood. Some important words were different among the Spanish-speaking countries, as he had learned from problems in communicating with Chileans, Argentines, Colombians, and Mexicans, and it was useful to know the word for a glass of beer.

Across the street he saw a young police officer checking the papers of a girl, who ended up walking down the street with him, evidently to the station. A few minutes later he noticed a girl crossing the street with an Asian man and heading into a street on the other side of the plaza.

But the main traffic on Montera, which cars couldn't enter, was a stream of people coming from and going to Gran Vía, many of them with shopping bags. At this hour, based on what he had read about the *madrileños*, they were on their way to meet friends for drinks and *tapas* before deciding what to do next in an evening that was only now beginning.

"Are you enjoying the show?" Raquel asked, appearing on the other side of the table.

"It's better than sitting on a plane," he told her.

As she sat down the waiter came over, and she ordered a *caña*.

He asked the waiter to bring him another.

"Did you get some rest?"

"Yeah. I feel better."

"You look better."

"You mean I looked like shit before?"

"Well, not exactly like shit," she said, smiling, "but something very close to it."

He smiled back.

"Oh, you can smile."

"Yeah, I can. But I'm not the smiley type."

"I noticed. What type are you?"

"The type who takes things seriously."

"That's good to know. What else would you like to tell me?"

"I don't know," he said, thinking. "I already told you I'm not doing this assignment for money."

"Why are you doing it?"

"I lost my fiancée in the World Trade Center."

"Oh, no," she said, shocked.

"They didn't tell you?"

"No. They didn't. I'm so sorry," she said with real feeling.

Never knowing how to respond when people said they were sorry, he asked: "What *did* they tell you?"

"They only told me you're an expert on money laundering."

"They must have told you I'm Dominican."

"They did. But it wasn't true."

He nodded, acknowledging how quickly she grasped things.

"Well, that's what they told me about you," she said, scanning his face. "What did they tell you about me?"

"They only told me you were an investigator with the Madrid police force. So I know you have experience, but I don't know why you're doing this."

"I lost my brother in 11-M."

"Your brother? Oh, my God." On March 11, 2004 a group of Islamic terrorists set off bombs on Madrid commuter trains at the morning rush hour, killing almost two hundred people and wounding more than two thousand. Three years later the people accused of being involved in the attack were still on trial, and it was still on the front page of *El Mundo*. "I'm so sorry."

"He was taking his usual train to work."

"Where did he work?"

"In the marketing department of a big international company. He was really an artist, but he had to make a living."

They were silent for a while, and then he said: "We both lost someone to terrorists, and the people who put us together knew that. They must have figured we'd have the same motive."

"Yes. They must have. But they could have been wrong. We might not have the same motive."

"What do you mean?"

"I mean you might want vengeance."

"I did want vengeance," he admitted, gazing past her. "But I knew from experience that if you get back at people, they'll get back at you, and it'll never end."

"It never will. So I don't want vengeance for my brother. I only want to stop them from killing people."

"That's all I want."

"Then we do have the same motive," she said, "so we should be able to work together."

"Partners," he told her, reaching for her hand.

She clasped his hand firmly. "*Compañeros.*"

Raquel offered him several options for eating dinner, and he chose the one that required walking to Plaza Santa Ana, where they could have *tapas* at various bars. So after paying the check they walked down Montera, staying in the center of the street to avoid the girls and the men who loitered in front of the sex shops. They arrived with the crowd at Puerta del Sol, where people were going in all directions. They paused beneath the bronze statue of the bear looking for food in a strawberry tree, which Raquel explained had marked the spot to build the city, and then they headed east on Carrera de San Jerónimo. At times it wasn't possible for them to walk side by side, so she went ahead and he followed, taking in the sights around them but periodically glancing at the back of her and being enthralled by the fluid, swaying motion.

They came to a round intersection, Plaza de Canalejas, and from there they headed south on Calle del Principe, which led them to Plaza Santa Ana. The large open space was bounded by the four walls of buildings around it, with an unusually tall white building on the west side, which Raquel said had a bar on top with a spectacular view of the city. The plaza itself was covered with tables and chairs belonging to the restaurants around it—they were grouped together by style and color so that you could tell which restaurant they belonged to. They were fully occupied, and there were people standing around evidently waiting for a table to become free.

Raquel took him around the plaza, not looking for a table but just giving him a tour of the scene, and then she led him down a narrow street that was lined with bars. She headed into one of the bars, which was packed with people, all of them standing with glasses in their hands. They parted for her and let her through, a few of them greeting her.

Standing next to her, Fenly saw women in uniforms with white caps working in the kitchen, responding to the brusque man behind the bar who shouted orders to them. Above the opening to the kitchen was the menu, with the dishes painted in white letters on a black board. On the bar were enormous jars of olives, and behind them were compartments of food divided into portions, ready to cook.

"What would you like?" Raquel asked.

"I don't know. What's good?"

"Everything's good. If you like smoked trout, they're famous for it. The fried eggplant is also a specialty. And they make a really great *revuelto de bacalao.*"

"What's in the *revuelto?*"

"Eggs, onions, and salt cod."

"Then let's have the trout, the eggplant, and the *revuelto.*"

"*Bueno.* Would you like another beer?

"No, thanks. I'll have a glass of red wine."

She ordered drinks and food from the man behind the bar, who treated her with great respect. He shouted the order to the women in the kitchen. He got their wine and placed a dish of green olives in front of them.

Raquel took an olive and popped it into her mouth.

"They seem to know you here," Fenly said.

"When I was a young cop," she said, "this area was my beat."

"How long ago was that?"

Deliberately, she finished eating the olive and removed the pit from her mouth and dropped it into the receptacle below the bar. "I'm twenty-eight if that's what you want to know."

"I was curious about that, but I wanted to know how long ago you were a young cop."

"Well, let's see. I joined the force when I was eighteen, so that would make it about ten years."

"When did you join this special team?"

"About three years ago."

"What did you do before then?"

"I worked in vice."

"Did vice include the girls on Montera?"

She nodded. "Yes. It included all the girls on the street."

"But if prostitution isn't illegal, what did you do?"

"As best I could, I protected the girls. And I made sure that their papers were in order."

"Are a lot of them immigrants?"

"More than ninety percent of them are immigrants."

"What do you do if they're illegal?"

"We send them back to where they came from."

"How do they get here?"

"They're brought here," she said with an edge in her voice, "by organizations that traffic in women."

"Did you go after those organizations?"

"Yes. We did. But they're like the organizations that traffic in drugs. They have so much money, and there's so much demand for their services, they're hard to stop. And even if you do stop one of them, another appears and takes its place."

"In that respect they're also like terrorist organizations."

"They are," she agreed. "I sometimes wonder if trying to stop those organizations will solve the problems."

"You mean prostitution, drugs, and terrorism."

"When we go after the organizations we're dealing only with the symptoms, not with the cause."

"You think the problems have a common cause?"

"I think they do. It's social injustice."

"You sound like my mentor."

"Who's your mentor?"

"A man who saved my life. He believes that if we all work for a better world, then we won't have terrorists."

"I think he's right. My brother believed that," she added with a look of sorrow.

"I want to believe it, but I'm not there yet."

"I understand. And in the meantime we have a job to do."

"We do," he said, knowing they couldn't talk about it here. "Could you tell me what the cops are doing on Montera?"

"It's a major pedestrian traffic area. It's a good place to stop people and check their papers."

"Before you arrived they were questioning a man who looked like a Muslim. Are they allowed to profile people?"

"Sure. Why not?"

"We couldn't do that in America."

"You don't check people who look like Muslims?"

"We can't just stop people on the street for no reason."

"We don't stop them for no reason," Raquel said. "We stop them to check their papers. If they're residents they should have identity cards. If they're foreigners they should have passports."

"We don't have identity cards. I mean, most people have social security cards, and many people have driver's licenses, but some people don't have any form of identification."

"They aren't required to have any?"

"No," he said. "Unless they want to board a plane."

At that moment the man behind the bar put a plate of fried eggplant in front of them.

"Let it cool for a moment," Raquel told him.

He held back from trying the eggplant and waited for her to go first. "What made you want to be a cop?"

"My father was a cop."

"Was he your role model?"

"He raised me. My mother died when I was five."

"I'm sorry," he said, imagining how that had affected her.

"Don't be sorry. There are kids with two parents who don't get the love I got from my father." Carefully, she picked up a piece of eggplant between the thumb and index finger of her left hand. Before taking a bite she said: "I hope you like to eat. For us it's a major activity."

"But you're not fat," he said, taking this opportunity to survey her body. She wasn't skinny, but she couldn't have weighed more than a hundred and twenty pounds.

"You won't see many fat people here. Except tourists."

"So what's the secret?"

"We eat a lot of small meals and never stuff ourselves," she said, reaching for another piece of eggplant. "We also like to talk, which burns energy."

"You must get a lot of exercise walking."

"In the city we do walk a lot. When I was growing up I could walk everywhere—to school, to church, to the grocery store. It's getting harder to do that."

"Where did you grow up?"

"In Lavapiés. It's south of here."

The man behind the bar put another plate in front of them. It was smoked trout on pieces of bread, each with a dollop of mayonnaise.

"Where do you live now?"

"I live in Malasaña."

"Where's that?"

"It's west of Chueca, where our office is located."

"Is it far from where I'm staying?"

"It's not far. You could walk there."

"Do you rent an apartment?"

"I own an apartment. I bought it before the prices went up."

"Then you've made money on it."

"I didn't buy it to make money," she said after swallowing the food in her mouth. "I bought it for a place to live."

"Do you live by yourself?"

"No." She kept him in suspense for a moment, and then with her eyes on the canapés she said: "I have a cat."

"A cat? What's its name?"

"Her name is Gabriela."

"I never knew a cat named that."

"How many cats have you known?"

"Not many. Dominicans don't have cats."

"I thought you were American."

"I grew up with Dominicans."

"You mean on the island?"

"No. In the Bronx."

"I never knew anyone from the Bronx."

"How many Americans have you known?"

"Not many. So now I have the opportunity to get to know one," Raquel said before he could say it.

After spending about an hour in the bar they moved on and went into another bar on the same street, where Raquel ordered wine for both of them and ham croquettes. They spent almost an hour there, and then they headed back toward Puerta del Sol.

"How are you feeling?" she asked as they walked along Calle Principe with a lot of other people.

"I'm okay. I'm still on New York time."

"Then you're not ready to go to bed?"

"No. I want to hear about our assignment."

"Well, I couldn't talk about it in those bars, but I know a place where we'll have privacy."

She took him from Puerta del Sol onto Calle del Carmen, which didn't allow cars, and finally into a narrow street called Mesonero Romanos, which had a small plaza with tables on it. There was enough room between the tables so you couldn't hear conversations at the other tables unless someone raised his voice. It was almost midnight, but there were people of all ages sitting at the tables, there were people walking in both directions on the narrow street, and there were people waiting to get into the flamenco club that adjoined the plaza.

"Does this city go all night?" Fenly asked after they had sat down at a table near the curb.

"Oh, yes," Raquel assured him with a show of pride. "There are places that are just opening now."

"But how do people get to work the next morning?"

"The people who stay out all night are young."

"The people around us aren't young."

"They won't stay out all night."

At that point a waiter came to serve them.

"Do you want something more to eat?" Raquel asked.

"No. I'm fine," Fenly said. He asked the waiter: "What kind of brandy do you have?"

The waiter reeled off a list, and then he said: "We also have Dominican rum."

"Do you have Brugal?"

"Yes. Of course."

"Then I'll have a Brugal without ice."

"I'll have a *chinchón*," Raquel said.

"How did he know I was Dominican?" Fenly asked her when the waiter had gone.

"From your accent."

"Not from the way I look?"

"Well, you're darker than most Spaniards, but we're a mix of just about everything—Celts, Romans, Germans, Moors—so you can't tell much from looking at us."

"You look Spanish."

"I might to you," Raquel said, "but people have stopped me on the street and asked me for directions in languages I don't understand."

"Do you understand English?"

"I studied it, and I can read it. But when English people ask me for directions I have trouble understanding them."

"What about Americans?"

"I have even more trouble understanding them. Americans mumble and swallow their words."

"I have trouble understanding people from the South."

"Then you know what I'm talking about."

When the waiter had brought their drinks and left them, Raquel leaned forward over the table. "Well, as you know, our assignment is to stop a terrorist attack."

"Before you go any further," he said, "can you tell me your source of information?"

"Sure I can. You probably know that the men accused of being involved in 11-M are still on trial—"

"I read that in the newspaper."

"A few days ago one of them offered us information in return for a more lenient sentence."

"What kind of sentence is he facing?"

"Almost certainly life in prison."

"And you're willing to bargain with him?"

"Why not? If his information helps us to stop an attack, then it's worth bargaining for."

"But what if he gave you false information?"

"If he did, we've been conned."

"It sounds like you've already made a deal with him."

"We have. And we already have his information."

"What did he tell you?" Fenly asked.

"He told us about an attack they're planning. If you look at a map," Raquel said, drawing an imaginary line on the table with her index finger, "you'll see that Spain is a natural bridge between Europe and North Africa. We were conquered by Islamic armies from North Africa, and we were under their rule for hundreds of years. We finally drove them out, but now after more than five hundred years they're coming back."

"You mean as immigrants."

She smiled. "Yes. But also as merchants and financiers."

"Are they involved in international trade?"

"They're involved in the drug trade. North Africa is a main source of drugs for Europe, and Spain is where these drugs enter the European market."

"So money from drugs changes hands in Spain."

"A lot of money. Some goes back to North Africa, some stays here, and some goes elsewhere. We're interested in the money that goes elsewhere."

"Where does it go?"

"We don't know. But we know what they're doing with it."

"What are they doing with it?"

"They're buying weapons."

"What kind of weapons?"

"Presumably weapons of mass destruction."

"What are they planning to do with these weapons?"

"They're planning to attack a target in New York City."

"Did he tell you the target?"

"He doesn't know."

"Well, we don't have to know," Fenly said. "If we could find the money we could follow it to the weapons, and we could stop them from being deployed."

"We could," Raquel said, "but we don't know where to look for the money."

"So my job is to find the money."

"That's your specialty, isn't it?"

"Yeah, but I can't guarantee success."

"You have to," she said urgently.

"You really believe what this guy told you?"

"I have an instinct about it."

"A cop's instinct?"

"A woman's instinct."

"Can we talk with him?"

"We can give the interrogators questions to ask him, and we can watch the interview."

"How soon could that happen?"

"Tomorrow if you're ready."

"I'll be ready. How much time do we have?"

She frowned. "He doesn't know the exact date, but he says the attack is scheduled to occur in about two weeks."

"Two weeks? Then we better get off our fucking butts."

From the look in her eyes he knew she had understood what he meant, but he also knew she wouldn't have put it quite that way in Castilian Spanish.

TWO

HE WENT TO bed around one, still on New York time, and he lay awake for a long time thinking about what Raquel had told him. From time to time he sat up and turned on the light next to the bed and made a note of something that had occurred to him. It was after three when he finally went to sleep.

He had trouble getting up at seven, but after figuring out how to use the stove he made a pot of coffee, which he drank before getting into the shower. It was harder to figure out how to use the shower, which had a flexible hose with a head at the end and a holder where you could station it, but it took him a while to get the head to spray in the right direction. His first attempts had left a puddle of water on the floor.

While eating the roll at the dining table he wrote out his questions on a pad, reviewed them, revised them, and got out his computer to type them, sitting at the desk. He read over the questions, made some corrections, and saved them in a file. Then, after finding the connection to the internet, he checked his personal email.

There was a message from his sister Jessi, saying she hoped he had a good trip and wishing he could have seen her daughter Jenny perform in the high school play. They lived in Dobbs Ferry, having left the Bronx in time for Jenny to benefit from better schools. It was hard to believe that Jenny was now a junior in high school, and it was gratifying to know that she was doing so well after her inauspicious start. Their family had come a long way from the island, where the grandparents were poor *campesinos* struggling just to feed themselves. Yesenia had become Jessi, and her daughter Jenny wasn't expected to speak Spanish since her last name was Johnson, not Rodriguez or García. In fact, the girl did speak a little Spanish so that she could communicate with her grandmother, who was finally learning English.

There was also a message from Stephen, wishing him well on his assignment and pretending that it was a consulting job, which was his cover. Except for his boss, Stephen was the only person back home who knew his real reason for being in Madrid. They had told him not to tell anyone, including his family, but he trusted Stephen, who had saved his life and become the father he never had. And Stephen understood the game since years ago he had been involved in military intelligence and the CIA. From his experience Stephen had formed a policy of never trusting the government.

Fenly wrote replies to both messages, describing his first night in Madrid. He emphasized the food since both Jessi and Stephen liked to eat. He didn't say a word about Raquel, which gave the impression that he had been alone. He had to remain conscious of the possibility that any messages he sent could be intercepted and mined for information.

Their meeting was at nine, and it was only a little after eight, so Fenly decided to kill the time by taking a walk around the neighborhood. On his way out he greeted the *portero*, who was busy sweeping the lobby. Instead of going to Gran Vía, he headed in the other direction, passing the theater, the Turkish restaurant, a beauty shop, a hotel, and a jewelry store on the other side of the street. At the corner, on the Plaza del Carmen, was a restaurant named Garbo, probably because there was a movie theater on the plaza. Across the plaza on the next street was a building with a sign that said: "Dance hall with orchestra." On the plaza they were doing what looked like a major construction project, with temporary buildings occupying almost half of the open area and spoiling the view of people who might want to sit at the tables in front of Garbo. There was no one sitting at the tables now, but a man was sweeping up around them, disturbing the pigeons who were scrounging for scraps of bread among the fallen olive pits.

He walked to the edge of the open area and confronted the temporary buildings, which evidently provided office space for the people working on the project, and then he turned around and faced the side of a building across the plaza. The windowless wall had been plastered over with a smooth coating, and on the surface was a graceful mural in the colors of the rainbow. On a sky-blue background was a statement that didn't look like graffiti. In script it said: "You cannot achieve peace through war. If you want peace, work for social justice."

In this statement he heard what Raquel had said in the bar last night, and he was struck by the coincidence. It was as if she had miraculously arranged for someone to reinforce her message by painting that mural in the early hours of the morning.

He crossed the plaza and walked up Calle de la Salud to Gran Vía, then headed east. There were already a lot of people on the avenue, but he couldn't see them very well since the sun was in his eyes, still low in the sky. Evidently because Spain was at the western edge of its time zone, the sun rose much later than it did in New York, and it set much later, which could be a reason why Spaniards stayed up so late.

He stopped at a kiosk and bought *El Mundo*. On the front page was an article about the trial of the men accused of being involved in 11-M. The bombing of the trains had occurred more than three years ago, but it was still at the forefront of public consciousness. There were still stories about 9-11 in the New York papers, but they tended to be about controversies over the delays in compensating families who had lost loved ones in the attack, or over the health problems of people who had worked at Ground Zero trying to rescue possible survivors, or over the proposals for rebuilding at the site. A recent poll had found that two-thirds of New Yorkers thought about 9-11 every day.

He returned to the apartment and got his computer and the map of Madrid that they had given him in New York. He had copied the map by areas of the city, enlarging each area so that he could easily read the names of streets and identify landmarks. This morning he needed the enlarged map of Chueca, the neighborhood where Raquel's office was located.

He went out again with his computer slung over his shoulder

and walked to Gran Vía, which he crossed with a thick crowd of people, hearing the chirp of the walk signal that told blind people it was safe to proceed. He headed up Fuencarral, noticing among the trendy boutiques a useful looking bakery. He passed Calle Infantas, Calle Pérez Gardós, and Calle Augusto Figueroa, and then started checking the numbers. He found the building with the number he was seeking and entered it. Like many other buildings in the area, it had been remodeled, and it had a security system. On the directory he found the company, Diseños en la Onda, and he pressed its button. With his hand on the door he waited for them to let him in.

When it didn't happen right way he wondered if he was too early, or if he had pressed the wrong button. He checked his watch, which said nine o'clock, and he was about to press the button again when the door buzzed.

He took the elevator to the third floor, where he found the door of the company's office. He pressed the button next to the door and waited again.

An attractive young woman opened the door and let him in.

"I'm Fenly Aquino," he told her.

"Could I see your identification?" she asked.

"Sure." He took out his passport and handed it to her.

She looked at his picture and then at him. "You're more attractive than your picture."

"You are too."

"I know," she said, though he couldn't have seen her picture. "I'll tell Señor Ezkarra you're here."

"Thanks."

As he waited he glanced around the reception area. There were framed pictures of designs on the walls and brochures about the company's services. It specialized in designing offices, though it would also do homes if the job was big enough. If he hadn't known that this was the office of a special team for counterterrorism, he would have been fooled.

The young woman returned and led him to an inner office, where he found Raquel and a man in his forties. The man, who had close-cut mostly gray hair and a tough-looking face, got up from his desk. He was tall and lean.

"Leandro Ezkarra," the man said, making eye contact and extending his hand over the desk.

"Fenly Aquino." As they shook hands Fenly could feel the strength behind the man's grip.

"Please sit down," Leandro said, indicating a chair next to Raquel, who had remained seated in front of the desk.

"Did you have a good night's sleep?" she asked.

"Better than I thought I would."

"I hope she didn't keep you up all night," Leandro said.

"From what I saw," Fenly said, "we ended the night as most people were getting started."

"You'll get used to our hours," Raquel said.

"Well, let me tell you something about myself," Leandro said, leaning back in his chair. "As you might guess from my last name, my family is from the Basque country. But I grew up in Madrid, and I've always considered myself a Spaniard, though I admire the culture and history of my origin. If you like to eat, you'll find that the Basque restaurants are the best in the city, and the most expensive."

"If we have time, I'll take you to one," Raquel offered.

"Like Raquel, I started my career with the municipal police, but then I asked to be assigned to a unit that dealt with Basque terrorism. Some people of my origin called me a traitor, and they tried to kill me more than once. They didn't understand that they would never achieve their goal by using violence."

"But aren't there situations," Fenly asked, "in which terrorists *can* achieve their goal by using violence?"

"There are," Leandro readily agreed, "depending on how the government responds. We have to remember that the purpose of a terrorist act is to provoke the government into responding in ways that will turn people against it. And when a government responds by killing innocent people, it loses moral authority, and people turn against it."

"Terrorists kill innocent people."

"But governments are held to a higher standard. They aren't supposed to kill innocent people."

"So what do you think about our government's response to the attack on the World Trade Center?"

"Your government did exactly what the terrorists wanted it to do. It invaded a major Arab country that had nothing to do with the attack on the World Trade Center, and it pursued a war on terror that has killed a lot of innocent people." Leandro paused as if he was giving Fenly an opportunity to challenge his statement, and then he continued. "Our government didn't respond that way to 11-M. It knew from experience with Basque terrorists not to play into the hands of these terrorists."

"But people turned against it."

"They turned against the party in power, and they promptly voted it out of office."

"As I recall, the party in power suggested that the Basques were responsible for the attack."

"That party tried to use the attack for political purposes. But it didn't respond by killing a lot of innocent people," Leandro said, "and it didn't invade an Arab country."

"Spain had troops in Iraq at the time," Fenly pointed out.

"We did have troops there. And our new government pulled them out. We never should have sent them there."

"What should you have done?"

"We should have worked to make a world where people have no reason for being terrorists."

"You sound like my mentor," Fenly said, conscious of having said the same thing to Raquel. He wondered if she had been influenced by Leandro, or if it had been the other way around. "He lived in Argentina during the Dirty War."

"Argentina is a good example," Leandro said. "The military government there killed a lot of innocent people, it lost moral authority, and people turned against it."

"Well, how does that apply to us?"

"In our efforts to stop this attack we're not going to violate our principles. For example, we're not going to torture this man to get more information from him."

"Okay," Fenly said. "When's our interview?"

"It's scheduled for eleven this morning."

"I'm ready with the questions I want to ask him."

"Do you have them down on paper?"

"I have them in my computer."

"You have them in your computer," Leandro said, mocking him. "What happened to paper?"

"We still have a lot of it," Raquel said.

"Before we get to my questions," Fenly said, "do you know anything about the money?"

"We know where it's coming from," Leandro said, "but we don't know how it's being laundered, and we don't know how it's leaving the country."

"If we can find out how it's leaving, then we can find out where it's going. But we have to identify one of the steps in the process before we can get anywhere."

"Well, let's hope this guy gives us more information. Will you print your list of questions so that I can read them?"

"Sure, if you have a printer."

"We have a printer," Raquel said, rising. "We even have phones in case someone calls and wants us to design an office."

A half hour later they were driven to the top security prison where the men on trial were being held. Though the driver was a trusted employee of the special team, they didn't talk in the car about the terrorist plot. Instead, they talked about Madrid, about the new municipal construction projects, about the political situation, and about sports.

"While you're here," Leandro told Fenly, "you can explain baseball to me."

"I'd be happy to. And you can explain soccer to me."

"Dominicans don't play soccer?"

"They do, but their main sport is baseball. And they're good at it. There are more than a hundred Dominicans playing in *las grandes ligas*."

"I guess that explains why there are no Dominicans playing on our soccer teams in Spain."

"I think there's one," Raquel said.

"If there is," Leandro said, "then it's more than the number of Spaniards playing on their baseball teams."

When they arrived at the prison they were greeted by a serious man in a dark gray suit, who led them down a corridor to a room with a one-way window into an interview room. A solid man in shirtsleeves joined them and took the sheets of paper on which they had printed the questions. After reading them he said: "*Bueno.* Let's see what we can get out of him."

The interrogator went into the interview room and sat down at the table. He set the sheets of paper with the questions in front of him with a file of other papers on each side.

A few minutes later a guard brought the accused man into the interview room and led him to the table. The man's head was shaven, which made him almost indistinguishable from other men whose heads were shaven. He moved carefully, and he looked tense as he sat down.

The interrogator didn't waste time in formalities. He asked the man to state his name, his date of birth, his place of birth, and his occupation. Presumably, this information was used to identify him for the recording of the interview.

"In a previous interview," the interrogator said, "you told us about a plot to attack a target in New York City. Would you please repeat what you told us?"

"Sure." The man repeated what they already knew.

The interrogator made some notes, and then he said: "Now, I'm going to ask you some questions."

"All right."

"Is the target a building?"

"I don't know."

"Well, let me mention some possibilities, and maybe one of them will jog your memory. The Empire State Building, the

Citigroup Building, Grand Central Station—" The interrogator read from a list of landmarks, taking his time.

At the end of the list the man said: "I don't know."

"You don't remember anything they said about the target?"

"They never said anything about the target."

"Are you sure it's in New York City?"

"Yes. I'm sure about that."

"All right." The interrogator paused. "Did they say what kind of weapons they're going to use?"

"They didn't say."

"Did they say anything about the attack?"

"They talked about an explosion."

"An explosion?" The interrogator reacted as if this were a new piece of information. "Are you sure about that?"

"Yes. I'm sure. They said that the explosion would be even more spectacular than the ones at the World Trade Center."

Fenly imagined them grinning with anticipated satisfaction as they talked about it, and he clenched his teeth in anger.

The interrogator made a note. "Does that help you remember anything they said about the target?"

"They never said anything about the target."

"But they did talk about an explosion."

The man nodded. "They also talked about how many people it would kill."

"Do you remember a number?"

"Yes. I remember them debating whether it would kill forty or fifty thousand people."

The interrogator remained impassive. "Did they talk about killing bankers or any particular occupation?"

"They only talked about killing Americans."

"Did they say why they wanted to kill Americans?"

"They said they wanted to kill Americans for creating Israel, for defiling our holy places, for declaring war on Islam, for invading Afghanistan, for invading Iraq—"

"All right," the interrogator said as if he didn't want to hear any more. "So they didn't say anything about the type of people they wanted to kill?"

"They didn't," the man said, shaking his head.

"Did they say how they planned to deliver the weapons? By plane, by missile, by suicide bomber?"

"They only talked about an explosion."

The interrogator checked his notes. "Did they say where they were going to buy the weapons?"

"No. They didn't," the man said.

"Did they ever mention Russia? China? Iran?"

"The only country they ever mentioned was America."

"Did they say how they were going to pay for the weapons?"

"No. But I assume that they were going to use drug money. That's the money we were going to launder."

"So the money was coming from drug dealers?"

"Yes. And it was going to a company."

"A company? How do you know?"

"They mentioned a company."

"Did they ever mention the name of this company?"

"No. But I think it was a French company."

"Why do you think that?"

"They called the people in the company frogs."

"Did they say what business it was in?"

"They didn't talk with me about that. They didn't want me to know about that part of the operation. I was only going to be involved in the money laundering."

"How were they going to launder the money?"

"I don't know the whole process. All I know is that I was going to pick up the money from a drug dealer and deliver it to another person."

"Can you tell us who this person was?"

"No. I was arrested before I started picking up the money."

The interrogator looked toward the window, gesturing as if to say he had run out of questions.

"Do you have any more questions?" Leandro asked Fenly.

"I can't think of any," Fenly said.

So they instructed the interrogator to wind up the interview.

"We appreciate your cooperation," the interrogator told the man. "But if what you've told us doesn't help us to prevent an attack, then the deal's off. So think carefully. Is there anything else you want to tell us?"

The man held his chin with his hand in concentration. After a long silence he said: "I can't think of anything."

"If you do, you'll let us know."

"Yes. I'll let you know."

When they returned from the prison Leandro asked the driver to let them out on Gran Vía at the corner of Calle Victor Hugo. From there they walked to a restaurant on Calle de la Libertad, where the headwaiter greeted Leandro as Señor Vásquez.

It was an old restaurant with a bar in front and tables in back. There were only a few patrons in the place since it wasn't yet two. From then until four, Raquel explained, it would be filled with people from business and government offices having a traditional lunch. And there wouldn't be any turnover.

The headwaiter showed them to a corner table which had a brass marker on it indicating that it was reserved, and he handed them menus.

Fenly perused the menu, unable to decide what to order.

"If you like meat," Leandro said, "then I can recommend the roast lamb. It's on the bone."

"That sounds good," Fenly said, closing his menu.

When they had ordered and been served bread, butter, a carafe of water, and a bottle of house red wine, they got down to business.

"I've observed two interviews with this guy," Leandro said, breaking a piece of bread. "And I still wonder if he's making up the whole thing to reduce his sentence."

"He could be doing that," Raquel said.

"Or he could be misleading us," Fenly said.

"That did occur to me," Leandro said. "When he explained why they wanted to kill Americans, I could feel some fervor. But I don't think he's committed to their view of the world."

"I don't either," Raquel said. "I think he went into it for the money, and now he wants to get out of it."

"If that's what he wants," Fenly said, "then the guy would tell us everything he knows. And he wouldn't mislead us."

"I only wish he knew more," Leandro said. "But I guess we're lucky that they talked as much as they did in front of him."

"They probably didn't expect him to be caught," Raquel said.

"If he hadn't been involved in 11-M," Leandro said, "he wouldn't have been caught. His big mistake was to get involved in more than one plot."

"If he did it for the money," Raquel said, "then it makes sense that he was involved in more than one plot."

"I guess it does," Leandro said.

"Well, we can decide to believe him," Fenly said, "or we can decide not to believe him."

"If we decide not to believe him and we're wrong," Leandro said, "imagine how we'll feel."

"That makes it an easy decision," Raquel said.

"I think we're entitled to an easy decision," Leandro said.

"All right. We believe him," Fenly said. "Now, what did we learn from that interview?"

Raquel said: "We learned that the weapons they're planning to use will make a spectacular explosion."

"We learned," Leandro said, "that they're hoping to kill forty to fifty thousand people."

"And we learned that they're using a French company to buy the weapons."

"That could help us find the money," Fenly said. "How many French companies are operating in Spain?"

"I have no idea," Leandro said.

"What else did we learn?"

"Nothing else new."

"Well, I learned something about the money laundering," Fenly told them, reaching for a piece of bread.

"What did you learn?"

"I learned that the people involved don't know the process

from one end to the other."

"Then we have to catch them at more than one step of the process," Raquel said.

"That's right. The only one who knows the whole process is the mastermind behind it."

"Did you learn anything else?" Leandro asked.

"I may have," Fenly said, taking some butter. "How long ago did they arrest this guy?"

"About three years ago. It was a few weeks after 11-M."

"Then it took them three years to accumulate the money they needed to buy the weapons."

"How much money do you think they needed?"

"Five to ten million dollars," Fenly guessed.

"If you split the difference," Leandro said, "that's seven and a half million dollars."

Fenly got out his calculator and used the back of the receipt from the grocery store to write down the results with a pencil that he always carried in his jacket. "That's five and a half million euros. To accumulate that amount of money over three years, they only had to launder about thirty-five thousand euros per week. And if they deposited that money in a bank over five business days, it wouldn't have been noticed."

At that point the waiter brought plates of salad, which he placed in front of them.

"Well, how can we pick up the trail of the money?" Leandro asked when the waiter had left.

"We have to imagine the whole process," Fenly said. "It starts with a drug dealer, and it ends with a weapons dealer. The next to last step is the French company, which pays the weapons dealer. And the second step is the person who picks up the cash from the drug dealer and delivers it to the next person. At some point in the process they have to deposit cash in a bank, and since there are limits on the amount of cash that they can deposit at one time without it being flagged, they've been making regular deposits in small amounts."

"You mean like a retail store would make," Raquel said.

"Yeah. Like the one I got this receipt from. Or any kind of retail operation."

"Well, we can't check the bank accounts of all the retail stores in Madrid," Leandro said.

"We don't have time for that," Fenly agreed. "But we can check the bank accounts of French companies operating in Spain."

"*Bueno.* We'll check those accounts."

"We should also try to catch them in the laundering process before they deposit the cash."

"I understand. But how could we do that?"

"By watching the people who might be couriers."

"We're already watching those people," Leandro said.

"But now we know what we're looking for," Raquel said.

"All right," Leandro said. "We're looking for people who are carrying five to ten thousand euros in cash. But how do we find them? We can't stop people and search them."

"We can't," Raquel said. "If the terrorists heard about it, they might accelerate their plan."

"And we don't want to stop the flow of money," Fenly said. "We want to follow it."

"I have a question," Leandro said. "If the attack is scheduled to occur in two weeks, then they've already bought the weapons. So why would they still be laundering money?"

"They might not be," Fenly said. "But they might still need money for other expenses."

"Let's hope they do. I'll tell the police what we're looking for."

"And I'll tell Antonio what we're looking for," Raquel said.

"I assume you're going to introduce Fenly to him."

"I was going to this afternoon."

"You mean after his siesta."

"I wasn't planning to have a siesta," Fenly said.

"You'll need one after the lamb," Leandro said. "And in any case, you should lie down for a while. We want to get you on Madrid time as soon as possible."

When they left the restaurant Leandro headed back to the office while Fenly and Raquel headed for Montera. He was planning to return to his apartment and lie down for a while, and she was planning to stop by the police station.

"Leandro seems like a good boss," Fenly said as they walked along. "How long have you worked for him?"

"Since I joined the special team," Raquel said. "He *is* a good boss. And he's like a father to me."

"Is your father still alive?"

"No. He died when I was twenty. He had a heart attack."

"Was your brother older or younger than you?"

"He was four years younger. He was only a baby when our mother died. So I helped to raise him."

"It must have been hard. You were only five then."

"It gave me a purpose. While other girls my age had dolls, I had my baby brother."

There were about a dozen police on the plaza near the Gran Vía metro station, one of whom was questioning a blond girl in a skimpy outfit. Another was talking with a short man who had the Indian features of people from the Andean countries. As he crossed the plaza after parting with his colleague Fenly wondered if the police might stop him to check his papers since he looked like an immigrant. But they ignored him, and he continued past McDonald's along Gran Vía, following two solid middle-aged women in skirts and cardigans and practical shoes, with one of them holding the other's arm companionably.

He turned on Tres Cruces and passed the grocery store, which had closed at two and would reopen at five. He saw no one in his building, and he entered his apartment ready to collapse, the time difference having caught up with him. But he couldn't lie down until he had reported to his boss, who would be waiting to hear from him.

It was ten in the morning in New York, a good time to call his boss, and Fenly spent the next half hour on the secure phone telling his boss what he had learned about the plot. His boss, a former FBI agent, was skeptical about the information since it was coming from a guy who had nothing to lose by making up a story. Like all such stories, it could never be disproven, and it could be a waste of time. By the end of the conversation Fenly agreed that in the absence of evidence that corroborated the guy's story, they should remain skeptical, and his boss agreed to keep an open mind.

He lay down on the bed and closed his eyes, succumbing to fatigue, though he didn't drop off to sleep right away. For some reason he started thinking about his father, who had left the family less than two years after he was born. He had no memory of his father, and he hadn't even seen a picture of him since his mother had destroyed all evidence of his father's existence. But during those years of growing up without a father Fenly had his own idea of what his father looked like, and he believed that he would recognize his father if he ever saw him.

Until later he didn't realize that his concept of his father was only a figment of his imagination. Until then his father was his role model, and he measured his behavior against standards that he ascribed to his father. His earliest arguments with his mother were over these standards of behavior. One such standard was the way you treated women. According to his father's standard, women were put on earth to serve men and make them happy. Obviously his mother had failed as a woman since his father had left her. It was all his mother's fault that he, Fenly, had to grow up without a father. If she had been a better woman, she would still have a husband.

His mother, who had nothing good to say about his father, insisted that Fenly treat her with respect. She also insisted that he treat his sister Yesenia with respect. Yesenia was two years older, and according to his mother Yesenia always did the right thing. In fact, she could do no wrong. Whenever there was any kind of dispute between Fenly and her, it was always his fault. And his mother was always urging him to follow his sister's example of never missing a Sunday of church, never missing a day of school, and never missing an opportunity to help her mother.

By the time he was ten he had had enough of living with his mother and his sister, and he decided to run away and join his father in Santo Domingo. That day he skipped school and rode the subway as close as he could get to JFK airport, which he knew about from listening to neighbors talk about going there and meeting people arriving from the home country, and he took the bus the rest of the way. His plan was simple. At the airport he would find a sympathetic man who would pay for his ticket and take him to Santo Domingo on the promise that his father would repay him.

He did find a sympathetic man, who could have been his grandfather, but the man put him into the custody of the police so that they could return him to his mother. Angry at the man for betraying him, and always hostile to police, he refused to give them his name, his address, or any information that would enable them to contact his mother. It was only when a tough cop threatened to lock him up in jail that he finally gave them the phone number of his uncle's bodega, where his mother could be reached. Since his family didn't have a phone, it was the number they gave for emergencies.

An hour later his mother arrived at the airport with his uncle, who had driven her there in the old car he used on special occasions. She couldn't have been worrying about him because he was supposed to have been in school, and the school didn't immediately report absences to the family, but she acted as if she had been worrying, and she did a number on him, saying: "How could you do such a thing to me?"

His uncle, his mother's brother, echoed her, saying: "How could you do such a thing to your mother?"

Of course he couldn't answer that question.

On the long drive back to the Bronx he sat in silence in the back seat, trying not to be moved by his mother's crying. It helped to imagine that his father would have been on his side and would have applauded his escapade.

He was jolted by the sound of a *merengue*—the ringtone of his cell phone. He had left the phone on the bedside table, and now he reached for it blindly.

"Hello?" he said with an uncleared throat.

"It's me," Raquel said from what sounded like a distance.

"What time is it?" he asked, trying to read his watch through the cobwebs of sleep.

"It's quarter after four, but something happened. How soon can you meet me at Arizona?"

"In fifteen minutes," he told her, suddenly awake.

"*Bueno*. I'll head there right away."

He got up and went to the bathroom, where he relieved himself and doused his face with cold water. He hadn't slept for very long, but he felt refreshed.

Outside, it was cloudy and the streets were wet from rain. It made him realize that he hadn't remembered to pack an umbrella. But he didn't need one right now since the rain had stopped. It had rained just enough to clean the streets.

He walked up Tres Cruces passing a group of rowdy girls who looked like American college students. They were probably here on their spring break.

On Gran Vía, in front of Zahara, a waiter was wiping off the tables and setting the chairs back upright, having leaned them forward against the tables so their seats wouldn't get wet. The seats were made of a plastic mesh, which wouldn't hold water.

The girls were standing on Montera as if nothing had happened. They must have huddled in doorways to avoid getting wet from the rain.

He approached Arizona and sat at a table that a waiter was still wiping off.

"What can I get you?" the waiter asked.

"A coffee," he said, "when you have a chance."

"I'll get it for you right away. You're my first customer since the rain ended."

He was sipping the coffee when Raquel joined him.

"Now," she informed him seriously, "we have a reason for

believing what that guy told us."

"We do? What?"

"They killed him. They poisoned his lunch."

"Do we have any idea who did it?"

She shook her head. "It could have been anyone who had access to the kitchen."

"But we have a list of all those people. Maybe we'll find a link among them."

"You *are* an American," she said, almost as a compliment. "You see an opportunity where I see a loss."

"It's not a loss. We got all the information he had, and now, as you said, we have a reason for believing what he told us. And we have another line of investigation."

"You think it'll lead anywhere?"

"No. But it could draw them out into the open."

"It could make them accelerate their plan."

"Let's hope they're not in a position to do that," Fenly said. "And let's hope our investigation slows them down."

Raquel reflected. "Well, I guess we do have one advantage. They don't know how much he told us. And if they think we know more than we do, they might give the game away."

"Yeah, they're on defense now."

"But they still have a lead."

"Oh, yeah. They do," Fenly agreed. "It's like they're ahead by five runs in the bottom of the ninth."

"Or," Raquel said, "it's like they're ahead by two goals with only five minutes remaining on the clock."

"It's more like that. In baseball the time never runs out. In soccer it does."

THREE

THEY LEFT ARIZONA and walked to an adjoining building, where Raquel opened the door with a key. Inside, he followed her up three flights of stairs.

They walked down a dim hallway and stopped at the door of an apartment. The smell of frying food pervaded the hallway, evidently coming from the restaurant below.

Raquel knocked three times on the door and then twice.

"I know that's hokey," she admitted, "but there's no peephole in the door, and we need some way of identifying ourselves."

"You could slip a note under the door."

"We could. But this is easier."

"Easier to copy. If I had my ear against the door across the hall, I could hear your signal."

"You wouldn't. We have agents across the hall."

The door opened, and a young man with bright eyes greeted Raquel effusively, saying: "*Hola, mi amor.*"

"*Hola, Tonio.*" She waited until they were in the apartment with the door closed before she introduced them. "Fenly, this is Antonio. He runs our street surveillance program. Antonio, this is Fenly. He's an expert on money laundering."

"Welcome to the team," Antonio said, checking him out. "You must have seen a lot of dirty money."

"I have," Fenly said. "The world's full of it."

"Come on. I'll show you around."

He followed Antonio, who started the tour by showing him the video cameras at the front windows of the apartment.

"They're aimed at different sections of the street," Antonio explained. "They cover Montera from the Gran Vía metro station to the passage that leads to Tres Cruces."

He had noted the passage, which was being remodeled—devoid of shops, it hadn't invited him to walk through.

"We take pictures of everyone who walks by."

"How many people walk by every day?"

"We never counted, but it must be half a million people."

Fenly looked out the nearest window and down at the street, where he recognized a waiter from Arizona. "Can't people see your cameras from the street?"

"They could if they had binoculars," Antonio said, "and if they knew where to look. But who would think of looking for cameras in an apartment?"

"People look at what's happening on the street," Raquel said.

"They don't look up unless someone points. I mean, like at a person about to jump out of a building, or something equally horrifying."

Having looked up and seen that happen, Fenly moved on to another subject. "What do you do with all the pictures?"

"We analyze them. We look for patterns of behavior."

"You mean like people walking by at the same time of day."

"Or meeting someone, or going into the same store, or eating at the same restaurant."

"Or going with a girl," Raquel added.

"Where do they go with the girls?"

"They have apartments on the side streets."

"The girls have apartments?"

"Their pimps have them," Antonio said. "The girls who belong to the same pimp use the same apartment."

"What if more than one of them wants to use the apartment at the same time?"

"They're near each other on the street, and they keep an eye on each other. If one of them has gone to the apartment and another has a client, then she strings him along until she sees that the first girl has finished."

"It doesn't take long," Raquel said.

"Based on our pictures," Antonio said derisively, "we estimate an average time of twenty minutes."

"Why do you want pictures of them?"

"Most of their clients are foreigners, and it helps us keep track of them."

"By recording their patterns of behavior?"

"Right. If we have a suspect and we know he goes with a girl on Thursdays, then we can watch for him and stop him."

"What about their Spanish clients?"

"We're not interested in them."

"The people who live in this neighborhood are interested in them," Raquel said. "They want to put up their own cameras and take pictures of them going with prostitutes."

"They do? What for?"

"They want to embarrass them by publishing their pictures in the local newspapers."

"They don't like having the girls on the street?"

"No, they don't like it. They have a neighborhood association that regularly lobbies the city government to get the girls off Montera."

"Could the government do that?"

"Of course they could. They could get the girls off Montera tomorrow if they wanted to."

"Then why don't they?"

"The girls would go somewhere else, and the people who live in that neighborhood would complain."

"So the government is less concerned about the people who live in this neighborhood than it is about the people who live in other neighborhoods?"

"I don't know," Antonio said. "The people who live in this neighborhood have a lot of money. You can pay a million euros for a two-bedroom apartment here."

"I think this neighborhood is less organized than other neighborhoods," Raquel said.

"There's also the fact," Antonio said, "that some businesses don't mind having prostitutes on the street."

"McDonald's must mind it," Fenly said. "They're standing in front of its windows."

"But the sex shops don't mind it," Antonio said.

"It attracts business for them," Raquel said.

"They need to resolve the legal status of prostitution," Antonio said. "But I don't know if they ever will. They've been debating it in a commission for almost three years."

"What are they debating about?"

"Well, the unions want to legalize prostitution so that the girls can have unions, a minimum wage, and health benefits. The socialists need the union vote, so you can guess their position. But the church is against legalization, and it has a lot of influence on the conservatives."

"And the feminists are divided," Raquel said. "They're against legalizing prostitution, which they regard as a form of slavery, but as long as we have it they want the girls to have the same rights as other workers."

"Don't forget the men," Antonio said as if he didn't belong to their gender. "If you made prostitution illegal, then you would have to punish men for having sex with prostitutes. And that would be very unpopular."

"So no one wants to touch it," Fenly said.

"No one does," Antonio said. "Well, you didn't come here to talk about prostitution, so why don't we get down to business. Would you like some coffee?"

"That would be great," Fenly said.

"How do you like it?"

"I like it black."

"I thought Americans liked cream in their coffee."

"Where did you get that idea?"

"I guess from Starbucks."

"Are they in Spain?"

"They're everywhere. Of course I've never gone to one, but I've seen people drinking coffee from Starbucks cups."

Fenly and Raquel sat down in chairs that looked as if they had come from the restaurant below, while Antonio went over to a kitchen area.

"You mentioned McDonald's," Antonio said, pouring coffee. "They're everywhere too."

"Have you ever eaten there?" Fenly asked.

"I couldn't," Antonio said with a shudder. "The décor is so tacky it would make me sick."

"You could take out the food," Raquel suggested.

"I have a place to take out food. Have you ever tried 100 Montaditos?"

"I never have. Are they any good?"

"Well, for one euro you can't go wrong."

"What kind of food is it?" Fenly asked, not sure what *montaditos* meant in Spain.

"They have a hundred different kinds of little sandwiches," Antonio said with enthusiasm, "all of them for one euro."

"The next time we meet," Raquel said, "we can order them for lunch."

Antonio brought coffee to Raquel and Fenly in mugs that were from different sets. He went back and got himself a coffee and sat down with them.

"We're looking for people," Raquel began, "who might be involved in laundering money. We think they're getting it from drug dealers and passing it to other people."

"Are they men or women?" Antonio asked.

"They could be either, but I think they're men."

"Well, if they're passing it on the street, then we should be able to spot them easily."

"They're probably not doing it on the street," Fenly said. "And they're probably not passing it directly."

"You mean whoever set this up doesn't want the people who receive the money to know where it's coming from."

"That's right. If one of them gets caught, he only knows his step in the process."

"How do you think they're carrying the money?"

"In briefcases, or else in envelopes under their shirts."

"If it's in envelopes under their shirts," Antonio said, "then they won't be easy to spot."

"You'll have to identify them from their behavior."

"What kind of behavior are we looking for?"

"Repetitive behavior," Raquel said.

"All right. What's the profile?"

"North African. We want you to search through all your files, going back three years, and look for repetitive behavior of North African males."

"You know," Antonio said after a moment, "there's a North African who meets Samira every Monday and Thursday."

"Does he go with her to the apartment?"

"He does the whole thing."

"How long ago did you notice this pattern?"

"Only a week ago. But then I looked back, and I found that he's been following this pattern for quite a while."

"Why didn't you notice it before?"

"He wears different outfits," Antonio explained. "They're like costumes, and unless you look at him very closely you wouldn't think it was the same man."

"It sounds like he's trying to avoid being identified," Fenly said, interested.

"We need to talk with Samira," Raquel said. "Could you see if she's on the street now?"

Antonio got up and headed toward the window.

"Samira works with us," Raquel told Fenly.

"You mean you employ her?"

"She's a volunteer. Her older sister, who cleaned bathrooms at Atocha Station, was killed in 11-M."

"She's there now," Antonio said.

"Then ask the police to take her to the station."

"I thought prostitution wasn't illegal," Fenly said.

"The police will ask her for her papers, which she doesn't have. She'll argue with them, and then they'll take her down Montera to the station."

"They have a police station on Montera?"

"Oh, yes. In fact, they're expanding it."

"I think they plan to inaugurate the new station in May," Antonio said, opening his cell phone.

"Are we going to talk with her there?"

"Yes. We never talk with her on the street. It might be noticed by the wrong people."

"Starting with her pimp," Antonio said.

"From her name," Fenly said, trying to organize his thoughts, "I assume this girl is North African."

"You're getting the hang of it," Raquel said.

"The hang of what?"

"Profiling."

"Should I ask your American colleague if he can profile me?" Antonio asked, striking a pose.

"Let's wait until he gets better at it," Raquel told him.

Antonio contacted the police, using code language, and they watched at the window while a young cop approached a brown girl and questioned her. When the girl started to argue with him, he gently took her by the arm and led her away.

They waited long enough to give the cop and the girl time to get to the station ahead of them.

Meanwhile, Antonio went into another room of the apartment and returned with a picture of a brown man, which had been enlarged. "That's the guy. If you show it to Samira, maybe she can tell you who he is."

It was their first lead, and Fenly knew from experience that the first lead often led nowhere. But they didn't have time for dead ends, so he hoped it would lead them somewhere.

Before going to the police station they stopped on the plaza, where Raquel showed the picture to a group of police. Despite his different costumes, they immediately recognized the guy as a regular client of the Moroccan girl. It had been a while since they had checked his papers, so none of them remembered his name, but they were sure that the girl would know it.

When they got to the station some construction workers were standing at the entrance, placidly having a discussion. Raquel stepped around them, attracting their eyes and momentarily interrupting their conversation.

Fenly followed her into the building and stopped with her at the checkpoint. The cop at the counter greeted her and asked him for some identification.

After scrutinizing his passport the cop said: "You're in good company, *señor*. Raquel's the best."

"Oh, you're just saying that to be nice," Raquel said.

"She's modest too," the cop added.

She led him down a hallway to a small office, where she introduced him to another cop. He took them into a holding room, where the girl from the street was sitting at a table. The cop left them and closed the door.

The girl, who had glowing black hair and sober black eyes, held her head high with a dignity that didn't go with her sleazy outfit, which included a short turquoise skirt.

"Hi, Samira," Raquel said. "How are you doing?"

Samira shrugged. "I'm doing all right."

"This is Fenly, a colleague from America."

Samira checked him out. "He doesn't look like an American."

"You mean he doesn't look like your American clients?"

"He doesn't at all. And I have a lot of them."

"I hope they treat you well."

"They do. At least they treat me better than Germans do."

They sat down at the table opposite the girl, who carefully rearranged herself in her chair.

"We're looking for a guy," Raquel explained, "who might be involved in money laundering. We believe he's North African, and we thought maybe you could help us find him."

"Just tell me how," Samira said obligingly.

"Our surveillance cameras have spotted a guy who sees you regularly. I have a picture of him." Raquel took it out of her shoulder bag and handed it to Samira.

Looking at it, the girl nodded in recognition. "That's Najib."

"Where's he from?"

"He's from Morocco."

"When do you see him?"

"On Monday and Thursday."

"How long have you been seeing him?"

Samira paused to think. "For about three years."

"Have there been any interruptions in this pattern?"

"A few times. But he's been a steady client."

"I understand that he wears a lot of different costumes."

"He likes to dress up and play different roles."

"What fun for you."

"It's better than cleaning bathrooms."

"Are you sure about that?"

"Yes. I've done both."

"Well, other than his dressing up and playing different roles," Raquel continued after a moment, "have you noticed anything in particular about him?"

"He's big on cleanliness."

"What do you mean?"

"Before we have sex he makes me go into the bathroom and use the bidet."

"Does he follow you into the bathroom?"

"No. He stays in the bedroom and listens for the sound of the water from the bidet."

"What if he doesn't hear it?"

"One time he didn't. I didn't think it was necessary, but when he didn't hear it he got very angry."

"Maybe his real purpose," Fenly said, "is to make sure you're not in the bedroom while he does something."

"Like what?" Samira asked.

"He could be hiding something in the bedroom."

"Hiding something?"

"The guy we're looking for is carrying money that he passes to another guy."

"Well, I've never seen Najib carrying anything."

"He could be carrying it under his shirt."

Samira opened her black eyes wide as if she had suddenly remembered something.

"What?" Raquel asked, leaning forward.

"One time my hand accidently brushed against his shirt, and I touched something that felt like a magazine. I asked him if it was pornographic, and he said it was."

"It could have been an envelope of money," Fenly said.

"If he was carrying it under his shirt," Samira said, "I would have seen it when he took off his clothes, which he always does in front of me."

"When you touched what felt like a magazine, did he take off his clothes right after that?"

"No. He made me go into the bathroom."

"So he could have hidden it *before* he took off his clothes."

"Well, I don't know where he could have hidden it. There's only a wardrobe, a bed, a small table, and two chairs."

"He could have hidden it in the wardrobe."

"But a client might have found it there."

"Then he could have hidden it under the bed."

Samira considered. "No one would look under the bed. I mean, except the cleaning woman."

"And the guy who picks up the money," Fenly said.

"If that's what they're doing," Raquel said, "then the guy who picks up the money must come right after Najib."

"Or soon after him," Fenly agreed.

"Do you have another client who comes every Monday and Thursday?" Raquel asked the girl.

"No. I don't. But another girl might."

"You mean another girl who belongs to the same pimp."

"That's right. We all use the same apartment."

"When you're done," Fenly asked the girl, "who leaves the apartment first?"

"We always leave together."

"Did you ever try to let him leave first?"

"A few times. But he always waited for me."

"He doesn't want her to look under the bed," Raquel said.

"Should I try to let him leave first?"

"No. You shouldn't change your behavior in any way."

"We don't want him to know we suspect what he's doing," Fenly said. "And we don't want to endanger you."

Samira looked as if she had guessed the purpose of their investigation. "How are they going to use this money?"

"We think they're going to use it to finance another attack."

"You think it's the people who killed my sister?"

"That's what we think."

"Well, I'm not afraid of them."

"You should be," Raquel warned the girl. "If they find out that you're helping us, they might kill you."

"I'll be careful, but I'm still not afraid of them," Samira said, holding her head high. "They talk about killing infidels, but they're the infidels. They act as if they don't know what the Koran says over and over."

"What does it say?" Fenly asked, though he had read it.

"God is merciful and forgiving."

As they walked up Montera from the police station Fenly asked: "How old is she?"

"She just turned fifteen," Raquel said.

"Fifteen? She looks a lot older."

"You would too."

Her tone of voice confirmed what he had sensed in Raquel's treatment of the girl. "I have the feeling that you have a special interest in Samira."

"I do," Raquel said. "I feel like she's my younger sister."

"Have you tried to help her find some other line of work?"

"I have. And I keep trying, but I can't find anything that pays as well. Her age is a problem, and also the fact that she's illegal."

"So why hasn't she been deported?"

"Because she's useful to us."

They entered the building where the surveillance office was located, and they headed up the stairs.

"I know that sounds awful, what I just said," Raquel told him. "It sounds like we're exploiting her. But if we sent her back to

Morocco she'd have an even worse life there. At least here she has a chance."

"A chance of what?"

"A chance of being saved." Raquel stopped at the landing to catch her breath.

"When I was growing up in the Bronx we lived in a five-floor walkup. It kept you in shape."

"I consider myself in shape, but for some reason these stairs seem steeper today."

"They seem steeper than they did in the Bronx."

They continued up the stairs, and when they arrived at the door of the apartment she gave the signal to Antonio, knocking three times and then twice.

Antonio opened the door and let them in, saying: "Would you like some oxygen?"

"No, thanks," Raquel said. "But I could use some coffee."

"Your timing is good. I just made some."

They sat at the table and brought Antonio up to date.

"So we're looking for the guy who picks up the money," Raquel concluded. "Someone who sees a girl who belongs to the same pimp as Samira."

"On Mondays and Thursdays," Fenly said.

"Well, that should be easy," Antonio said. "We can look at pictures and find that pattern."

"Do we know how many girls belong to Samira's pimp?"

"There are four others on Montera," Raquel said.

"And we know who they are," Antonio said.

Raquel nodded. "Two are Romanian, one is Bulgarian, and one is Russian."

"How did the Russian get into the country?" Fenly asked.

"She was brought here by a Spanish businessman, who gave her a job in his company. You know what I mean."

"And he got tired of her?"

"I think she got tired of him."

"If we each took one of the girls," Antonio said, "we could do the job efficiently."

"There are four girls," Fenly said, "and only three of us."

"José will help us." Antonio got up and went to a door that led into what must have been a bedroom. He opened the door and said: "José? Could you join us? We have a project."

A young man with spiky hair, which had blond highlights, came out of the room and ambled toward them. He had several piercings in each ear.

"José, this is Fenly, and you know Raquel."

Fenly shook hands with the young man, whose grip was lackadaisical.

"José is our technology guy," Antonio said. "He understands everything about cameras and computers and other electronic equipment. He lives in cyber world."

"It's a good place to live," José said, still standing.

"Please sit down," Antonio said. "I'll explain the project."

José sat down and listened and made a few suggestions on how to perform the task efficiently.

They agreed to start at the previous week and to work backwards until one of them found the same guy meeting a girl on Monday and Thursday. Then they would all concentrate on that girl and look for confirmation of the pattern.

It took José about a half hour to produce enough pictures for them to get started. He had a lot of equipment in the room from which he had emerged—cameras, enlargers, copiers, scanners, and other devices that Fenly didn't recognize.

Sitting at the table, they worked until eleven o'clock without finding the pattern. At that point Antonio said: "Let's take a break and have supper."

"We could do a takeout from McDonald's," José suggested.

"You see what's happening to the next generation?" Antonio said. "It's being corrupted by American junk food."

"They make good French fries," José said.

"Well, I don't want a meal of French fries. I want some real Spanish food."

"We don't have time to go out and eat," Raquel said.

"I'm not suggesting that. I'm suggesting that we do a takeout from 100 Montaditos."

"That's fine with me," José said.

Antonio had a menu from the restaurant. It had a hundred different items, and to order an item you only had to check it and indicate how many you wanted. The menu also had beer, wine, and other beverages.

They told Antonio what they wanted as he read down the list of items. He explained that the sandwiches were small, so each of them would need at least three.

When they were done they had a variety of sandwiches made of ham, cheese, meat, shrimp, and other ingredients. Antonio volunteered to go and get them since it was his idea, and it didn't take him long. He returned within fifteen minutes.

"Now, that's fast food," Fenly said in admiration.

"Faster than McDonald's," Antonio said. "And much better. Just wait and see."

The sandwiches were in containers, so they didn't need plates.

"This is good," Fenly said after taking a bite of a little baguette with ham inside it.

"At least they give you chips," José said.

"We're not making any progress," Raquel said, referring to their project.

"If the pattern we're looking for existed," Fenly said, "we would have found it by now."

"Maybe the pattern is Tuesday and Friday," Antonio said.

"No, it can't be," Raquel said. "If they left the money in the apartment overnight, the cleaning woman would find it under the bed in the morning."

"I agree," Fenly said. "It has to be Monday and Thursday."

"But maybe he doesn't always go with the same girl," José said, munching on a chip.

"What do you mean?" Antonio said.

"To pick up the money, he has to go to the same apartment. But he doesn't have to go there with the same girl."

"You're right," Fenly said. "He only has to go with one of these girls, and he could go with a different girl on Monday and Thursday."

"Which makes it hard to spot the pattern," Raquel said.

"I wonder why the other guy doesn't do that," José said.

"He makes it hard to spot the pattern," Antonio said, "by meeting Samira in different costumes."

"He figured out a way to meet the same girl without being spotted," Fenly said. "He probably likes her."

"We need to start over again," Raquel said after wiping her mouth with a paper napkin. "We need to sort the pictures by the guys, instead of by the girls."

"We can do that," Antonio said, "but it'll take longer. There are a lot of guys."

"Well, let's start with last week. The three of us can look at the pictures while José is sorting for the previous weeks."

Once they had the first set of pictures it took them less than a half hour to find a guy who fit the pattern. Raquel found him, and Antonio asked José to search back through the records and find every picture of this guy meeting a girl.

It was after one when they spread the pictures on the table.

"Monday and Thursday," José said, "going back three years. And he never met the same girl in the same week."

"We got him," Antonio said, clapping his hands. "Now, what do we do with him?"

"We don't arrest him," Fenly said. "We need to tail him and see where he takes the money."

"Well, we missed him tonight," Raquel said.

"He might not deliver the money tonight. He might wait until tomorrow."

"We can have the police look for him tomorrow. And if they spot him, they can tail him."

"If they don't spot him, we'll have to wait until Thursday."

"Does that mean we can go home now?" José asked.

"You're not going home this early," Antonio said.

"I am. I'm too tired from last night to go out clubbing."

"Your generation doesn't have the stamina that ours had."

Fenly smiled. He figured that Antonio was in his early thirties and that José was in his early twenties. The difference in their ages probably wasn't more than ten years, which didn't seem long enough to delimit generations.

"I'm going home," Raquel said, stifling a yawn.

"You mean you're going to abandon us?" Antonio asked.

"If you want, we could send you reinforcements."

"We don't need reinforcements. We need motivation."

"All right." Raquel approached him and put her arms around him and hugged him. "Does that help?"

"It helps a lot. I didn't get enough of that from my mother."

"What about me?" José asked.

She hugged him too. "Now, can I go home?"

"Yes, you can go," Antonio said. "*Hasta mañana.*"

Fenly followed her out of the apartment and down the stairs. He walked with her to the Gran Vía metro station, where they said goodnight and arranged to meet at nine the next morning in the office of the design company. He watched her descend into the metro. A lone woman wouldn't take the subway at this hour in New York, but this was Madrid, and Raquel was a former cop, so she could take of herself.

When her head disappeared he turned and headed across the plaza toward the girls who were standing in front of McDonald's. He didn't see Samira, but he recognized a few of the other girls from looking at their pictures. It was bad enough that they were being used to satisfy the lust of uncaring men, but evidently they were also being used to carry out a plot of insane men to kill thousands of people. These girls were the same age as his niece, whose main goal in life now was to have a boyfriend.

It was too late to call New York, so before going to bed he sent an email telling his boss that they now had evidence that corroborated the guy's story. He hoped his boss wouldn't suggest that it could have been accidental food poisoning.

He hated his mother, who wouldn't buy him the sneakers he wanted. She didn't understand how important they were. She didn't realize that his current sneakers, which she had bought at a discount store, were strictly for losers, and that if he didn't have the cool sneakers his friends all had, then he would be a loser.

"We can't afford them," his mother told him.

"We can afford to buy clothes for Jessi," he pointed out.

"Well, she's a girl. She needs clothes. And I don't spend a lot on them. In fact, I could buy a lot of clothes for the price of those sneakers."

"It's all I'm asking for. You don't have to buy anything else for me. Only the sneakers."

"I have to buy food for you."

"No, you don't. I just won't eat."

"You have to eat, but you can live without those sneakers."

"I can't live without them."

"You mean you'll die if you don't get them?"

"I might," he said. "I might kill myself."

"Don't talk like that. It's sinful."

"It's sinful not to buy me the sneakers. You'll go to hell for not buying them."

"Then I'll be the first person to go to hell," his mother said, "for not buying sneakers."

"Lend me the money," he pleaded with her.

"It would take you years to pay me back, and in the meantime we'd be short of money."

In desperation he fired his last, best shot. "If Papi were here, he'd buy them for me."

"He's not here," his mother fired back. "And even if he were, he wouldn't have the money."

"Yes, he would. He's a rich man."

"In your imagination he is. He probably doesn't even own a pair of shoes."

"You're making that up because you hate him."

"I don't hate him. I just don't have any use for him."

"Well, if Papi were here," Fenly argued, "he'd buy me those sneakers. I know he would."

"I don't have time to argue with you," his mother said with finality. "I have work to do. And you have homework to do."

"They didn't give us any homework."

"They gave your sister homework when she was your age."

"Maybe they did. But things have changed."

"Then go and do something, but don't bother me again about those sneakers. You hear?"

He heard, and the only conclusion he could draw was that his mother didn't love him.

He did go and do something. He went to the mall in White Plains and found the sneakers. He put them on and walked around the store in them to see how they felt, and then when no one was looking he simply walked out of the store in them, leaving his loser sneakers behind. But as he went through the doorway an alarm went off. He started running, and he tried to get out of the mall, but they were waiting for him at the exit, and they put him in a holding area while they called his mother.

She arrived with his uncle, who had driven her there. She pleaded with them, and she pleaded with the store manager, who got the shoes back undamaged, and they finally let him off without charging him, but they warned him that if they ever caught him stealing again they would prosecute him to the full extent of the law.

"You know what means?" his mother asked him as they drove home. "They'll put you in jail for ten years."

"Or even longer," his uncle said.

He knew they were trying to scare him, and it didn't work. He resolved to be smarter the next time and not get caught.

Awakened by the sound of a *merengue*, Fenly reached for his cell phone. It was quarter of four in the morning, so he knew without being told that something had happened.

"I'm sorry to wake you at this hour," Raquel said.

"No, that's all right." He was relieved that it wasn't his sister calling with bad news.

"Can you meet me at the plaza on Mesonero Romanos?"

"Sure. I'll be right there."

He dressed quickly and left the building.

As he hurried to the plaza he passed a couple returning home from a night at the clubs.

Raquel was waiting for him on the plaza, plainly visible in the bluish light from the sign of the Hotel Regente. She was holding two unmarked paper cups. "I brought coffee for you."

"Thanks. Where did you get it at this hour?"

"From a place on Gran Vía that stays open all night."

He pried the lid off the cup and found that the coffee was too hot to drink, so he held it and waited.

"One of the girls was killed this morning."

"Oh, my God," he said, imagining how Raquel felt.

"She was one of the Romanian girls. Her name was Lina. She was strangled with her stocking."

"Where was she killed?"

"In the apartment."

"When did it happen?"

"Around three this morning. The next girl who went to the apartment found her there."

"How old was she?"

"Her papers said she was legal age, but they were probably forged by the organization that brought her here. I think she was only about fourteen."

"Oh, my God," he repeated in utter dismay.

"Let the little children come to me," Raquel recited sadly, "and do not hinder them, for the kingdom of God belongs to such as these."

He reached out and put his hand on her shoulder.

Tears streamed down her cheeks as she asked: "Why does God allow such things to happen?"

He had asked this question many times, but no one had ever

given him a helpful answer, so all he could do was put his arms around Raquel and draw her close and hold her.

After a while she pulled herself together and said: "Antonio and José are looking for a picture of the last guy who went with Lina. When they find his picture we're going after that son of a bitch. And we're going to get him."

FOUR

THEY WENT TO the surveillance office, where Antonio and José were examining pictures. José didn't look fully awake, but he was applying himself to the task.

"Help yourself to some coffee," Antonio said.

"I need some more," Raquel said, heading toward the kitchen area. "How's it going?"

"We're moving along. The pictures we're looking at now were taken at three this morning."

"Was there much activity?"

"You'd be surprised."

"Well, if you don't see Lina on the street, then you don't have to go any further."

"We haven't seen her since quarter of three."

"Then you have what we're looking for." Raquel brought her mug of coffee over to the table where they were sitting. "Show me the last guy who went with her."

Antonio handed her a picture, saying: "Guess what. It was the guy who picks up the money."

"But he went with her earlier last night," Raquel said, staring at the picture. "Are you sure it's the same guy?"

"It's the same guy," José said.

"He must have had some unfinished business," Antonio said.

"He might have guessed that we're after him," Fenly said.

"He might have," Raquel said, still staring at the picture. "But it could be unrelated to us. There are guys who use these girls for purposes other than sex."

"If this guy's using them to launder money, he wouldn't kill one of them on a sadistic impulse."

"You never know what a guy will do."

Fenly was abashed by that statement, which carried the weight of her experience.

"What would you like us to do now?" Antonio asked.

Raquel put the picture into her shoulder bag, saying: "We'll stick to our plan. Watch for this guy, and if you spot him ask the police to tail him."

"You don't want the police to arrest him?"

"Not yet. We want to see where he goes with the money."

"What if he goes with another girl?"

"That's a good question," Raquel said with a worried look.

"If he follows his schedule," Fenly said, "he won't go with another girl until this Thursday."

"All right," Antonio said. "We'll watch for this guy, and if we spot him we'll ask the police to tail him."

Raquel said nothing as they left the apartment and descended to the street and crossed Gran Vía.

"You're concerned about the girls," Fenly said as they walked up Fuencarral.

"I know it doesn't make any sense," Raquel said, "but I feel responsible for them."

"You're too young to be their mother."

"I don't feel like their mother."

"What do you feel like?"

"I feel like their guardian angel."

"That's not your job."

"Well, someone has to worry about them."

"Doesn't God worry about them?"

"I believe He does, but the only evidence I have for that is that I worry about them."

"So you're His agent here on earth?"

"Whether or not we like it," Raquel said, "we're all His agents here on earth. We're all responsible for each other."

"I guess we are," Fenly said, beginning to see where the events of his life had been driving him.

They found Leandro at his desk with a legal pad in front of him on which he had drawn a diagram. They sat down and brought him up to date.

"So we know who killed this poor girl," Leandro said, gazing at the picture that Raquel had handed him. "Do we have any idea why he killed her?"

"We have some ideas," Raquel said tautly.

"Could you tell me what they are?"

"Well, one idea is that this guy likes to hurt girls."

"You say he's been with three other girls who belong to the same pimp. Do we know if he hurt any of them before?"

"We never got a complaint about him. And he's been seeing them regularly for three years."

"Then that idea doesn't fly," Leandro told her.

"Another idea is that he found out that we're after him."

"How would he have found out?"

"I don't see how, but he could have."

"All right. And why would he have killed the girl because he found out that we're after him?"

"To eliminate a witness."

"If that's the case, then this pimp's other girls are in danger."

"They are. And I'm concerned about them."

"Let's come back to that later," Leandro said. "Do you have any other ideas?"

"I have an idea," Fenly said.

"You do? Let's hear it."

"The girl saw him picking up the money."

"Now, that has possibilities," Leandro said. "Tell me how you think it happened."

"I assume that after they had sex the girl would go into the bathroom." Fenly looked to Raquel for confirmation.

"Yes. She would use the bidet."

"While she was in the bathroom he would find the envelope under the bed and get dressed and put it safely under his shirt. But last night she came out of the bathroom before he expected, and she saw the envelope."

"That could have happened," Leandro said. "But she wouldn't have known what was in the envelope."

"She could have guessed that it contained money or drugs, and she could have told him that if he didn't give her a piece of the action, she'd report him to the police. But he couldn't give her a piece of the action since the money wasn't his, so he didn't see any choice but to kill her."

"Why didn't he kill her then?"

"The next couple would have found her a few minutes later. So he promised to return and give her some money."

"We'll use your idea as a working hypothesis," Leandro said after reflecting. He turned to Raquel. "Now let's go back to your concern about this pimp's other girls. If the guy's not eliminating witnesses, then they're not in danger."

"They are if they do what this girl did."

"Then we have to warn them."

"What are we going to tell them? Not to ask for a piece of the action if they see the guy pick up an envelope?"

"Let's think about it," Leandro said, tapping his fingers on the desk. "We can't tell them he was the guy who killed this girl."

"We can tell them to stay in the bathroom and give the guy plenty of time to get dressed," Fenly suggested.

Leandro looked at him quizzically. "And what would be the reason for that?"

"I don't know. Maybe the guy has a problem with people watching him get dressed."

"But the girls must see him get *un*dressed."

"That's different."

"It is," Raquel agreed. "Getting dressed is more personal."

"More personal?" Leandro looked from one of them to the other. "I don't see that, but I'll take your word for it."

"I guess we've ruled out telling them not to go with the guy," Raquel said after a silence.

"Unless we can spot the guy before then," Leandro said, "we have to let a girl go with him this Thursday so that we can put a tail on him and see where he goes with the money."

"Well, maybe we'll spot the guy today."

"Maybe we will. But if we don't, then we have to let a girl go with him to that apartment."

Raquel sighed. "I know we do."

"I don't see any other way. Do you, Fenly?"

"No," Fenly said, wishing for Raquel's sake that he did see another way. "We have to let him pick up the money."

"I think we should plant a microphone in the apartment," Raquel suggested, "so that we could hear if a girl's in danger."

"How would we do that?" Leandro asked.

"I don't know. We could ask Samira."

"It could get her into trouble with her pimp."

"She can deal with her pimp."

"It could put her at risk with the guys who are laundering the money," Leandro pointed out.

"We'll tell her not to go with the guy who killed Lina."

"What about Najib?"

"I don't think he would hurt her," Raquel said. "He has some kind of relationship with her."

"And Najib has no connection with the guy who killed Lina," Fenly said. "If you think about it, they found an ingenious way to make sure that the guy who collected the drug money would never see the guy he passed it to."

"I admire their ingenuity," Leandro said dryly. "So what have we decided to do?"

"We've decided," Raquel said, "to tell the girls to give the guy plenty of time to get dressed. And we've decided to talk with Samira about planting a microphone in the apartment."

"Does that satisfy your concern about the girls?"

"The only thing that would satisfy my concern about them is to get them off the street."

"In another world," Leandro muttered.

"Did we put a tail on Najib?" Fenly asked.

"We did that last night."

"Has the tail reported back?"

"No. We should hear from him later today."

"And we're going to put a tail on the guy who killed Lina."

"As soon as we spot him."

"What about the French company?"

"We have a preliminary report," Leandro said. "But so far we haven't found a company whose remittances match the patterns we described."

"How far have we gone?"

"About halfway down the list."

"If we can follow the trail of the money that the guy picks up," Fenly said, "then it'll lead us to the company. But we should keep going through that list."

"You mean in case he doesn't pick up any more money."

"Yeah. They might have all the money they need. But so far it looks like they still need money."

"For their commissions," Raquel said.

"Imagine doing this kind of thing for money," Leandro said, scowling in disgust. "It really makes you wonder how low human beings can go."

"From what I've seen," Raquel attested, "there's no limit."

"So how do you live with that?"

"I keep reminding myself that there's no limit to how *high* human beings can go."

"I'll try that the next time I get depressed."

"I will too," Fenly said with a growing appreciation of his partner.

They got the police to take Samira down to the station so that they could talk with her. They met her in the same holding room.

Raquel opened the conversation by saying: "I assume you know what happened to Lina."

"Yes. I know," Samira said. "The poor girl."

"We're trying to find the guy who did it. But at the same time we're keeping an eye on another guy." Raquel took out the picture. "Do you recognize him?"

"I've seen him, but I've never gone with him. He never asked me to go with him."

"Well, if he does ask you, don't go with him."

"Why not?" Samira asked.

"We heard he abuses Muslim girls."

"Do Muslim girls complain about him?"

"They say he beats them."

"Then I won't go with him. Thanks for warning me."

"I want you to warn the other girls. I mean, the ones who belong to your pimp. They've all gone with him, and they haven't been abused by him. But according to my information he has a problem with people watching him get dressed."

"That's one problem I haven't seen, but I can believe it."

"He goes berserk if a girl sees him putting on his clothes, and he becomes violent. So tell the girls to stay in the bathroom after they've had sex with him and give him plenty of time to get dressed. If they do, they'll be in no danger."

"All right. I'll tell them," Samira said. "How badly does he beat the Muslim girls?"

"A few of them have had to go to the hospital."

"Why haven't you arrested him?"

"None of those girls will testify against him. They don't want their families to know what they do for a living."

Samira nodded as if she understood. "Do they know why he beats them?"

"They think he's punishing them for being whores."

"And he only does that with Muslim girls?"

"He doesn't care what infidels do."

"A defender of the faith," Samira said. "I hate that type of male. It's the same type that becomes a terrorist."

"It is," Raquel agreed. "You know, after what happened last night I'm concerned about you."

"I know you are. So find the guy who killed Lina."

"We're trying to, but in the meantime you're in danger."

"We're always in danger. You never know what a guy will do. But after what happened we'll be more careful."

"That's not enough. You need to be protected."

"Our pimp is supposed to protect us."

"He didn't do such a good job of protecting Lina."

"The police didn't either."

"You're right," Raquel readily admitted. "But you can enable the police to protect you."

"We can? How?"

"You can let us plant a microphone in that apartment, so you could shout for help if you were in danger."

"A microphone?" Samira laughed. "If the guys ever heard about it, they wouldn't go with us. They'd be afraid of having their sessions with us recorded."

"That wouldn't be legal. But it would be legal to have a microphone for security purposes."

"What would prevent it from being used illegally?"

"You have my word that it wouldn't be. It would only be there to protect you."

"Well, let me think about it," Samira said. "And let me talk with the other girls who use the apartment. We couldn't do a thing like that without their agreement."

"Fair enough," Raquel said, "and be sure to warn them about this guy's problem."

"I will. Don't worry."

When Samira had left them Fenly said: "I liked the way you gave her a reason not to go with him, while you made it safe for the other girls to go with him. That was creative."

"Thank you. But I didn't invent it."

"There *is* a guy who beats Muslim girls?"

"There was such a guy."

"What happened to him?"

"We nailed him. And we deported him to Egypt."

"Where he's now plotting to get back at you."

"Whatever we do," Raquel said, "there's someone plotting to get back at us. Just think what the world would be like if all the energy that now goes into getting vengeance went into working for social justice."

"You know, you don't talk like a cop."

"How do you know what cops talk like?"

"I had a lot of dealings with them."

"You talk like a perpetrator."

"I was. I was a bad kid."

"Did you go to jail?"

"No. I should have, but I was lucky."

"Let's have lunch, and you can tell me about it."

"Are you sure you want to hear about it?"

"Yes. I'm sure," Raquel said. "I want to take advantage of this rare opportunity to get to know an American."

By the time he was fifteen Fenly was a member of a local gang that performed a role in drug distribution, extorted money from store owners, mugged strangers, and ruthlessly defended its territory from rival gangs. It had made him feel like somebody to be accepted into the gang, especially since he and another kid who lived down the block were the youngest members. The others were all sixteen and seventeen.

His mother didn't know about his involvement in these activities until an extorted store owner complained to the police, identifying Fenly as a member of the gang. Though they returned the money to the store owner, he pressed charges to the point where the boys were given probation and ordered to report weekly to an officer.

"I don't know what to do with you," his mother said when they got home from the court. "I've tried everything."

"No, you haven't," he retorted.

"What haven't I tried?"

"You haven't tried letting me live with my father."

"I couldn't do that," his mother said, shaking her head. "It wouldn't be good for you."

"How do you know? You never tried it."

"How could I try it? I never hear from him, and I don't know how to contact him."

"Someone must know how to contact him."

His mother reflected. "All right. I'll see if I can find him. But I don't think it's a good idea."

Through his uncle, who knew someone who had recently seen his father, she got an address in Santo Domingo, and she wrote a letter to his father.

A few weeks later she got a response, and she showed him what his father had written. It was one sentence, scrawled almost illegibly, saying: "I don't think it's a good idea."

The fact that it was the same thing his mother had said, in the same words, made him suspicious. He wondered if his mother had only pretended to write to his father and had gotten someone in Santo Domingo to send a reply that she had dictated. He was angered by the possibility that she had done this, and he was hurt by the possibility, however remote, that his father had rejected the idea. He reacted by skipping school, missing appointments with his probation officer, and getting more involved in gang activities.

One night in the middle of summer, as he was roaming the neighborhood with two other members of the gang, they spotted a white man walking ahead of them. The man was wearing khaki pants and a blue checked shirt with the sleeves rolled up to the middle of his forearms. And he was carrying a briefcase.

"He looks like a businessman," Ramón said.

"Yeah. I'll bet he has a lot of money," Lázaro said.

They quickened their pace and caught up with the man before he reached the corner of the block, at which point Fenly said in English: "Hey, mister, you have the time?"

"Sure," the man said, stopping. He was in his mid-forties, with short dark hair tinged with gray and dark eyes. Except for his clothes he could have been Latino. After checking his watch the man said in Spanish: "It's ten thirty-five."

"What are you doing on this street?" Ramón asked in Spanish.

"I'm walking to the subway," the man replied. He was fluent in Spanish, but he had a funny accent. It sounded Italian.

"This is our street," Lázaro said. "You need our permission to walk on it."

The man smiled. "You mean you want to collect a toll?"

"You can call it that. It's all your money."

"All my money? That's not much." The man reached into a pocket in the back of his pants and brought out a wallet, which he opened. He counted the bills and then told them: "It looks like I have sixty dollars."

"You have more than that," Ramón said.

"Not on me," the man said.

At that point Lázaro pulled out a switchblade knife and sprung it open menacingly. "You better find more money, man, or I'll cut your throat."

"I don't have more," the man said calmly, looking directly at Lázaro. "So I guess you'll have to cut my throat."

There was something about him that made Lázaro hesitate. Was he an undercover cop, ready to pull a gun on them? Was he an important drug dealer with a band of gunmen lurking right around the corner? Was he an expert in martial arts?

"You know," the man told them, "if you value money more than human life, then you have your priorities wrong."

"We don't need a fucking lecture from you," Fenly said, feeling uncomfortable.

"You need a lot of things from me. You just don't know it."

"You talk like a priest," Ramón said.

"I'm not a priest." The man pulled a card out of his wallet. "I run a community center in the neighborhood."

Fenly, who was closest to him, took the card and glanced at it. The man's name was Stephen Wyatt, which didn't sound Italian.

"I'll bet his briefcase is full of money," Lázaro said.

Stephen opened his briefcase and showed them its contents, which included a yellow legal pad with writing on it and several brochures. The man handed a brochure to Fenly, saying: "This will explain what we do."

"We don't give a fucking shit what you do," Ramón said. "We want your money."

Stephen offered him the bills from his wallet. "Here. Take it."

Ramón snatched it. "Now, give us the rest."

"There isn't any more."

Lázaro waved the knife at him.

Stephen didn't flinch. He acted as if he was protected by an invisible shield.

"I think he's telling the truth," Fenly said.

"I think he's giving us a load of bullshit," Ramón said.

"We have his money. Let him go."

"You're acting like a pussy."

"We should carve him," Lázaro said.

"What'll that prove?"

"It'll prove we own this territory."

"It'll send a clear message," Ramón said, "that *gringos* aren't welcome in our neighborhood."

"But he's helping our community. And he speaks Spanish."

"I don't care. I think we should carve him," Lázaro said, "and take his money."

"Before you carve me," Stephen told them, "you should think about the consequences."

"There won't be any consequences for us," Ramón said. "If you're dead, you won't be able to identify us."

"You'll identify yourselves."

"What do you mean?"

"You'll know who you are and what you did."

"Come on," Fenly urged them. "Let's not mess with him."

"Are you afraid of him?" Lázaro asked.

"No. I'm not. I just don't want to mess with him."

"But he could go to the police."

"I don't think he will."

"I won't," Stephen said, "on one condition."

"You're not in a position to make conditions," Lázaro told him, brandishing the knife.

"Yes, I am. You have my card. I expect to see you all at the center." With that he turned his back to them like a matador turning his back to a bull, and he started walking away from them. He didn't even glance over his shoulder.

Lázaro stood there as if he were unable to move.

"Well, I'll be damned," Ramón said in admiration. "He sure has a pair of *cojones.*"

Fenly watched the man go with the feeling that something important had happened to him.

Toward the end of the summer, on a hot night, a rival gang challenged their authority in a block at the edge of their territory.

A battle ensued with knives and clubs. When it became clear that the rival gang was losing, one of its members produced a gun and fired at Ramón. The bullet hit him in his right eye, and he tumbled forward, bleeding profusely.

The rival gang fled, and Fenly's gang fled too, except for him and Lázaro, who went into a nearby building and called for help.

Fenly was kneeling next to Ramón when the police arrived. Since Ramón was already dead, there was nothing they could do for him, but they wanted to catch the guy who had killed him, so they took Fenly and Lázaro to the station for questioning.

Neither of them could give the police a description of the killer. It had happened so fast, and their attention had turned immediately to Ramón. And they didn't want to help the police catch the guy. They wanted to catch the guy themselves. They wanted vengeance.

Their gang extorted enough money from store owners to buy some guns, and they were planning to invade the territory of the rival gang and kill the guy. But after going along with them Fenly began to have reservations. The image of Ramón lying in a pool of blood kept appearing in his mind, and he felt revulsion at the thought that they were going to kill someone.

When he raised questions about the plan his fellow gang members easily parried them, armed with a code of conduct that had governed human behavior for millennia, and he didn't have any arguments to use against them.

As the day of the invasion approached he was still revolted by the thought of what they were going to do, but he felt he had no choice. If he didn't join them, then he would be a traitor. It would be as if he joined the rival gang and fought against them. And that would leave him without a place in the world.

The night before, while pacing the cluttered room that served as a living, dining, and family room as well as a place for him to sleep, the only bedroom being shared by his mother and his sister, Fenly remembered the man they had mugged back in July. He remembered the man saying he expected to see them at the community center. Of course they hadn't gone there. It wouldn't have been cool. But he had kept the man's card, and he tried to remember where he had put it. He knew he had hidden it, not wanting to give his mother any ideas—like the time she had wanted him to meet with a priest for counseling.

Since his only private places in the apartment were the section of a closet and the drawers in a chest where he kept his clothes, it had to be in one of the drawers. So he ran his hand under his tee-shirts and found it.

Gazing at the card, which had the man's name, the name of his center, an address, and a phone number, he decided that at this point he had nothing to lose.

The next morning he walked to the community center. It was in a former warehouse that covered half the block. Inside, he was greeted by a pretty Latina who made him feel welcome. She asked him to wait, inviting him to sit in the reception area while she tried to locate Mr. Wyatt.

As he waited he picked up from the adjoining table a brochure that described the activities of the center, which included English classes, immigration services, tax counseling, family counseling, a program for completing a high school equivalent diploma, a day care center, a charter school for grades one through five, and a sports program. The only activity that interested him was the sports program, though he had never played an organized sport.

When the man appeared, wearing khaki pants and a checked shirt with the sleeves rolled up, Fenly recognized him. He got up, hastily putting the brochure back on the table as if he had been caught with it.

"I'm glad to see you," the man said with a welcoming smile. "Come on. We can talk in my office."

He followed the man through a door and down a corridor and into an office, which had a work area and a sitting area. One wall was lined with shelves of books, and centered on another wall was a framed quotation: "The Lord sent me to bring glad tidings to the poor, to proclaim liberty to captives."

Following his eyes, the man said: "A friend gave that to me. He's a priest, but as I told you and your friends, I'm not a priest. And I'm not an evangelical minister."

"What are you?"

"I'm a guy with a mission. You can call me Stephen. What can I call you?"

"Fenly," he said self-consciously.

"Would you prefer to speak in Spanish?"

"Yes." He felt that it would give him greater privacy.

"So we'll speak in Spanish," Stephen said with the accent that sounded Italian. "Tell me what's on your mind."

"If I do," Fenly said, "you won't tell anyone, will you?"

"Whatever you tell me is strictly confidential."

"Well, you said you'd go to the police if we didn't come here," Fenly reminded him.

"I shouldn't have said that. It seemed like the right thing to say at the time, but later I realized that it wasn't. I shouldn't have used a threat to get you to come here. And obviously," Stephen added, "it didn't work."

"I'm in a mess," Fenly said, trusting him.

"Does it have to do with your gang?"

"Yeah. One of the guys who mugged you that night was killed in a fight with another gang. A guy shot him, right in the eye, and he bled all over."

"So your gang wants vengeance."

"How did you know?"

"It's human nature. You killed one of our guys, so now we have to kill one of your guys."

"They're ready to do it," Fenly said. "But I don't want to go along with them."

"Why not?" Stephen asked him.

"The thought of killing makes me sick. I mean, they didn't watch Ramón die like I did. And they didn't have his blood on their jeans like I did."

"Have you tried to talk them out of it?"

"Yeah. But they won't listen. And I don't have any arguments to use against them."

"What about the fact that it's wrong to take a human life?"

Fenly shrugged. "We don't get into things like that."

"What things do you get into?"

"Territory. Money. Proving you're *macho*."

Stephen nodded. "Where's your family from?"

"Santo Domingo." He used the name of the capital city as most of them did to indicate the whole country.

"What does your father do for a living?"

"I don't know. I just know that he makes a lot of money."

"Do you have a good relationship with him?"

"I haven't seen him since I was two."

"Where does he live?"

"Santo Domingo."

"Does he help your mother?"

"He doesn't do a thing for her."

"So she does everything."

"Yeah. She does." He felt that he was being led toward a new understanding of the situation.

"Where does she work?"

"She works at my uncle's bodega."

"How old are you?"

"I'm fifteen."

"Are you the only child?"

"No. I have a sister. She's seventeen. Her name is Yesenia. We call her Jessi."

"Tell me about her."

"There's nothing to tell," Fenly said. "My sister's perfect."

"And you're the bad one," Stephen said. "That's how you get attention."

"What do you mean?"

"You get attention by being the bad one. You feel you can't compete with your sister, so you don't play that game. You play another game."

"I don't want attention."

"Then what do you want?"

"I want respect."

"Then you have to do something to earn it. And being in a gang doesn't earn respect."

"It earns respect from the other members."

"Do you really care what they think about you?"

"I don't know. I thought I did."

"But you're wondering now. You're wondering if you want the respect of guys who would kill someone for vengeance."

"I am," Fenly admitted. "But if I don't go along with them, I'm nowhere."

"I understand," Stephen said. "It's hard to let go of something if you don't have anything else to hang onto."

"I don't have anything else."

"Well, I could offer you something."

"You could? What?"

"I could offer you a job here. It doesn't pay much, but it'll give you satisfaction."

"Doing what?"

"Helping your community. Your first assignment would be to help me stop your gang from killing someone."

"You promised not to tell the police."

"We're not going to involve the police."

"Then how would we stop them?"

"By talking with them."

"They won't talk with you."

"I think they will. I think you can get them to come here."

"I don't think I can. I'm not their leader."

"You're going to be their leader," Stephen said. "You're going to set an example for them, and they're going to follow your example."

"I need to think about it," Fenly said, unconvinced.

"I have the feeling that you don't have time to think about it."

"You're right. I don't. They're planning to attack tonight."

"Then you better get them here today."

"All of them?"

"No. Just the leaders."

"We have two leaders. You met one of them."

"The guy with the knife?"

"Yeah. Lázaro. And he's the one who wants the most to get back at them."

"Then he's the best one to talk with."

"What would you tell him?"

"I'll tell him that vengeance won't give him any satisfaction."

"How do you know?"

"It's a long story, and you'll both hear it."

"But why would he believe you?"

"Because he'll know I'm speaking from experience."

Fenly had heard older people, including his mother and his uncle, say that they were speaking from experience, and it hadn't given him enough reason to believe them. But he had a different feeling about Stephen, so he finally said: "Okay. I'll try to get Lázaro to come here."

"Were you successful?" Raquel asked after sipping her coffee. They were in a restaurant on Libertad, at a corner table, where they had spent the past two hours.

"Yeah, but it wasn't easy. The hardest part was getting Lázaro to talk with Stephen."

"How did you convince him?"

"I reminded him what Ramón had said about Stephen."

"You mean about his pair of *cojones?*"

"Yeah. That did it. Lázaro was willing to listen because he had respect for Stephen. And he ended up playing for our basketball team, the one we started at the center."

"What happened to him?"

"He's a teacher and a basketball coach at a high school in the Bronx. He's married, and he has three children who wouldn't think about joining a gang."

"Isn't that supposed to happen in America?"

"It is," Fenly said, "but it doesn't always happen. It didn't happen for Ramón."

At that point her cell phone rang. She answered, listened, and said: "We're about to leave. We'll be there in ten minutes."

Fenly was already signaling for the check.

"That was Leandro. Something has happened."

"He didn't tell you what?"

"Not over the phone. He'll tell us when we get to the office."

When they got there they learned that the pimp whom Lina and Samira belonged to had been killed.

FIVE

"THEY FOUND HIM outside the building where he lived," Leandro told them, referring to the pimp. "The killer must have followed him."

"Well, it wasn't Najib," Raquel said.

"No. Unless our tail on him took a lunch break."

"He wouldn't have done that."

"I'm just kidding. I'm trying to deal with all these murders." Leandro looked at Fenly and asked: "Did you bring them with you from New York?"

"What do you mean?"

"In this city we have less than fifty murders a year, and we've had *three* since you got here. That's an average of one murder per day. At that rate we're going to catch up with New York."

"You still have a long way to go. We have about five hundred murders a year."

"Are most of them gang killings?"

"Most of them involve two guys in a conflict that escalates into violence, with at least one of them having a gun."

"Is it easy to get a gun?"

"Yeah. It's too easy."

"I think whoever killed Lina," Raquel said, redirecting them, "also killed her pimp."

"I think so too," Leandro said.

"Her pimp may have known who killed her."

"He may have. But how could he have known? Is he watching his girls with surveillance cameras?"

"Maybe not with cameras, but he's watching them."

"He could have seen the last guy who went with Lina," Fenly

said. "And when she didn't come back to the street, he could have gone and checked on her."

"So he found her body," Leandro said. "But how would he have found the guy who killed her?"

"He could have followed him before," Raquel suggested.

"Why would he have followed him?"

"The guy was a regular client of his girls. He might have been setting him up for blackmail."

"You mean for having sex with prostitutes?"

"Respectable guys wouldn't want people to know about it. And when the pimp figured out that this guy had killed Lina, he had something much bigger on him."

"That makes sense. But it doesn't get us anywhere."

"It does," Fenly said. "It supports our belief that the same guy killed both of them."

"Well, we have a picture of him, and the police are looking for evidence at the crime scenes that would tell us who he is."

"We can't count on their finding anything," Raquel said.

"I know we can't," Leandro said. "And we can't count on his meeting a girl this Thursday."

"Without a pimp," Fenly asked, "what happens to the girls?"

"They'll work without one," Raquel said, "until another pimp moves in and takes over."

"So it'll be business as usual?"

"Yeah, though of course the girls will be upset by what happened to their pimp."

"Enough to take a day off for mourning?" Leandro asked.

"Enough to take a day off," Raquel said.

Leandro rubbed his chin. "Well, let's try to get into this guy's head. Last night a girl caught him picking up the money and tried to blackmail him, so he killed her. And today her pimp tried to blackmail him for killing her, so he killed the guy. Will that make him change his behavior?"

"It'll make him wary of blackmailers," Fenly said.

"Who else could blackmail him?"

"One of the girls," Raquel suggested.

"But you warned them."

"We asked Samira to warn them."

"You think she did?"

"I'm sure she did. But they don't always listen."

"None of the young people listen," Leandro said. "They have their ears plugged into music all the time."

"Maybe after two murders," Raquel said hopefully, "they'll be more inclined to listen."

"You should talk with Samira and find out what they know."

"By now they must know what happened to their pimp."

"They may have known before we did."

"They're good at picking up signals."

"I wish we could pick up this guy's signal."

"I think I know where you're going with that," Raquel said, frowning, "and I don't like it."

"Are you suggesting," Fenly asked, "that we ask the next girl who goes with this guy to plant a tracker on him?"

"I was going to suggest it," Leandro said, "but Raquel got there ahead of me."

"Is it feasible?"

"It's feasible, but it's dangerous."

"You mean for the girl."

"For the whole operation. If they find out at this stage that we're tracking them, they could burn their bridges."

"I couldn't ask a girl to do that," Raquel said, shaking her head. "What if he caught her?"

"We know what would happen. So let's rule it out."

"We should plant the microphone in the apartment. I mean, if the girls agree to let us do it."

"If they agree, who would do it?"

"I could do it," Fenly said. "I could go there with Samira and pretend to be her client."

"I like that idea," Raquel said, "as long as you only pretend to be her client."

"Don't worry."

At that moment the phone on Leandro's desk rang. He picked

it up and concluded a short conversation by saying: "Please show him in."

Raquel raised her head in anticipation.

"It's our tail on Najib," Leandro said. "He has something to report to us."

A young man with black hair, wearing jeans and a black pullover, entered the office. Like many of the men his age he looked as if he had been up all night and hadn't shaved, so there was nothing remarkable about him.

Leandro introduced him as Mateo.

There were no extra chairs in the office, so Mateo delivered his report to them standing. "I know where he lives, and I know where he hangs out. But the interesting thing is that he had a meeting with a drug dealer."

"Where was this meeting?" Leandro asked.

"In a small café off Hortaleza."

"How do you know it was a drug dealer?"

"I know the guy. I helped the police arrest him once."

"Why isn't he in jail?"

Mateo shrugged. "He must have a good lawyer."

"What kind of drugs does he deal?" Raquel asked.

"The stuff from Morocco."

"What kind of volume?"

"Enough to hire a good lawyer."

"Who's tailing him now?"

"Simón. We're alternating."

"Twelve hour shifts?"

Mateo nodded.

"Did the drug dealer give him anything?" Raquel asked.

"He could have. They were sitting in a corner, and the dealer could have slipped him something under the table."

"It's Tuesday," Leandro said. "Would they have given him the money so soon?"

"Why wouldn't they?" Fenly asked.

"The longer he has the money on him, the more risk that he'll get caught with it."

"The only way he'll get caught with the money," Raquel said, "is if the police stop him to check his papers. And they have no reason to stop him. They all know him."

"I thought this guy dressed in different costumes."

"He does, but the police still recognize him."

"Whoever set up this operation," Fenly said, "must have seen Najib hanging out on Montera, and that made him an ideal candidate for his role."

Leandro nodded, and then he asked Mateo: "Where did he go after meeting with the dealer?"

"He went home," Mateo said. "Simón relieved me there."

"You said you know the drug dealer."

"We have his name, and we know where to find him."

"So we don't need to tail him. But keep a close eye on Najib," Leandro instructed the young man. "We don't want to let him out of our sight."

"Understood," Mateo said.

"And thanks for this information. It confirms that we're on the right track."

When Mateo had gone they reviewed their plan. They would look for the guy who had killed Lina and had also probably killed her pimp. If they spotted him before Thursday they would put a tail on him. If they didn't they would wait for him to go with a girl to the apartment on Thursday, and they would tail him after he came out and see where he delivered the money. If he didn't show up on Thursday, then that stage of the trail would be lost, and their only hope would be to find the French company, which they knew was a long shot.

As they waited for Samira in a holding room of the police station, Fenly asked: "Where do we get the microphone?"

"I already have it," Raquel said.

"When did you get it?"

"Leandro gave it to me while you were in the men's room."

"He doesn't waste any time."

"He doesn't." She smiled at him mischievously. "You think Leandro should have waited and given it to you while I was in the women's room?"

"No, you're the one who had the idea."

"Well, it's not a bad idea, and we only have to monitor the apartment when that guy is there. But we can't tell Samira who he is. If we do, then none of the girls will go with him. Though they should be grateful to him for one thing," Raquel added. "Their pimp was an asshole."

"You mean he fit our stereotypical view of pimps?"

"They're all assholes. But that pimp was one of the worst."

"Then why did those girls work for him?"

"They don't have much choice. It's not like they can interview candidates for the job."

At that moment Samira appeared, looking as if she were fed up. "Whenever you bring me here I lose money."

"I'll pay for your time," Raquel offered.

"You don't have to do that. Just stop bringing me here so often." Samira slumped morosely in the chair.

"So what do your colleagues say about what happened to your pimp?" Raquel asked her.

"They say he had it coming."

"What do they think about our idea of planting a microphone in the apartment?"

"They like the idea."

"*Bueno.* Then we'll do it."

"If you want, I can plant it for you."

"I don't want to get you too involved in this," Raquel said. "My colleague here will plant the microphone."

"How will he get into the apartment?"

"He'll go there with you."

"Will he pay me for my time?"

"Of course he will."

"I won't take long," Fenly said.

Samira smiled. "I never heard a guy admit that before."

"So let's do it now," Raquel said. "About fifteen minutes after you leave here, Fenly will walk up Montera. As he passes you, proposition him, and then take him to the apartment."

"I like the way you do business," Samira said, rising. "Do you want to be our new pimp?"

"No, thanks. I wouldn't be good at it. I'd set you all free."

When the girl had left, Raquel showed him the device. It was small enough to hide in your hand, but it had a powerful transmitter inside. She explained how he could stick it on the back of a chest or a wardrobe, and it would pick up any sound in the room.

He waited fifteen minutes, and then he walked up Montera, seeing the street from a whole new perspective. He passed the girls who lined the street, pretending to check them out but not stopping until he got to Samira. Aware of the fact that he was being watched not only by people on the street but also by Antonio's cameras, he engaged in a conversation with Samira, who opened by asking: "Would you like to have a good time?"

"Yeah. What can you do for me?"

"I can do everything."

"What do you charge?"

"For you only fifty euros."

He had no idea whether that was a good price or not, but he nodded, saying: "Okay. We're on. Where do we go?"

"Just follow me," Samira said, taking his hand.

She led him across the street and around the tables in front of Arizona and into Calle del Caballero de Gracia. He noticed that there was a church on the street, and he made a mental note of it. A few doors further down the street she stopped and used a key to open the outer door of a building.

On the second floor she unlocked the door of an apartment and let him in. It was a studio, with a door that evidently led into a bathroom. The main piece of furniture was a queen size bed that sagged in the middle. There was one bedside table with a lamp on it and a wardrobe against the wall to the right of the window. There were two chairs that looked as if they were in temporary positions.

The *persiana* was raised about a foot, and the window was open, but the air in the room was still laden with the rank smell of human effluents—an odor of despair that no perfume, no spray could cover.

"You could hide that thing in the wardrobe," Samira told him, stopping in front of it.

"Do your clients use it?"

"Some of them use it to hang up their jackets. But most of them leave their clothes on a chair, or on the floor."

"Why do you do this?"

"To make money."

"There are other ways to make money."

"I know, but they don't pay as well."

"You mean for work that a girl your age is allowed to do."

"You know what they pay for taking care of children?"

"If they pay less for taking care of children," Fenly said, "then the world has its priorities wrong."

"What world do you come from?"

"The same world you do."

"You're not from Morocco."

"I'm from the Bronx."

"I never heard of it," Samira said, "but I'm sure it's not as bad as Morocco."

"It's not. But it has poor neighborhoods."

"And you grew up in one of them?"

"Yeah. I grew up in a ghetto."

"How did you get out?"

"Someone helped me."

"Well, no one helped me."

"Raquel wants to help you."

"She can't help me."

"Why can't she?"

"She doesn't have money."

"She could get money."

"Come on," Samira urged him. "Plant that microphone. If I'd known you were going to lecture me, I would have charged you a lot more."

He went to the wardrobe and reached behind it and found a good place to stick the device. After checking to make sure it wouldn't fall he said: "Okay. It's planted."

"Then let's go. I hear someone coming up the stairs."

On the way down they passed a girl on her way up with a client, a balding man in a gray suit who averted his eyes as if he hoped it would make him invisible.

Pausing on the sidewalk with Samira, he said: "You should be in school."

"If I was in school, I wouldn't have money to pay for my rent, to pay for my food, to pay for my clothes, or to pay for my other expenses. I have no one to support me."

"What happened to your parents?"

"I don't know what happened to my father, but I can tell you what happened to my mother. She was hit by a bus on a street in Rabat, and she was crippled."

"Does she get help from the government?"

"No. The government doesn't do shit for her."

"Then how does she survive?"

"Her daughter supports her," Samira said, turning to go.

School started the week after his meeting with Stephen, and Fenly was now a freshman at the high school where kids in his neighborhood were assigned. The school was like an extension of the streets, so he felt at home there. He even recognized some members of the rival gang, who stuck together just as members of his gang stuck together. The school was open territory, but neither gang wanted it. If the school belonged to anyone it belonged to the girls, who occupied its rooms and halls as if they owned it.

Every day after school Fenly and Lázaro went to the center, where they did odd jobs to help Stephen and learned to play basketball. The center had a full-sized gym, which kids from the neighborhood used intensively. They organized themselves into teams and played without supervision until around four-thirty, when a tall black man arrived at the gym. He came to the center directly from work, wearing a suit, and he changed into sweats and joined them on the court, where he performed the dual roles of coach and referee. From the kids who played there every day he would select a team to represent the center in a neighborhood league, so they had a goal—to make the team.

Fenly and Lázaro had shot baskets but had never played in an organized format, so they were in a new element. The coach told them that they had talent but needed to work on passing, defending, and being team players. He kept stressing that he wasn't interested in brilliant solo play but in routine team play. The game, he said, was all about teamwork.

Fenly could see that Lázaro had more talent than he had, and he wasn't surprised when his friend made the starting lineup. He was happy to make the final cut as a second string forward. At least he would get to play in the games.

On the day that the coach posted the roster on a bulletin board outside the gym Stephen asked Fenly to come into the office, where they sat and talked.

"I see you made the roster," Stephen said.

"Yeah," Fenly said, proud of this accomplishment.

"You have talent for the sport."

"I don't have as much as Lázaro."

"But you also have talent in other areas."

"I do? What areas?"

"Areas that require education."

"Well, I'm going to school."

"What are you learning?"

He shrugged. "I don't know."

"What subjects are you taking?"

"English, math, and other subjects."

"Do they give you homework?"

"They give us reading assignments, but no one does them."

"Do they give you any writing assignments?" Stephen asked. "Or math assignments?"

"No. If they did, they'd have to correct them."

"Have you ever had an aptitude test?"

"What's that?"

"It's a test to see how much talent you have in these areas."

"What's the point of it?"

"To place you at a level where you'll be challenged."

"I think I'm being challenged enough."

"In life, yeah. But not in school."

"How can you tell?"

"From experience," Stephen said. "I'm a teacher. My students are a few years older than you, but they're coming from similar backgrounds."

"Where do you teach?"

"At St. Catherine. It's a college in Yonkers."

"I heard of that," he said politely. In fact, he hadn't. The only college he had ever heard of was the Rensselaer Polytechnic Institute, where his sister wanted to go.

"I want you to take an aptitude test," Stephen told him. "If I'm right about you, then we should think about getting you into a better high school."

"My sister goes to a better high school."

"What school does she go to?"

"The Bronx High School of Science."

"That's an excellent school. She must be bright."

"She's a brain," he said without admiration.

"Well, if your sister's bright, then there's a good chance that you're bright too."

"My mother doesn't think I'm bright."

"You can't blame her. You've done some stupid things."

"I guess I have. But she never said I was bright enough to get into the Bronx High School of Science."

"Did she ever say you *weren't* bright enough?"

He thought about it. "I guess she didn't."

"Where did your sister get the idea of applying to the Bronx High School of Science?"

"From a teacher, I think."

Stephen nodded as if he had expected this answer. "She got the idea from someone who knew about the school and could tell she had the talent."

"You mean," Fenly said, "she didn't get it from her mother."

"You can't get everything from your mother."

He realized that he had blamed his mother for not being able to give him everything, even before the emblematic sneakers.

"Or from your father," Stephen added as if to head him off from going there.

"Then where can I get the things I need?"

"You're never going to get everything you need, so the only solution is not to think about what you need but to think about what other people need."

"Other people?"

"There *are* other people in the world. People who have a harder time than you. People who don't have your talent for basketball and don't have your brains."

"So what are you saying?" he asked uncomfortably.

"I'm saying you'll be happier if you stop thinking about yourself and start thinking about other people, beginning with your mother."

"You don't know her."

"I don't have to know her."

He tried to understand. "You mean I should stop giving her a hard time and start helping her."

"That's right. You should try to make her life less difficult."

"Well, what about this test you want me to take? What does it have to do with her?"

"It would show your mother that you want to do something with your life."

"Is that what she needs?"

"Where you're concerned, yes."

"How do you know?"

"I've known a lot of mothers, including my own."

It was hard to imagine this older guy having a mother. "Were you a fuckup?"

"I wasn't a fuckup, but when I was your age I did some things that made my mother's life more difficult."

"Were you poor?"

"No. We were far from poor. But mothers are mothers, and kids are kids. The income level doesn't matter."

"If you have more money, you can buy more things."

"It's not about things."

"What's it about?"

"It's about people. It's about caring for other people and not thinking about yourself."

"So who am I taking this test for? My mother or myself?"

"For both of you. I think you'll find," Stephen told him after a pause, "that when you do things for other people, you also do them for yourself."

"He wants you to take an aptitude test?" his mother asked. They had finished eating dinner, and they were still sitting at the table. Jessi had excused herself to go and study. "Why?"

"To find out how bright I am."

"We know you're bright."

"How do you know?"

"You're my son. We have brains in the family."

"Then why aren't we rich?"

"Because I haven't used my brain any more than you have."

For a moment he thought about this statement, and then he asked: "Does Papi have brains?"

"He has shit for brains."

"Then why did you marry him?"

"I fell for him. I didn't use my brain."

"Are you sorry you married him?"

His mother sighed. "If I hadn't married him, I wouldn't have you and Jessi. So I'm not sorry. I'm just sorry that he turned out to be such a bum."

"Why did he leave us?"

"He ran off with another woman."

"He did? Is he still with her?"

"No. He left her for another woman."

"Does he have other children?"

"Not that I know of."

"Then why doesn't he send us money?"

"Because he doesn't have any."

"I heard he made a lot of money."

"That's what he tells people, but it's a load of bullshit."

"Well, I don't know if I should believe you."

"Believe what you want, but I'm telling you the truth. Your papi is a worthless bum. And my greatest fear is that you'll turn out exactly like him."

"You never told me that before."

"I didn't? Well, maybe I should have. Maybe I should have told you a lot of things before." His mother stared at the table for a long time, saying nothing. Finally she said: "So this man wants you to take a test to find out how bright you are."

"Yeah. He says I can take it at school."

"Then why didn't the school have you take it?"

"I don't know." He remembered skipping school on a day when they were supposed to take some kind of test, which could have been the one they were talking about.

"Who is this man anyway?"

"I told you. He runs a community center."

"Where does he live?"

"In Westchester."

"This man hasn't touched you, has he?" his mother asked suspiciously.

"No. He's not like that."

"How do you know?"

"He has a wife."

"That doesn't prove anything."

"Well, he's not a *maricón.*"

"Then why is he interested in you?"

"He wants to help me."

"I'd like to meet him."

"Fine. You can come and watch me play."

"Play what?" his mother asked.

"Basketball," he said proudly. "I made the team."

"You did? That's great." His mother gave him a rare smile. "I didn't know you played basketball."

When they got up from the table he said: "I'll help you wash the dishes."

His mother looked at him as if she wondered what had gotten into him, but she accepted his offer, saying: "*Gracias*. I really would like to meet this man."

"Did everything go all right?" Raquel asked, joining him at a table in front of Arizona.

"Yeah. I stuck the mike on the back of a wardrobe."

"As soon as he goes into the building we'll have a cop across the street with a listening device, ready to respond."

"I wish it was tonight. I hate having to wait until Thursday."

"I do too," Raquel said. "And there's nothing more we can do in the meantime."

"I think we have the bases covered."

"Bases covered? We wouldn't say that."

"What would you say? We have the bull surrounded?"

"No. We'd use an expression from a sport."

"Isn't bullfighting a sport?"

"No. It's a ceremony."

"A ceremony? Well, maybe we can go to a bullfight and you can explain it to me."

"The bullfighting season doesn't start until the middle of May. If you're here that long we could go then. But what are we going to do now?" It was nine in the morning.

"You could show me the city."

"You think we can take some time off?"

"Sure—as long as we keep our eye on the bull."

"You mean the ball."

He laughed. "Yeah. I'm ready for a drink."

They had a few glasses of wine at Arizona, and then she led him down Montera to Puerta del Sol and over Calle Mayor to Plaza Mayor. They paused and surveyed the hordes of people sitting at tables while she explained the historical significance of the plaza, including the fact that they once held bullfights there. Then, saying it was a place for tourists now, she led him through an archway and down some stairs and down Calle de Toledo and over to Calle de la Cava Baja, which was lined with bars and restaurants. After passing several of them she led him into a *tasca* that was packed with people mostly in their twenties. Some of the people recognized her and made way for her, so that she could get to the bar and order.

"Were you assigned to this area too?" Fenly asked when they had been served.

"No, this is where I came to play," Raquel said.

"You don't play anymore?"

"No. I stopped playing three years ago."

He didn't have to say that he had stopped playing almost six years ago. He could tell they were on the same wavelength.

They wandered the area going from bar to bar, drinking wine and occasionally eating *tapas*. They ended up in a Cuban place, which claimed to make the best *mojitos* in the city and also had a live band that played a variety of Latin music, including *salsas, merengues,* and *bachatas.* They started dancing to a *salsa*, which Raquel knew how to do, and he taught her how to do the *merengue* and the *bachata.*

It was after three when they returned to Calle Mayor, where they got a taxi. He told the driver that the first stop was in Malasaña and the second was at Gran Vía metro station.

As the driver shifted into forward Raquel said: "We don't have to go to Malasaña first. I'll get home safely."

"I'm trying to be a gentleman."

"You don't have to try. You *are* one."

"My mother tried to raise me well, but I always gave her a hard time—until I woke up."

"At least you woke up. Some people never wake up."

"What time is our meeting with Leandro?"

"It's at nine," she said. "You can take a *siesta* after lunch."

"I'll need it," he said, wondering how they got things done in this country.

Their meeting with Leandro was short, and they spent the rest of the morning at the Prado, where Raquel took him around and showed him the highlights. He lingered by the dark paintings of Goya, especially the one of the two primitive males beating the shit out of each other.

"I find this painting very upsetting," Raquel said.

"I know what you mean," Fenly said. "It reminds me of the time I saw two guys get into a fight over a parking spot. One guy was backing into it, and the other guy came from behind him and drove into the spot. They got out of their cars and yelled at each other. They pushed each other, they hit each other with their fists, and finally they got tire irons out of their trunks and whacked each other."

"What did you do?"

"I didn't do anything. I just watched them. I was about ten at the time. I thought it was normal male behavior."

"It is," she said. "Come on. I'll show you my favorite."

She led him to *Virgin with a Rosary* by Murillo. After standing in front of it for a moment of silence Raquel said: "The first time I saw this painting I thought it was my mother."

"Did your mother look like her?"

"Something like her. She had dark hair and dark eyes like her. His other Virgins look like ideal women, but this one looks like a real woman. A real mother."

They had lunch at a restaurant on Calle Ventura de la Vega which had an extensive *menu del día*. For only eleven euros you got a first course, a main course, a dessert, a glass of wine, and a coffee. As a main course Fenly had roast shoulder of lamb and Raquel had Dover sole.

As they left the restaurant Raquel said: "There's one more painting you should see. It's at the Reina Sofía."

"Sure," he said, going along with her.

They walked to the museum and inside they went directly to the painting. It was *Guernica*, the painting by Pablo Picasso that showed the horrors of bombing civilians in a war. It was based on a specific bombing in the Spanish Civil War, but it could have been any war.

"This was my brother's favorite painting," Raquel said. "If he had lived, he would have done a painting of what happened at Atocha. But he did do a painting about war."

"Where is it?"

"On the wall of a building near Plaza del Carmen."

"Your brother did that painting?"

"You've seen it?"

"Yeah. I walk by it all the time. I know the statement by heart now. Is that his statement?"

"You cannot achieve peace through war. If you want peace, work for social justice," Raquel recited. "Those are his words. But the idea is from every religion in the world. That's the meaning of the rainbow colors."

"Do you believe in that idea?"

"Yes. I do. But I'm not living by it."

"I'm not either. But we can't live by it now. We have to stop a terrorist attack."

"Well, maybe after we stop this attack," Raquel said hopefully, "we can live by it."

"Maybe," Fenly said, confronting the horror of war that the painting so forcefully conveyed.

The next morning they reviewed the plan with Leandro, and they spent the rest of the day making sure that everything was in place. If anything went wrong they wouldn't have another opportunity to tail the guy who picked up the money until Monday—if then.

They went directly from the meeting with Leandro to the surveillance office, which would be their base of operations. Sitting at the table and drinking coffee, they reviewed the plan in detail with Antonio and José.

"As soon as you spot Najib on the street," Raquel said, "you should be on the alert."

"I collected data from our pictures of him," José said. "His mean time of arrival is eleven ten, and the standard deviation is twenty minutes."

"So you know when to watch for him."

"The other guy arrives about an hour later."

"An hour later?" Antonio said. "Najib takes that long?"

"No, he only takes about twenty minutes."

"Then why is there so much time between them?"

"They want to make sure," Fenly said, "that the guy who picks up the money never runs into Najib."

"If Najib hides the envelope under the bed," Raquel said, "they don't have to worry about anyone finding it."

"I guess they don't want to take any chances," Antonio said.

"They didn't take any chances with Lina," Fenly said. "The guy who killed her waited until three in the morning, when no one would come to the apartment for a while."

"And no one did come for a half hour," Raquel said.

"How late do the girls stay on the street?" Fenly asked.

"A few of them stay there all night," José told him.

"To catch the early commuters," Antonio said.

"*Bueno*," Raquel said. "As soon as you spot the other guy you should signal me, and I'll contact the police."

"What will they do?" Antonio asked.

"The cop with the listening device will watch them go into Caballero de Gracia. He won't follow them until he sees them go into the building. And then he'll position himself across the street, ready to respond if the girl calls for help."

"If the guy only does his business as usual, won't it spook him when he comes out and sees a cop across the street?"

"The cop will be in plainclothes. He'll be standing there with the tail. They'll be acting like they're drunk, and they'll be arguing about soccer."

"You mean the cop will be a fan of Real Madrid and the tail will be a fan of Barcelona?"

"Actually, they'll be arguing about whether that goal by Messi yesterday was as great as the goal scored by Maradona in the 1986 World Cup."

"It was nowhere near as great," Antonio said.

"It was even greater," José said.

The two of them launched into a serious comparison, citing

technical, aesthetic, and other reasons why one goal was greater than the other.

Raquel let them argue for a while, and then she said: "You'll never settle that. So let's get back to business."

"It's a really great idea," Antonio said, "to have them arguing about that goal."

"It wasn't my idea," Raquel said. "It was my boss's."

"So when the guy sees them," José said, "he won't think twice about them. He'll go on his way unsuspecting, and the tail will follow him."

"That's what will happen. *Si Dios quiere.*"

After a pause Antonio asked: "Where will you guys be?"

"We'll be sitting at a table in front of Arizona."

"You can watch it all from there."

"Almost all," José said, referring to what might happen in the apartment.

They were at a table in front of Arizona by shortly before ten. They ate some *tapas* to keep them going but avoided drinking wine. Their interlude of play was over.

At five minutes before eleven, well within the standard deviation of his arrival times, Najib came walking around the corner from Gran Vía, passed the girls in front of McDonald's, and stopped at Samira.

They talked, using their hands, and then they came across Montera and headed into Caballero de Gracia.

"Well, let's see how long it takes him," Raquel said, checking her watch.

"You mean Najib?"

"No. The guy who picks up the money."

It took him an hour and ten minutes. From studying the guy's picture they both recognized him even from a distance. His identity was confirmed by a signal from Antonio, which beeped on the device that Raquel had set on the table. She used the device to signal to a cop in plainclothes who was loitering near the Gran Vía metro station.

The guy stopped and talked with a girl who belonged to Samira's late pimp. The girl, the other Romanian, chatted with the guy and waited for the girl who had gone to the apartment ahead of her to finish with the client.

When that girl returned, the girl with the guy who picked up the money led him across Montera. They passed about ten feet from where Raquel and Fenly were sitting.

"You know what?" Raquel said when they were beyond the range of hearing. "I think this guy's an American."

"You do? What gave you that idea?"

"Americans have something about them, and he had it."

"I thought you haven't known many Americans."

"I haven't. But I've arrested a lot of them."

"For drunk and disorderly conduct?"

"How did you guess?"

"It's the kind of trouble Americans get into."

"Yeah, you and the Irish and the English and the Germans."

"Don't forget the Canadians and the Russians."

"How could I forget them? You know what you all have in common? You all live in cold climates."

"Which makes us depressed?"

"Whatever it does, it makes you drunk and disorderly."

The loitering cop went into Caballero de Gracia, which meant that the couple had entered the building.

"Please don't let that guy hurt her," Raquel said, clasping her hands and raising her eyes in an attitude of prayer.

"Don't worry," Fenly said. "She knows what to do. And if anything happens, the cop will be there in a split second."

"I don't like using them."

"I don't either, but we have no choice."

"We say that to justify a lot of things, but most of the time we do have a choice."

"In this situation we don't. We have no other way of tracking that money."

Raquel stared anxiously toward Caballero de Gracia.

More than twenty minutes later the guy who picked up the money returned ahead of the girl, who they hoped was still in the bathroom waiting for him to get dressed.

The guy walked to Gran Vía, followed by a nondescript man.

As soon as they were out of sight Raquel got up and hurried toward the street where the guy had come from.

Before she got there the girl appeared, and it was clear from Raquel's body language that she was relieved. She waited for the girl and patted her shoulder, expressing her gratitude for what the girl had unwittingly done for them.

SIX

THE NEXT MORNING they met with Leandro, who already had some information for them.

"Our tail followed him home," Leandro told them, "so we know where he lives."

"Where does he live?" Raquel asked.

"In your area. Malasaña."

"Do we know the guy's name?" Fenly asked.

"No. He lives in a building that has eight apartments, so we have eight possible names."

"Are any of the names American?" Raquel asked.

Leandro looked at a paper on his desk. "There's a Smith."

"That's like García," Fenly said.

"What do you mean?"

"Smith is the most common last name in America."

"I read that García was going to become the most common last name in America," Leandro said.

"Either that or Rodriguez," Fenly said.

"So it's probably a fictitious name," Leandro said.

"Is that all the tail had to report?" Raquel asked.

"No. There's more. The guy—let's call him Smith—went out early this morning and took the metro to Gran Vía. From there he walked to an exchange office."

"An exchange office?" Fenly said, excited.

Leandro nodded. "It wasn't open yet, but the owner let him in, and they went into a back office, where they stayed for a half hour. Then Smith came out and walked to Calle de Tetuán, where he had a coffee. Then he went home."

"So that's where the guy delivered the money."

"You mean at the exchange office."

"I didn't mean at the coffee bar."

"An exchange office makes sense. It's a business that handles a lot of cash legitimately."

"It's a perfect conduit for laundering money."

"Exchange offices are regulated," Leandro said. "But people can always find ways around the regulations."

"If I had access to their bank account," Fenly said, "I could track the money."

"We're one step ahead of you. We sent a man over there after they opened. He bought a check, which has the name of their bank on it. And if you give me another half hour, you'll have remote access to their account."

"Where can I work?"

"You can work at your apartment. We have a tight security system there."

"It's as good as the military's," Raquel said.

"It's better," Leandro said.

"What about Smith?" Fenly asked. "I assume we're going to keep tailing him."

"We won't let him out of our sight."

"I don't want this guy to get away," Raquel said.

"He won't. Don't worry. But we don't want to spook them. And we could learn more by tailing him."

"Have we learned any more by tailing Najib?"

"We haven't yet. We're going to follow up on the drug dealer, but right now we have to focus on tracking the money."

They agreed on that priority.

A half hour later a computer geek on the special team, who could have been any nationality, gave Fenly the codes that would give him remote access to the exchange office's bank account, and Fenly went back to his apartment.

He sat at the dining table with his computer and tried the codes. They actually worked. Knowing so much about software systems, he was always a little surprised when they worked. People who didn't understand all the things that could go wrong with systems expected them to work and got angry or frustrated when they didn't.

He spent the next three hours examining transactions in the company's account. He examined the cash deposits, both in euros and in foreign currency, and he examined the payments and transfers. He found deposits that were large enough to include the money that they believed was being laundered, and he found transfers out of the country that were large enough to include that money. But he didn't find what he was looking for—payments to a French company or transfers to Russia, China, or Iran. So there was another step in the process.

He was wondering what they should do next when he heard the buzzer from the entrance of the building. It was Raquel, who had dropped by to see how he was doing.

He let Raquel into the building and opened the door of the apartment and waited for her to emerge from the elevator.

She was carrying a bag that looked familiar. As she entered the apartment she said: "I've brought something to eat. I thought you might be hungry."

"Thanks," he said, recognizing the bag from 100 Montaditos. He got two plates out of the cabinet over the stove and led her into the room where he had been working. They sat at the opposite end of the table from the computer.

"Those are ham and cheese," she said, pointing to two of the little sandwiches. "You said you liked them."

He took one of the sandwiches and put it onto his plate.

She waited for him to start eating.

"Well, I haven't found anything unusual in the account," he told her after taking a bite of his sandwich. "The transactions all look as if they were done in the normal course of business. There were deposits of foreign currency from people who changed money, and there were deposits in euros from people who sent money back home."

"You mean people like Samira."

"There were transfers to Morocco that could have been hers," Fenly said, knowing how she supported her mother.

"There should be a lot of transfers to Latin America," Raquel said, "especially Ecuador."

"Why Ecuador?"

"Almost thirty percent of the immigrants in Madrid are Ecuadorians."

"I did see a lot of transfers going to Ecuador, but I didn't pay much attention to them. I was looking for payments to a French company or transfers to Russia, China, or Iran. And I didn't find any, so there's another step in the process."

Raquel considered. "If a lot of transfers are going to Ecuador, they could be used to hide the money."

"Yeah. They could. And Ecuador would be convenient since its currency is the dollar."

"Where in Ecuador were the transfers going?"

"They were going to a bank in Guayaquil."

"They were all going to the same bank?"

"It's normal to use only one bank as a correspondent."

"Then you should focus on the bank there."

"I will, but I need more information. The account just shows the amount of the transfer and the name of the bank that received the money. It doesn't show where the money went at the other end of the transaction."

"The bank here would have that information, wouldn't it?"

"Yeah. It has to tell the bank in Ecuador what to do with the money at the other end."

"Well, you can get that information."

"I can if someone authorizes the bank to give it to me."

"Leandro will do that. What else should we do?"

"While we're following the money we should also work on the people who are involved in the process."

"If we make a move, it'll tip them off."

"I think they already know we're after them."

"I think so too," Raquel said. "Then we should start with the owner of the exchange office."

"I agree," Fenly said. "He has a bigger role than Najib or Smith. And he's a step closer to where the money goes."

"So let's go and talk with Leandro."

They polished off the last *montaditos* and left the apartment and headed for Chueca.

Without any preparation Fenly took the aptitude test under the supervision of a guidance counselor at his school, and he was surprised by the results, which placed him within the top five percentile in the nation.

Encouraged by Stephen, he took the admissions test for specialized public high schools, which assessed his ability to comprehend English prose, his ability to reach a reasoned conclusion for a verbal problem, and his problem-solving skills in mathematics. He did extremely well on the test, but there were other qualifications, including a good record of school attendance and good behavior. Evidently his work at the community center and a strong recommendation from Stephen helped to overcome those deficiencies, and in February he learned from his guidance counselor that he had been admitted to the Bronx High School of Science.

He entered as a sophomore. His sister was a senior, the top student in her class, and every time he had a teacher who had had her as a student he heard how wonderful his sister was, and he felt that he could never be as good. When he told Stephen about this feeling, Stephen advised him not to worry about being as good as someone else, but to be as good as he was capable of being. That would be enough. He applied this advice not only to school, where he couldn't compete with his sister, but also to basketball, where he couldn't compete with Lázaro, and in both situations he came out fine. The basketball team won the league championship, and he was accepted by Princeton.

He hadn't thought of applying to Princeton. He had planned to follow in the footsteps of his sister, who had gone to Rensselaer, but Stephen, an alumnus of Princeton, encouraged him to apply there. His guidance counselor firmly supported Stephen's assertion that Princeton had a top engineering school and helped him with the application, but advised him to apply also to several less competitive schools, implying that despite his academic record the chances of his getting into Princeton were slim. It didn't help that three other students in his class, who were excellent students, were applying to Princeton.

When he got into Princeton he wondered how much the decision to accept him might have been influenced by his being a minority and by Stephen's letter of recommendation, so he went to Princeton with the contradictory feelings of being a token minority and being a favored alumni legacy, instead of being there on his own merit.

The second feeling went away when he realized how many students came from privileged backgrounds, but the first feeling was aroused on more than one occasion.

Though his tuition, room, and board were fully covered by a scholarship, he still needed spending money, so he worked in the cafeteria cleaning tables and cooking short orders. It wasn't a bad job, and he could easily schedule his work hours around his classes. It also wasn't a bad place to meet people, especially girls, who eyed him across the counter while he scrambled eggs and fried bacon and made toast and grilled hamburgers.

One day in his freshman year, while he was cleaning tables, he overheard two men in suits who didn't look like faculty talking over coffee.

"They've given us a higher goal for minorities," the older man said as if he wasn't happy about it.

"Oh, no. It's hard enough to make the goal we have," the younger man said.

"Yeah, finding qualified women was easy."

"Where are we going to find more minorities?"

"In the high schools. There aren't enough of them anywhere else. If you find a black kid at Exeter, he has fifty other colleges after him."

"But there aren't many in the good suburban high schools."

"They're in the urban high schools," the older man said.

"How can we recruit from those schools?" the younger man asked. "A kid with an A average in one of those schools might have failed in a good school."

"There're huge differences between schools."

"How are the specialized public high schools in New York? Are they any good?"

"They're very good. They produce some good students."

"So if we had two applicants, a minority from a specialized public high school and a non-minority from a top private school, which applicant would we select?"

"If they had comparable test scores, we'd select them both."

"Well, what if the minority applicant had lower test scores, and we could accept only one of them?"

"We'd accept the more qualified applicant.

"You didn't answer my question."

"I can't. I'd need to know more about the applicants."

"So there *would* be room for judgment."

"There's always room for judgment."

"Then you can't tell me that if we have a higher goal for minorities, we wouldn't favor the minority applicant."

"It's a goal, not a quota. We don't have quotas."

"We have them for legacies."

"That's different."

Another incident occurred during the fall of his sophomore year. By then he had scored with a number of girls, who evidently were attracted to him because he was a minority—and maybe because their parents wouldn't have approved of him. With their encouragement he had learned to play the role of a badass Latino from the Bronx, and they loved it. They kept him so busy servicing them that his grade point average dipped a little before recovering.

One evening he was in the library, at a lower level, resting in a comfortable chair from his exertions that afternoon with a vigorous blond from Wisconsin, when he overheard two girls talking among the stacks.

"What do you find attractive about him?" one girl asked.

"He has a great body. It's lean and hard and sinewy, not plump or soft or hulky."

"Do you like the color of his skin?"

"Yeah. It's like dark roast coffee with cream in it."

"Is there anything else you like about him?"

"What else is there?"

"Brains, for example."

"If he didn't have brains, they wouldn't have admitted him to Princeton."

"They could have lowered their standards for him."

"You mean because he's a minority?"

"They do that everywhere."

"Well, he's as bright as anyone here. But I don't care about his brains. I just want a guy to fuck me. And Fenly knows how to fuck me."

For many students at Princeton the most traumatic experience was the process of being selected for an eating club, which they called Bicker. It occurred at the end of the fall semester of your sophomore year. In theory, the process assured that everyone who wanted to join a club was selected by one or assigned to one, but in fact there were people who ended up in a social limbo and having to make other arrangements for their meals.

Fenly didn't worry about Bicker. Though he wasn't a member of an athletic team or a political club or any other organized group, a lot of his classmates were attracted to him, not only the girls, and the top clubs competed fiercely to sign him up. He joined the club that agreed to take his roommate, who otherwise wouldn't have gotten a bid there.

The end of Bicker was celebrated by parties at the clubs, where the level of drinking was higher than usual. Fenly and his roommate were feeling no pain when they returned to their dormitory. While his roommate staggered up the stairs Fenly stopped in the bathroom, where he found a guy who lived down the hall from them standing in front of the mirror above the sinks. He noticed that the guy was crying, but he had an urgent need to relieve himself, so he reeled up to a urinal and unzipped the fly of his pants.

"I hope you're happy," the guy said as if he didn't mean it.

"What?" Fenly said, trying not to miss the urinal.

"It must have been great to know you could get into any club you wanted."

"I didn't know that."

"Yeah, you did. You knew they all wanted a token minority."

"That's not why they wanted me."

"Yeah, it was. Why else would they have wanted you?"

"I'm a cool guy," he said, zipping up.

"You're not a cool guy. You're a token minority."

"I'm sorry," he said, turning away from the urinal, "but you can't blame me for what happened to you."

"I can blame you for taking my place."

"What do you mean?"

"If they hadn't been forced to take a minority, they would have taken me."

"They weren't forced to take a minority."

"Yeah, they were. You don't know how it works."

He washed his hands and wiped them on his pants and glared into the mirror at the guy. He wanted to smack him for arousing the doubts that were always there in the back of his mind and for spoiling his night of celebration.

But then he heard a voice advising him not to and telling him that the guy wasn't worth it.

"If it makes you feel better," he said, facing the guy in the mirror, "you can believe whatever you want. But I don't see how it could make you feel better."

"That's because you've never been in my position."

"Oh, now you want me to feel sorry for you?"

"I only want you to understand."

"Where did you go to high school?"

"I went to a private school."

"Which school?"

"Andover."

"What does your father do for a living?"

"He's a lawyer in New York."

"Where do you live?"

"On Park Avenue."

"You know where I live?"

"No. Where?"

"I live in the Bronx."

"The Bronx?"

"Yeah. Have you ever been there?"

"No. I haven't."

"Well, you should go there and see what it's like. Then maybe *you* could understand, and maybe you could be happy that I got into the club."

"I would be happy if we both got into it."

"Would you want to be in a club that has minorities?"

"It only has a token minority."

Again Fenly wanted to smack him, but again he heard that voice, and he realized that he wasn't going to get anywhere with this guy. "I gotta go to bed. Goodnight."

"Goodnight," the guy said, still staring at himself in the mirror. It was as if he were hoping that the next morning he would awake and find that his not getting into a club had only been a nightmare.

A month later he got a phone call from his mother, who said: "I want you to come home this weekend."

"Why?" he asked. It flashed across his mind that his father might have reappeared. "Has something happened?"

"Yes. It's your sister."

"What happened to her?"

"I'd rather not say over the phone."

"It's a private line. No one's listening."

"Your sister's pregnant," his mother sobbed.

"What? Are you sure?"

"Yes. I'm sure. I had her tested."

"But she's supposed to graduate this June."

"She's not going to. She dropped out of college."

He should have felt vindicated. After all those years of his being the bad one and his sister being the good one, he should have felt some satisfaction. But he didn't feel anything like that. Instead, he felt sorry for his mother in a way that he never had before. He even felt sorry for his sister. "I'll be there on Friday. I don't have a class."

He took the dinky to Princeton Junction, then the train to Penn Station, and from there he took the subway home. He had been home for Christmas, and so had Jessi, but he hadn't noticed any sign of trouble. She had been her usual superior self.

He found her sitting at the kitchen table looking as if she had been convicted of a crime.

"Where's Mom?" he asked.

"She's at the bodega."

He opened the refrigerator and found a Presidente and opened it. He took a swig and sat down at the table, asking: "How're you doing?"

"Okay," she said glumly.

"I assume you didn't plan this."

"No. I didn't plan it."

"Then how did it happen?"

"I had sex with a guy."

"You weren't on the pill?"

"I didn't plan to have sex with him. In fact, it was the first time I ever had sex with anyone."

"Oh, man. What were you thinking?"

The tears started flowing. "I wasn't thinking. For once in my life I didn't want to think. I just wanted to feel something."

"I don't understand."

"You would if you were in my position. You don't know what it was like always having to be the good one. It's easy to be a fuckup, but it's hard to be good."

"So you felt like being bad for a change?"

"Yeah," she said, wiping a tear away from her cheek.

"Do you love this guy?"

She shook her head. "He's attractive, and he has a good body, but I'm not interested in him."

"You mean you just wanted him to fuck you?"

"Yeah. Is that so hard to understand?"

"No," he said, thinking of the girls he had overheard talking at Princeton. "I do understand. But I don't understand why you weren't on the pill."

"I didn't plan to have sex with him," his sister repeated.

"What are you going to do?" he asked her.

"I'm going to have the baby of course."

"What about the guy?"

"He doesn't know."

"Are you going to tell him?"

"No. I'm not."

"Why not?"

"I don't want to marry this guy. I don't love him, and also he reminds me of Papi."

"You remember Papi?"

"A little. I was four when he left."

"You never told me anything about him."

"We never talked."

"I guess we didn't. So how did this guy remind you of Papi?"

"He acted like women were put on earth to serve him."

"Is that how Papi acted?"

"That's how I remember him."

"Do you remember anything else about him?"

"Yeah. He smelled like rum and cigars."

"How did you know at the time it was rum?"

"I didn't. Mom told me later what it was."

"So she might have influenced your memory of him."

"She might have," Jessi said, "but it doesn't matter. That's how I remember him."

He envied her having a memory of their father, even if it wasn't a good one. "If you're not going to marry the guy, then how are you going to raise the baby?"

"I'm going to get a job, and Mom will help me for a while. And then I'm going to finish college."

"That's good. It would be a waste if you didn't."

"I know. You don't have to tell me that."

"Is there any way I can help?"

"Yeah. Mom told me you know a man who runs a community center in the neighborhood. Maybe I could work there."

"Doing what?"

"Taking care of children."

Fenly thought about it, and then he said: "He might be able to find you a better job than that. He has a lot of contacts in the business world."

"That would be great. You can tell him I almost have a degree in software engineering."

"Okay. I was going to see him anyway."

The next day he introduced his sister to Stephen, who got her a job at IBM. She worked there for two years before going back to college, and when she did IBM paid for it.

"Let's see if I have this right," Leandro said. "Smith delivers the cash to the exchange office, which deposits the money in its bank account and instructs its bank to transfer the money to a bank in Ecuador."

"That's right," Fenly said.

"How does the exchange office account for the cash?"

"The same way they account for the cash they get from immigrants who send money home to their families."

"But this cash didn't come from immigrants."

"It didn't, but they can pretend it did. They can use fictional names for the money transfers."

"Wouldn't they get caught?" Leandro asked.

"A lot of people who send money home are here illegally," Raquel said. "They're not in the system, so it would be hard to tell if the names were real or fictional."

"I guess it would be."

"An auditor checks the records of the exchange office," Fenly said, "he verifies that its transactions have been documented, and then he signs off."

"And no one's going to worry about a hundred euros here or there," Leandro said.

"No one except us."

"So what happens when the money gets to Ecuador?"

"That's what we have to find out. We can ask the bank here, but they're only going to tell us that the money was transferred to Ecuador for payment to a list of people there."

"They probably don't know where it's going."

"They probably don't," Fenly agreed. "But someone inside the bank in Ecuador knows where it's going."

"Then we have to talk with that bank," Leandro said.

"We do. But in the meantime Raquel and I think we should question the owner of the exchange office."

"What would you hope to get from him?"

"A description of the guy who set up the process."

"What if he never met that guy?"

"He must have met him," Raquel said. "And if we could find him we could move a lot faster."

"At the rate we're tracking the money," Fenly said, "it could take us more than a week to find out where it went, and we don't have much more than a week."

"If we question one of these guys," Leandro said, "we should question all of them."

"I agree," Raquel said. "We should question all of them at the same time, so they can't warn each other."

"As soon as we start questioning them," Leandro pointed out, "the guy who set up the process will hear about it."

"That could help us," Fenly said.

"How could it help us?"

"It could draw him out into the open."

"Why would he come out into the open?"

"To stop these guys from talking to us."

"But what if they don't know about the plot?"

"He still might want to stop them from talking to us," Raquel said. "I mean, if they can identify him."

"*Bueno*," Leandro said. "We question these guys, we learn as much as we can from them, we try to get a description of the guy who set up the process, and then we let them go to draw that guy out into the open."

"That's the idea," Fenly said.

"You don't mind using them as bait?"

"I mind using anyone as bait. But I'd rather use these guys for that purpose than anyone else."

"I'm with you there," Leandro said, nodding.

SEVEN

WITHIN AN HOUR Fenly was sitting at a metal desk in the transfer department of the bank, attended by a woman with a pleasant smile, who was introduced to him as the supervisor of outgoing foreign transfers.

She gave him access to the instructions that were sent with the money to the bank in Ecuador, and he spent the next two hours examining them. He would have liked to find the name of a French company, but he found what he expected—lists of individuals to be paid by the bank in Ecuador. So he looked for patterns among the recipients of the payments.

He limited his examination to transfers made on Tuesdays and Fridays, the days after the money was picked up, and he sorted the names of the recipients in alphabetical order. It didn't tell him anything other than the fact that a lot of recipients had the last names of García, Hernandez, López, Martinez, and Rodriguez, as he should have expected.

Most interesting, he found that the list of people receiving money on a given Tuesday or Friday was repeated four weeks later, so there were only eight lists of people who received money with uncanny regularity.

The recipients all had addresses, but they didn't have phone numbers, so the bank would have to notify them by mail that money had arrived for them and then wait for them to claim it. But if they were fictitious people they wouldn't ever claim the money, and it would go elsewhere.

When he examined the amounts of money being transferred, he found that the most common amount was a hundred euros, and that there was no amount larger than two hundred euros, so the amounts were small enough to avoid attention.

Estimating the volume of payments over the past three years at an average amount of one hundred fifty euros, he came up with a total of about five million euros.

That was enough to buy what they needed.

When he returned to the office in Chueca he found Raquel and Leandro sitting in the conference room with two men. He recognized one of them as the tail on Najib who had reported the meeting with the drug dealer.

"We've picked them up," Leandro said. "They're at the police station on Montera."

"That's convenient for us."

"I didn't want to drive anywhere in rush hour traffic."

It was seven-thirty. By that time in New York the rush hour was ending, but in Madrid it was only beginning.

"When are we going to question them?"

"Now. We were waiting for you."

"I found what I expected," Fenly said. "I need to talk with the bank in Ecuador."

"We already contacted them," Leandro said. "You can talk with them later tonight."

"How many hours are they behind us?"

"Seven. If you call them at eleven our time, they should be back from lunch by then."

"So let's go and question these guys."

Leandro thanked the two men, who had guided the police to Najib and Smith, and then they all left the office.

They walked to the police station, where they sat behind a one-way glass while an inspector questioned the owner of the exchange office. He was in his mid-fifties with thinning hair and a drooping mustache. His name was Moreno.

After getting the usual personal information the inspector asked: "Do you know a man named Smith?"

"No," Moreno said, shaking his head.

"Well, maybe we have the wrong name," the inspector said almost apologetically. "But this morning you opened your office early and let in a man who went with you into your back office. Do you remember that?"

"It didn't happen."

"We have a witness who will testify that it did happen."

"Maybe it did. But there's no law against opening my office early and letting someone in."

"There's a law against money laundering."

"I'm not involved in money laundering."

"We have evidence that you are, and if you don't cooperate with us, you could spend up to twenty years in jail."

"I don't know anything about it."

"Then I'll tell you about it," the inspector said, leaning toward him. "Every Tuesday and Friday a man delivers cash to your office. You deposit the cash in your account, and you ask your bank to send the money to a bank in Ecuador with instructions to pay a list of people there. It looks like a normal transaction, but the people on that list are fictitious. They don't exist, and they don't receive the money. Does that sound familiar?"

Moreno averted his sad eyes.

"I didn't hear your answer," the inspector said.

"I didn't say anything," Moreno said.

"You don't have to say anything. But as I said, if you don't cooperate with us—"

"All right," Moreno said as if he didn't want to hear again how many years he could spend in jail. "I'll tell you what I know."

"You won't regret it," the inspector said, sitting back in his chair and relieving the pressure on Moreno. "Now, let's start over. Do you know a man named Smith?"

"Yeah. He's the guy who delivers money to me every Tuesday and Friday."

"What nationality is he?"

"He's an American."

"How do you know?"

"He has an American accent."

"You mean when he speaks Spanish?"

"Yeah. He's fluent in Spanish, but he still has an accent."

"Then he must have lived here for a while."

"I don't know how long he's lived here, but he's been coming to my office for about three years."

"Delivering money?"

"Yeah," Moreno said hoarsely. "On Tuesday and Friday."

The inspector paused. "How did you meet him?"

"Another American introduced him to me."

"How do you know he was American?"

"I know how Americans talk."

"How do they talk?"

"They talk like they own the world."

"They do. Now, which of these guys did you meet first?"

"I met them at the same time."

"How did it happen?"

"They came to my office after I'd closed," Moreno recalled. "I'd put the sign on the door saying I was closed, but they ignored it. They acted like it didn't apply to them. That's another reason why I know they're Americans."

"What did they do?"

"They rapped on the door and insisted that I open it. They wouldn't go away, so I finally let them in."

"You weren't concerned that they might rob you?"

"They didn't look like robbers."

"What did they look like?"

"Businessmen. I thought they might make me an offer to buy my business."

"Did you want to sell it?"

"At the right price. I wanted to retire and go to the Canary Islands and live in peace."

"So you let them in, and then what happened?"

"They asked if there was somewhere we could talk, and I led them into the back office. They got right down to business, and they explained what they wanted me to do. It sounded like an easy way to make some extra money, so I agreed to do it."

"What's your cut?"

"Six percent."

"That's not a bad deal."

"They offered me three," Moreno said, "I asked for eight, and we settled at six."

"They must be Americans. If they were English, you never would have gotten above four."

Moreno momentarily looked proud of himself.

"So how many times did you see this guy?"

"The guy who introduced me to Smith? Just that one time."

"Do you know his name?"

"I don't know his last name, but Smith mentioned his first name while they were talking to each other in English."

"He did? What is it?"

"Daryl. And that's his real name."

"How do you know?" the inspector asked.

"Daryl told him not to mention his name again."

"You understand English?"

"More than I let on."

"Well, that must give you an advantage in your business."

"It does," Moreno said, looking pleased with himself.

"Did Daryl mention Smith's first name?"

"Yes. It's John."

"John Smith. That's probably a fictitious name."

Moreno shrugged. "I wouldn't know."

"Can you tell us anything more about Daryl?"

"I can give you a description."

"After three years?"

"I'm very good at remembering faces. It helps in my business. And I have a hobby," Moreno said. "It's something I want to do full time after I retire."

"What's your hobby?"

"Sketching faces."

The inspector leaned forward, maintaining his composure but betraying more than a flicker of interest. "Whose faces?"

"The faces of people who do business with me."

"I assume they don't sit for a portrait."

"No. I do it from memory."

"What happens with the sketches?"

"I keep them. You never know when they might be useful."

"You know what I'm going to ask you next."

"You're going to ask me if I have a sketch of Daryl."

"And you're going to tell me?"

"I'm going to tell you I might," Moreno said, "if you can make it worth my while."

"If you have one," the inspector said, "we could find it. We could tear apart your office."

"It's not in my office."

"We could tear apart your home."

"It's not at my home."

The inspector nodded as if he could see how Moreno had gotten six percent. "So let's talk about how we can make it worth your while."

After the interview they returned to the office in Chueca, where Fenly called the bank in Ecuador. He started with the president, who after a brief conversation turned him over to the internal auditor. He explained what he was looking for, and he agreed to email the dates of the transfers and the names of the recipients. The auditor said he would get started right away but would probably not have anything to report until Monday.

Fenly sent an email to the auditor, attaching the information on the transfers, and then he joined Raquel and Leandro in the latter's office.

"While you were talking with the bank," Leandro said, "I was talking with the inspector who interviewed Moreno. He thinks he can make a deal with the guy. So we could have a sketch of Daryl by tomorrow morning."

"Moreno could give us a sketch of anyone."

"I know he could. But we can verify his sketch. The police are going to make sketches based on descriptions from Smith and Najib, and we can see how they compare with the sketch that Moreno gives us."

"Well, let's hope those guys are good at remembering faces. They might not have seen Daryl in three years."

"I wonder about that," Raquel said. "I know he's smart, but imagine having an operation that runs so smoothly that you never have to worry about it."

"I can't imagine such an operation," Leandro said.

"I can't either," Fenly said, remembering the screw-ups where he had worked.

"Something must have gone wrong at some point," Raquel said, "and Daryl must have had to deal with it."

"He must keep an eye on the operation," Leandro said.

"If he does," Fenly said, "then he could keep an eye on us."

"So maybe it's a good thing we picked up those guys."

"Before he killed them," Raquel said, completing the thought.

Fenly saw another possibility. "If he's keeping an eye on his couriers, he could have killed Lina."

"Smith was the last guy to go with her," Leandro said.

"I know he was, but suppose Smith came out of the building and Daryl was standing across the street. Our cameras wouldn't have spotted him. They're aimed at Montera."

Leandro rubbed his chin reflectively. "You think Smith told Daryl about the problem with Lina?"

"He could have, and Daryl could have come back with him at three in the morning."

"If that's what happened," Raquel said, "then Smith saw Daryl recently, and he could give us a good description."

"Good enough," Fenly said, "to verify Moreno's sketch."

"I'll call the inspector," Leandro said, reaching for the phone. "I'll ask him to pursue that line of questioning with Smith. And then I'm going home."

"What time would you like to meet tomorrow?"

"Let's say eleven. We won't have anything before then."

Fenly and Raquel left the office and walked to the plaza on Mesonero Romanos. They sat at a table where they could talk privately. They ordered drinks and a *tortilla*.

"You don't look happy," Raquel said.

"I'm thinking about those two Americans."

"You mean Smith and Daryl."

"I can't understand why they would get involved in a plot to attack their own country."

"Maybe they're only involved in the money laundering. Maybe they don't know what the money's being used for."

"Maybe Smith doesn't know. He's only a courier, picking up money in one place and delivering it to another place. But the guy who set up the laundering process would know what the money's being used for, wouldn't he?"

"Not necessarily," Raquel said.

"Then who does know?"

"Some pervert like Osama bin Laden."

"I like your word for him. Did you see those video shots of him after the attack? He was holding a rifle, fondling it like he was jerking off."

"I remember seeing that. It made me think of the perverts I encountered in my job."

"Well, let's assume that some pervert like Osama bin Laden is behind the whole thing, and that Daryl is simply laundering the money. Let's assume that Daryl gets fifteen percent, minus the six percent he pays Moreno and minus what he pays Smith and Najib, say two percent for each of them. So he would get two hundred fifty thousand euros over three years."

"That doesn't sound bad."

He refrained from telling her what kind of bonuses he received while he was on Wall Street. "It's not bad, but it's not enough money for killing people."

"No amount of money is enough for killing people," Raquel said. "Though I've seen people killed for ten euros."

"I've seen people killed for nothing," he said, remembering what had happened to Ramón.

"So you don't think he's doing it for money."

"I think the other guys are, but I don't think he is."

"Then what's he doing it for?"

"I don't know. I just have the feeling that he's doing it for some other reason."

"Maybe he's doing it for vengeance."

"If he is, then he knows what the money's being used for."

"He knows it's not being used to help the poor."

"He knows they have something evil in mind for America. And maybe that's enough for him. Maybe he doesn't know exactly what they plan to do."

"Then it won't help that much to catch him."

"That's why we have to keep following the money."

They were both tired, so after they finished their drinks and the *tortilla* they headed home. Raquel took the metro to Malasaña, and Fenly walked to his apartment building.

Before going to bed he watched CNN for a while. They were still following the story of the kid who had massacred thirty-two people at Virginia Tech. They showed some footage of video tape that the kid had taken of himself, explaining why he had done it and bringing God into it, portraying himself as a savior. Fenly supposed that the guys who steered the planes into the towers of the World Trade Center saw themselves as saviors, and he wondered if the guys who were planning the next attack on America saw themselves as saviors.

If you saw yourself as a savior, then you could justify anything. But were such people really capable of using their rational faculties to justify things? Were they not like kids playing video games in which they blasted hundreds of people without a second thought? Did the kid at Virginia Tech know the difference between the real people he was killing and the digital people in video games? Did the guys steering the planes into the Twin Towers know the difference? Did they know the value of a human life?

The kid who massacred the people at Virginia Tech was from an immigrant family, and his parents were working hard to make a better life for their children. Though Fenly had something in common with that kid, he couldn't imagine himself going on a murderous rampage. Despite his being a juvenile delinquent, something had prevented him from becoming a gang leader, a drug dealer, or a terrorist. As he looked back he could see that for him the turning point had been watching Ramón bleed to death. It had shown him what happened to real people when they got shot with real bullets.

At the end of his sophomore year Fenly changed his major from engineering to economics. He had finally taken the required course in economics, and much to his surprise it had turned him on. When the professor explained game theory a whole new world opened up, and with this professor as his advisor he wrote his senior thesis on the applications of game theory to resource acquisition strategies in a market characterized by imperfect competition. The thesis not only won him an award, but it also got him a job offer from a major oil company.

He graduated Phi Beta Kappa and Summa cum Laude from Princeton with his mother, his sister, and Stephen attending the ceremony. When he saw them together he realized that he owed something to each of them, including his sister who had proven that a girl with a single parent who hadn't gone beyond eighth grade could get into the Bronx High School of Science and into Rensselaer and then after dropping out to have a baby go back and finish college and start working on a master's degree while holding a job at IBM. Without his sister leading the way he might never have imagined that he could do it.

He turned down the job at the oil company and went to the Wharton School for a master's in finance. Upon completing this degree he had job offers from Exxon, Citicorp, Morgan Stanley, and other notable firms, and by then it barely occurred to him that they might want to hire him because he was a minority. After some deliberation he accepted a job with a major securities dealer, which offered him a bonus as well as a salary and an opportunity to use his mind in devising strategies for trading, positioning, and risk management. The company's office was on an upper floor in the south tower of the World Trade Center.

Three years later he got his first seven-figure bonus. He bought a two-bedroom condo for himself in Tribeca. He bought a condo for his mother in Yonkers in a neighborhood where the main language was Spanish. He helped his sister buy a house in Yorktown within ten minutes of where she worked. And he donated money to Stephen's center.

A week after his twenty-sixth birthday he was relaxing in his apartment, listening to music, when he heard the buzzer from the entrance of the building. It was Sunday evening, and he wasn't expecting anyone, so he assumed that someone had pressed the wrong button. But the buzzer sounded again and again, and he finally went to the intercom to see who it was.

"Hello? Who is it?" he said in English.

"*Tu padre*," said a voice that he didn't recognize.

"Hey, that's not funny."

"It's not a joke," the voice said in Spanish. "Let me in."

He hesitated, wondering if it was a thief who gained entrance to buildings by claiming to be the father of people who lived in them. "Prove you're my father."

"Your name is Fenly. You were born in 1973."

"What's my sister's name, and when was she born?"

"Yesenia. She was born in 1971."

He pressed the button to open the door, still having doubts. He went and got a baseball bat that his uncle had given him years ago. With the bat in hand he opened the door to his apartment and looked toward the elevator.

A man in a shabby raincoat got out of the elevator. When he spotted Fenly he grinned widely, revealing neglected teeth. He staggered toward Fenly.

"Son," he said, extending his arms for an *abrazo*.

Fenly raised the bat in warning.

Seeing it, the man was shocked. "Is this any way to greet your father?"

"I still don't know if you *are* my father."

"You don't? All right." The man unbuttoned the top of his raincoat and reached into an inner pocket and pulled out a Dominican passport, which he opened and held out to Fenly. "Now, look at that. What does it say?"

"Franklyn Aquino," Fenly read.

"That's me, your father."

Fenly examined the picture in the passport and then the man. The man in the picture looked better than the man standing before him, but they were undoubtedly the same man.

"So are you going to let me into your apartment?"

"Yeah," he said reluctantly, stepping back.

As he let the man pass he smelled rum.

He closed the door, still holding the bat, and watched the man go into the living room.

"You have a nice place," the man said, glancing around.

"Why did you come here?" Fenly asked.

"I came to see you."

"You haven't come to see me since you left twenty-four years ago. Why now?"

"I would have come sooner," the man said, unbuttoning his raincoat the rest of the way, "but I didn't have the money to buy a plane ticket."

"I thought you were rich."

"Who told you that?"

"I heard it from people in the neighborhood."

"I don't know where they got that idea."

"Someone must have given it to them."

"I used to be rich," the man said, "but I trusted a man to manage my money, and he swindled me out of everything I had. So now I have nothing."

"And you heard that I was making a lot of money."

"I did hear that. It made me feel proud of you."

"You must have heard some other things that made you feel proud of me. So why didn't you come to see me before?"

"I told you. I didn't have the money to buy a plane ticket."

"You just said you used to be rich. You had the money then."

"I had trouble getting a visa," the man said lamely.

"Why would you have had trouble getting a visa? You were an American resident."

"I lost my rights when I went back to Santo Domingo."

"So how did you get a visa now?"

"It wasn't easy. It took me a year. You have no idea how hard it was, not only to get the visa but also to get the money for the plane ticket."

Fenly said nothing. He realized that the man standing in his living room was the person his mother had always described, not the person he had imagined.

"Do you mind if I sit down?" the man asked.

"No. Go ahead."

The man removed his raincoat and draped it over a chair and then sat down on the sofa without leaning back. He was wearing khaki pants and a navy blue jacket that could have been a uniform. His white shirt looked as if he had slept in it.

"When did you arrive?" Fenly asked.

"Yesterday evening."

"Where are you staying?"

"At a friend's place in Alta Manhattan."

"You still have friends here?"

"Well, this guy goes back and forth. His family lives there, but he keeps an apartment here for his business activities."

"Are you involved in his business activities?"

"Oh, no. I'm not involved in anything."

"Do you have a job?"

"I work now and then at the hotels."

"So you're on vacation now?"

The man smiled. "Yeah. I'm on vacation."

"How long do you plan to stay?"

"Until I get what I came for."

"You mean money."

"Well, children are supposed to take care of their parents."

"Parents are supposed to take care of their children."

"I gave you life. If it weren't for me you wouldn't exist, and you wouldn't be where you are now."

"I almost didn't make it."

"But you did make it."

"No thanks to you."

The man leaned back into the sofa. "I hear you bought a house for your mother."

"She deserved it."

"And you helped your sister buy a house."

"She deserved it too."

"Then you should buy a house for me."

"Why should I?"

"You remember the parable about the prodigal father?"

"I remember the one about the prodigal son."

"It's the same idea," the man said. "I was lost to you, and now I've been found."

Fenly shook his head in wonder, realizing that the man was clever and knew how to take advantage of a situation. "What do you need?"

"I don't need much. On the island I could build a palace for twenty thousand dollars, and I could live like a king for three hundred dollars a month."

It wasn't a lot, considering that Fenly made three hundred dollars an hour, and he could write a check for twenty thousand. "Is that the deal?"

"That's the deal. You give me that, and I'll get lost again."

"I wouldn't ask you to get lost again."

"But you'd want me to," the man told him.

"I don't know what I'd want you to do," Fenly said. "I don't know you."

"You don't want to know me. Take my word for it."

"Well, I should decide if I want to know you."

The man shrugged. "I don't care. I just want the money."

The next morning he went out and bought a newspaper and got some things at the grocery store, including a fresh roll for breakfast. Back in the apartment, he made a pot of coffee and sat at the table, eating and reading the newspaper, which continued to run a story on the front page about the trial of the people accused of being involved in 11-M.

He took a shower and dressed and left the apartment and walked to Gran Vía. There were fewer people on the street, and most of them were probably shopping since it was Saturday. He waited for the light and crossed Gran Vía with the shoppers, following two middle-aged women in conservative skirts and sensible shoes, who represented a different generation from the girls in tight jeans and stylish footwear. The women headed left on

Gran Vía, and Fenly headed straight on Fuencarral, following a young gay couple, who bounced along with their arms around each other's waist.

He found Leandro in his office with papers spread out in front of him on the surface of his desk.

"Would you like some coffee?" Leandro asked.

"No, thanks. I just had some," Fenly said.

"Well, come around and look at these."

Fenly went around the desk so that he was standing next to where Leandro was sitting. The papers on the desk were sketches. There were three of them, with the one in the middle the most finished, the most professional.

"What do you see?" Leandro asked.

"I see three sketches of the same person."

"The one in the middle was done by Moreno, and the ones on the left and the right were done by a police artist, based on descriptions by Smith and Najib."

"Is the one on the right based on the description by Smith?"

"Yeah. How did you guess?"

"It's closer to the one by Moreno," Fenly said, "and Smith saw Daryl more recently."

"You mean we think he saw him more recently."

"You're right. We don't know that."

"A major challenge when you're doing an investigation is maintaining the distinction between what you know and what you only think you know."

"Well, we know what this guy looks like now."

"We do know that. And we're giving this sketch to every police unit in Spain."

"What else are you doing with it?"

"We're sending it to all the international agencies, including yours, in the hope that they can identify him and tell us something about him."

At that moment Raquel appeared with two cups of coffee. She handed one of them to Leandro and told Fenly: "If you want coffee, you can have this one."

"No, thanks," he told her.

"I was just telling Fenly what we're doing with the sketch," Leandro said.

"Could I see it?" Raquel asked, having sat down in front of the desk.

Leandro handed it to her.

Fenly came around the desk and sat down next to her.

After gazing at the sketch for a while she said: "You can tell this guy's an American."

"You can? How?" Leandro asked.

"It's there at the surface, everything he is."

"Are you saying that Americans have no depth?" Fenly asked.

"I'm saying that you can see in their faces what they are."

"Can you see in my face what I am?"

"I'm not talking about you," Raquel said. "I'm talking about typical Americans."

"You got yourself out of that one deftly," Leandro said. "And right into another one."

"I'm not typical?" Fenly teased her.

"You know what I mean," Raquel told him. "I mean typical Americans, like the ones you see in the movies. Good looking and short on brains."

"Well, this guy isn't short on brains," Leandro said.

"Maybe he isn't, but he looks like he is."

"The better to fool people like you."

"I do see what you mean," Fenly said, looking at the sketch. "You could spot him on the street as an American."

"That's what I'm hoping the police will do," Leandro said.

"As soon as we're done," Raquel said, "I want to show this sketch to Samira."

"We're done," Leandro said, "except for one thing. Are we still going to let these guys go?"

"I don't see what we would gain by holding them," Fenly said. "They can't tell us anything about the attack."

"But if we catch Daryl, they can testify against him. If he kills them, they can't."

"Then we have a choice," Raquel said, "between using these

guys as witnesses and using them as bait."

"Which could be a choice," Leandro said, "between bringing Daryl to justice and stopping the attack."

"If that's the choice," Fenly said, "it's a no brainer. Our top priority is to stop the attack."

"I agree," Raquel said.

"Then we'll let them go," Leandro said, "and hope that Daryl comes after them."

Before they left the office Raquel contacted a policewoman on Montera and asked her to bring Samira to the station.

When they got there Samira was in the holding room.

"Did you catch the guy?" the girl asked them.

"We think we did," Raquel said. "But we're going to leave the microphone in the apartment, just in case."

"I don't mind."

Raquel took a copy of the sketch out of her shoulder bag and handed it to the girl. "Have you ever seen this guy?"

Samira examined the sketch and said: "Yes."

"Where have you seen him?"

"On the street."

"Have you ever gone with him?"

"No. I never have."

"Have you seen him go with another girl?"

"No. At first I thought he was a pimp, but I asked around, and no one belongs to him."

"So what does he do?"

"He walks up and down Montera. And he hangs out by the metro station."

"Have you ever seen him go into a building?"

"I've seen him go into McDonald's. And I've seen him go into the street where we have the apartment."

"Really? Did you see him go there last Tuesday?"

"You mean the night that Lina was killed?"

"Yes. Try to remember."

Samira frowned. "I can't remember."

"*Bueno.* You can go now. Thanks for your help. And please be careful," Raquel added.

When the girl had gone Fenly said: "I think this guy might live on Montera."

"It would make sense. He could watch the street from his apartment and keep an eye on his couriers."

"And we could keep an eye on him."

They exchanged a mutual look, and they raced out of the police station with the same thought in mind.

EIGHT

"IT'S NICE TO see you," Antonio said after opening the door. "Where have you been?"

"We've been working," Raquel said.

"Well, we've been idle, so I hope you have something for us to do." Antonio led them to the table, on top of which there were pictures of a flamboyant blond woman.

"Who's she?" Raquel asked.

"Guess," Antonio said.

"A famous singer?"

"No. A famous drag queen."

"What was she doing on Montera?"

"Hoping someone would take her picture."

"We do have something for you to do," Raquel said. She took the sketch out of her bag and handed it to Antonio.

"Who's he?" Antonio asked.

"We think he's the mastermind."

"He doesn't look like a mastermind."

"What does he look like?"

"A dumb American."

"Have you ever seen him?" Raquel asked.

"I don't know. I've seen people who look like him."

"Well, we want you to go through all your pictures and see if you can find him."

"You think he hangs out on Montera?"

"I think he lives here," Fenly said.

"Why would he want to live on Montera?"

"To keep an eye on his couriers."

"We want any pictures you have of him," Raquel said, "but we especially want a picture that shows where he lives."

"You mean a picture of him going into a building."

"Let's look at the possibilities."

Joined by José, they went to a window and looked across the street. Within their view there were several possible buildings with apartments above the stores.

"If he lives above McDonald's," Antonio said, "he's already being punished for his sins. Imagine going to bed with the smell of their French fries."

"That's my idea of heaven," José said.

Raquel stepped back from the window and phoned her police contact and asked him not only to watch all the buildings on Montera but also to show the sketch of Daryl to all the *porteros*.

When she returned to the window Antonio said: "I assume that while we're looking for his picture, you want us to watch for him on the street."

"We want to find him one way or another."

"What about the other guys?"

"We picked them up for questioning, but we let them go."

"We're hoping he'll come after them," Fenly explained.

Antonio nodded as if he understood. "Then we'll watch for them. We might spot him following one of them."

"I hope we do," Raquel said, turning from the window.

Since at this point there was nothing else they could do, Raquel and Fenly joined Antonio and José at the table, and for the next two hours they scanned the pictures, each of them covering a different period of time. In particular they looked for pictures of people going into buildings across the street.

Around two-thirty José asked: "Is anyone hungry?"

"I am," Raquel said. "I skipped breakfast."

"Does anyone feel like a Big Mac?"

"Yuck," Antonio said. "Let's stick with the *montaditos*."

"They only have chips, not French fries."

"Chips are just as bad for you, so they should satisfy your self-destructive urge."

"I vote for the *montaditos*," Raquel told them.

Antonio got up and found a menu from 100 Montaditos and filled out their order and read it back to them.

José volunteered to go and get it.

"You know," Raquel said while they were waiting for him to return, "they're all beginning to look alike to me."

"I thought his face was distinctively American," Fenly said.

"It is, but they're all beginning to look American."

"I know what you mean," Antonio said. "The whole world is beginning to look American. On every corner of every city you see a McDonald's or a Starbucks or one of those chains. Thank God for 100 Montaditos."

"But they're a Spanish version of fast food," Raquel said.

"Who said that fast food was American?"

"I guess it's not. We've always had *tapas* in Spain. When did McDonald's start in America?"

"I think it started in the sixties," Fenly said. "I know it was around before I was born, though we didn't have them in my neighborhood."

"What did you have?"

"Places where you could get *cuchifritos.*"

"*Cuchifritos?*" Antonio said warily.

"Yeah, fried things like pork skin and stuffed potato balls."

"Is that Dominican food?" Raquel asked.

"It's really Puerto Rican, but they were in the Bronx first so we ate their food."

"Our *cuchifritos* are fried lamb or fried goat meat."

"The latest thing here is Turkish food," Antonio said. "We have kebab places everywhere."

"Are there a lot of Turks here?"

"You'd think there were millions, but there aren't that many. It's like all the Turks have kebab places."

José returned with a large bag from 100 Montaditos and a small bag from McDonald's, which he set on the table in front of himself and opened with glee.

"I wondered why you volunteered to get the food," Antonio said, waving away the smell of French fries.

"If I'm going to work all night on this project," José said, "I need something to keep me going."

They took a break to eat, and then they resumed looking at the pictures.

A half hour later Raquel got a call from her police contact.

Fenly could tell from her expression as she listened that the police had nothing to report. When she was finished he asked: "Did they show the sketch to the *porteros?*"

"They showed it to the *porteros* they could find. It's Saturday, so most of them are off."

"I should have been a *portero,*" José said, flipping a picture.

"Can you fix a broken washing machine?"

José shook his head. "I don't know mechanical things, I only know electronics."

"Then you could never be a *portero.*"

Shortly after six Antonio slapped his hand on the table.

The others looked up.

"I found him. I have him going into a building."

Taking the picture with him, Antonio got up and headed for the window.

The others got up and followed him.

"It's that building," Antonio said, pointing to an old building directly across the street from them.

They looked at the picture.

A man in a suit was opening the door with his head turned to talk with someone.

"Let's blow that up and make sure," Raquel said.

They followed Antonio into the other room, where José sat down at his computer and found the picture in a file. He enlarged it, printed it, and handed it to Antonio.

"That's him," Antonio said.

"It's lucky he turned to talk with someone," Fenly said. "If he hadn't, we wouldn't have seen his face."

"Let's see who it was," José said. He expanded the scene and printed a picture.

"It's one of the girls," Raquel said.

"It's the one who stands in front of that building," Antonio said. "A Romanian girl."

"He was probably telling her to stand somewhere else."

"Like he has no use for prostitutes."

"I'll ask Leandro what he wants to do," Raquel said, stepping back from the window.

They waited while she called Leandro and talked with him. After telling her boss what they had found she mainly listened without comments, so it was hard to guess what he was saying. When she had finished they looked at her expectantly.

"He said we should watch for him and not take our eyes off that building."

"I could have told you that," Antonio sniffed.

Raquel ignored him. "He considered going into the building and waiting for him, but he doesn't want to spook him, so for now we'll wait outside."

"He could be in his apartment," Fenly said.

"He could be. But sooner or later he has to come out."

"Maybe he only comes out at night."

"Like a vampire," José said.

"A lot of people who aren't vampires," Antonio said, "only come out at night."

"Leandro will talk to the rental agent," Raquel resumed, "and find out which apartment he's in."

"The *portero* would know," Antonio said.

"The *portero* is probably off today."

"The lucky guy," José said.

Raquel called her police contact and told him which building to watch. By now it was almost seven.

"Let's go down to Arizona," Fenly suggested, "so that we can have a front row seat."

"That's a good idea," Raquel said.

They left Antonio and José, who would watch the building and scan Montera with their cameras. If they spotted Daryl, they would contact Raquel.

At Arizona they found a table and ordered coffee.

Fenly gazed across the street and spotted the girl that Daryl had been talking with. She had blond hair, a short skirt, and long legs. She loitered in front of the building to the left of its entrance, swaying toward a likely prospect when he walked by and evidently propositioning him. The guy appraised her and kept going.

"I wonder what it feels like," Fenly said.

"What do you mean?" Raquel asked.

"Being rejected by a guy you've propositioned."

"You've never been rejected?"

"Yeah. I have." He remembered his first date with Camila. "But they must be rejected a hundred times per day."

"A salesman experiences the same thing."

"How do you know?"

"I dated a salesman. He had good days and bad days."

"But this is different. They're selling themselves."

"He was selling himself too."

"Well, he wasn't selling his body."

"He was selling his personality. I think it's harder to detach yourself from your personality than from your body."

"Maybe it is, but I don't know."

"I don't know either," Raquel said. "I'm just telling you what the girls have told me."

"You said that when you worked in vice you tried to protect them. Is that what your bosses wanted you to do?"

"They wanted me to maintain order. But if a girl got hurt, it would be in the newspapers, so they went along with the idea of protecting the girls."

"They wanted to protect themselves."

"That's all they ever want."

"I guess it is," Fenly said, thinking about the guy he worked for. "Above a certain level it's always political."

"So my bosses let me protect the girls," Raquel said, picking up where they had left off. "But when I tried to do more for them I ran into obstacles."

"What did you try to do for them?"

"I tried to help them find other ways to make a living."

"What kind of obstacles did you run into?"

"Bureaucratic obstacles."

"Yeah, I can imagine."

"I also ran into the myth that prostitution is a necessary evil, though they didn't call it that."

"What did they call it?"

"They called it a safety valve for men. They said it allows men to blow off steam without affecting society."

"But it does affect society."

"It does," she said with deep feeling. "It corrupts people, it spreads disease, and it degrades the girls to a level where they lose the spirit that makes us human."

"Did you ever consider being a social worker?"

"Yes. I was seriously considering it. But then came 11-M, and everything changed."

They observed a moment of silence, keeping their eyes on the entrance of the building, along with Antonio, José, and the cops on the plaza.

"I wish I could get Samira off the street."

"I could give her enough money to live on and support her mother while she learns a new profession."

"Why would you do that? You don't even know her."

"I know how you feel about her."

Raquel took her eye off the building for a moment and gazed with concern at Samira, who was standing in her usual place on the street. "I do want to help her."

"Then think about it."

She looked at him as if she were seeing him as a true friend. "I will. *Gracias.*"

They sat there watching the entrance of the building until the waiter started collecting the chairs and piling them around a tree. At that point they paid the check and went to see how Antonio and José were doing.

Antonio was staring at a monitor, and José was taking a break, playing a game on a hand-held device, completely engrossed in it.

"What a totally depressing way to spend a Saturday night," Antonio complained.

"It's too early for anything to be happening," Raquel said, "so you're not missing anything."

"If he doesn't appear by three, I will."

"If he doesn't, you can go. The police will still be watching the building."

"I think José was right. This guy's a vampire."

To be supportive they stayed with Antonio and José until after three. By then it was too late for public transportation, so Raquel shared a taxi with the two guys, who also lived in Malasaña.

Crossing the street, Fenly noticed that the Romanian girl was still standing in front of the building where Daryl lived.

He was waiting in the elevator, which would rise like a rocket for eighty floors before stopping, when a girl strolled in. She was wearing a green dress with a white sweater draped over her shoulders. She had flowing dark hair and dark eyes, which had an expression that warned you not to take her lightly. She looked right through him with those eyes and then turned her back to him and faced the closing door.

He gazed at her head, observing the rich color of her hair and inhaling a soft perfume that made him think of spring. He was still reeling from their frontal encounter, feeling as if he had accidently touched a live wire. He had learned in a physics course that you could create a magnetic charge with electricity, and this girl had done that with him, attracting him by an unseen force of nature. Glancing down, he noticed the curve below her waist that formed the part of her body closest to him, and then the tapering of her legs into a pair of high heels.

When the elevator stopped at his floor he didn't get out but stood in place as if his feet were riveted to the floor. She stepped to her right to let him pass, but he shifted with her, staying behind her. When she got out he followed her.

She walked ahead of him to the door of an office that said Pan American Trading Company, and she went in, apparently unaware of him.

He faced the closed door, resisting the urge to pursue her and wondering what to do. He knew where she worked, but he didn't know her name, so he couldn't call the company and ask to speak with her. He considered standing outside the door until it was time for her to go home, but it was only two in the afternoon, and what would he do for three or four hours? How would he explain his presence there?

But if he went back to his office and worked until five, what if he missed her? What if this was her last day of work? How would he ever find her again?

He finally decided to return at quarter of five. If she was a secretary she would have to stay until then, and if she was something else she would have to stay longer. He would wait in the hallway until she appeared.

So he went back to work, checking his watch every half hour and missing a number of good opportunities to make money that afternoon. But he didn't care. All he could think about was the girl, whose face he kept recalling and embellishing. Without a doubt she was Latina, and from her prominent cheekbones and her straight thick hair he could tell she had Indian blood in her, not African as he did. Based on his experience with a Colombian girl at college, who could never get enough sex, he hoped that she was Colombian.

At quarter of five he was standing in the hallway of her floor as if he were waiting for the elevator. It wasn't long before two girls emerged from the office, speaking in Spanish. They were attractive girls, but not like her. They smiled at him disarmingly and stopped in front of the elevator.

"Are you going down?" one of them asked when the elevator stopped for them.

"No, thanks. I'm waiting for someone."

"Okay," the girl said, and she followed her colleague into the elevator, telling her about a great place to buy shoes.

He went through the same routine with about twenty other people who came out of the office, and by five-thirty he began to wonder if he had missed her.

Then finally the door opened and she appeared.

She was more attractive than he remembered, and when she looked at him, not through him, he felt a stronger charge than before. At the same time he felt the counteracting force of a gold cross that hung around her neck on a fine gold chain, which he hadn't noticed when she came into the elevator, maybe because it was hidden by her sweater.

"Are you waiting for someone?" the girl asked in English, though he could tell from her accent that her first language had been Spanish.

"Yes," he said shakily.

"Well, you don't have to wait outside."

"I know, but—" He stopped, not knowing what to say.

"If you want, I could tell them you're here."

"I was waiting for you," he admitted.

"For me?" She looked confused. "Do I know you?"

"No. But you must have seen me."

She furrowed her brow, shaking her head. "I don't remember seeing you before."

"I was in the elevator when you came back from lunch."

"You were? I'm sorry. I was lost in thought."

He wondered what she had been thinking about, but he knew it would be premature to ask.

As if she had gathered her senses, she asked: "Do you work in this building?"

"Yeah. I do." He told her the company he worked for.

"Could I please see some identification?"

"Are you a cop?" he joked with her.

"I'm serious," the girl said. "I'm standing here alone in the hallway, talking with a complete stranger, and how do I know what you have in mind?"

"I wanted to meet you. That's all." He took out his wallet and found his company ID and showed it to her. At that moment he understood what his father must have felt like being threatened by a bat and asked to identify himself.

She examined the ID, and then she asked him in Spanish: "Why were you waiting for me?"

"The moment I saw you I fell in love with you."

She made a sour face. "Yeah, sure you did."

"I did. I swear to God. I never felt this way about a girl."

"I'm not a girl," she corrected him. "I'm a woman."

"I never felt this way about a woman."

"And you think that because you feel that way, you have the right to meet me?"

From that he knew she was not only a woman but also a lady. "I don't have the right to meet you. I don't have the right to breathe the same air, or to walk the same earth, or to feel the warmth of the same sun."

"I didn't expect a *piropo* like that from a Dominican."

"How do you know I'm Dominican?"

"You look Dominican, you sound Dominican, and anyone with a name like Fenly has to be Dominican."

"So what are you?"

"Colombian," she said with pride.

"Well, I may be Dominican, but I'm not a *campesino*," he told her. "I went to Princeton."

"Then you're a gentleman."

"I try to be one."

By now two men had come out of the office, talking about baseball. They were Latinos, and from the names of the players they mentioned they were Yankees fans.

"Hi, Camila," one of them said, revealing her name.

Fenly thought it fit her, though he wouldn't have guessed it.

When the elevator stopped they all got in, and they all observed the taboo about talking in the elevator. They dropped like a stone in silence.

Down in the lobby, which was flooded with people, Camila said: "Well, it was nice meeting you, Fenly."

"Wait," he told her. "You can't just walk away."

"Why can't I?" she asked, cocking her head.

"Because you and I are bound together by destiny."

She smiled at him indulgently. "Well, that line may work on other girls— "

"I thought you were a woman."

"I am. But I can refer to myself as a girl."

"You can, but I can't?"

"There's a double standard."

"Okay. I can handle that."

"So let me repeat my question. Why can't I just walk away?"

"Because you don't want to walk away."

"Why don't I?" she asked, humoring him.

"Because you're attracted to me."

"I'm attracted to a lot of people, but what's special about you? I mean, besides the fact that you went to Princeton?"

"I make a lot of money."

"There's nothing special about that."

"Well—" He thought hard, feeling that his life depended on how he answered her question. "I contribute time and money to a community center."

"Where?" she asked as if she might be interested.

"In the Bronx, where I was born and raised."

"What's the name of the center?"

He told her.

"Really? Can you tell me the name of the man who runs it?"

"Stephen Wyatt."

She covered her mouth with her hand before it opened too wide. "You're kidding."

"I'm not. Do you know him?"

"He's my mentor."

"Where?"

"At St. Catherine College."

"You go to St. Catherine in Yonkers?"

"Yes. It's not Princeton, but it's a good college."

"I know it is. We just hired a guy from there. What are you studying?"

"International business."

"When do you expect to graduate?"

"In May of 2001."

So she was nineteen or twenty. "Do you live in Yonkers?"

"I've lived there since we came to this country."

"How long ago was that?"

"Seven years ago."

She didn't act like someone from the *barrio*, so he wondered why her family had left Colombia, but he could find out later. In the meantime they were standing in an open area with people flowing by them in all directions.

"How do you get home?" he asked her.

"By train from Grand Central."

"Well, I could go with you to Grand Central, and we could have a drink there."

"I can't tonight. I have a paper due tomorrow."

"You haven't finished it?"

"I have, but I want to improve it."

"Then how about tomorrow?"

"I have a class. But I could meet you after work on Friday."

"Do you have a card?"

She dug into her pocketbook and found one, almost dropping her cell phone in the process.

The card said: "Camila Flores, Transport Assistant."

"Thanks. So I'll see you after work on Friday. I'll call you to confirm the time."

She looked him over as if to make sure that she wasn't making a big mistake, and then she said: "Okay."

He watched her join the stream of people who were heading toward the subway.

For reassurance he checked her card. For luck he kissed it.

After work on Friday they met in the lobby of the building, and they walked to a place on Greenwich Street. It was an Argentine restaurant that Stephen had introduced him to, and he mentioned that fact shortly after he and Camila sat down.

"I asked Mr. Wyatt about you," she told him.

"You did?" He was curious. "What did he say about me?"

"He gave you a very good reference."

"That's nice. But it doesn't answer my question."

"Well—" She paused, leaving him in suspense for a while. "He said you cared about other people, and that you were good to your family."

"He didn't say I was smart?"

"He did, but I already knew that."

"How did you know?"

"You have to be smart to get into Princeton."

"Would you have changed your mind about going out with me if he hadn't given me a good reference?"

"Yes. I would have."

"Then you trust his judgment."

"I absolutely do. I'm still in college because of him."

"You mean you almost dropped out?"

"I almost did. I didn't think I could work full time and go to college, but he convinced me that I could do it. And he helped me through a bad time."

"What was happening?"

She hesitated. "My mother was sick, she couldn't work, and we didn't have enough money to live on. I was going to get a second job, but Mr. Wyatt found her a doctor and paid for her medical expenses, and she got better."

"Where was your father?"

Her face clouded. "He was killed before we left Colombia."

"I'm sorry," he said, wishing he hadn't asked.

"I didn't expect to get into this so soon."

"It's all right. Tell me about it."

She took a deep breath and composed herself. "My family had a ranch in Colombia. We weren't rich, but we were well off. Unfortunately, we were in an area where there was a lot of fighting between the guerrillas and the paramilitary. And one day the guerrillas came and took our cattle. My father decided that it wasn't safe for us in the country, and that we should move into the city. We were driving there with as many things as we could carry in a trailer when the paramilitary stopped us and accused my father of being a guerrilla. They killed him, and they took our car, and they left us with the trailer—my mother, my brothers, our housekeeper, and me."

"I'm sorry," he said, reaching for her hand.

She withdrew it to wipe away her tears, and then she held it out of range, resting on her cross.

"How old were you?"

"Twelve."

"How old were your brothers?"

"Nine and seven."

"And you all came to America then?"

"All except our housekeeper. She had family in the city, and she stayed with them."

"How did you happen to go to Yonkers?"

"My mother had a cousin there. We stayed with her for a while until we could buy our own house. We sold our land in Colombia," she explained, "and we finally got the money out."

"What did you live on?"

"Not much. My mother got a job at a daycare center. She didn't speak a word of English, so her opportunities were limited. But after she learned enough English, her cousin got her a job at the post office."

"Is that where she works now?"

"Yes. She had to go on medical leave while she was sick, but she's back there now."

"What about your brothers?"

"They're going to school. One's in high school, and the other's in middle school. Unfortunately, they don't have good public schools in Yonkers."

"They don't have good public schools in the Bronx. But I went to the Bronx High School of Science."

"That's a good school."

"My sister went there too. She led the way."

"So you have an older sister."

"Yeah. Her name is Yesenia. We call her Jessi."

"That must be a popular name with Dominicans. I've known three Yesenias."

"Did you go to a Yonkers high school?"

"No. I went to Sacred Heart. I got a scholarship."

"Why doesn't your brother go there?"

"His grades are terrible," she said. "He has the brains, but he never studies. He never helps my mother, and he always causes trouble for her. Boys don't get it."

"They don't," he agreed, remembering how he had been as a teenager. "I didn't get it for a long time."

They had dinner at the restaurant, talking continuously, and he felt that things were going so well that when he had paid the check he said: "I live near here. I have a great view. Why don't you come and see it?"

"Oh, I don't know." She checked her watch as if she were looking for a way out. "I better not. I don't want to miss the nine-twenty train."

"I have a car. I could drive you home."

"I wouldn't want you to go out of your way."

"I wouldn't be going out of my way. I'd be going with you."

She hesitated. "I really shouldn't."

"Come on," he urged her. "You'll get home sooner than if you took the train."

"Well, all right," she finally said. "But no funny business. *Me entiendes bien?*"

"Don't worry," he told her.

They walked to his building and went up in the elevator to his floor. In the apartment he led her to the window, where you could see the Twin Towers all lit up and buildings across the river in New Jersey. If you looked hard, and had good eyes, you could make out the Statue of Liberty in the harbor.

"It *is* a great view," she said softly.

"I told you. I didn't bring you here under false pretenses."

She turned to him, smiling. "No. You didn't."

Impelled by the force that had attracted him to her the moment he saw her come into the elevator, he closed the distance between them and kissed her.

At first she didn't respond at all, but then with reserve she kissed him back.

Without thinking, he did what he usually did with a girl. He grabbed her ass and pulled her toward him.

With both hands she pushed him away, saying: "What do you think you're doing?"

"Nothing. I was just kissing you."

"You weren't just kissing me, you were grabbing my ass."

"I'm sorry. I did that without thinking."

"I'm sure you did. Well, I don't want to be with someone who does things like that without thinking." She moved around him and headed for the door.

"I said I'd drive you home," he said, following her.

"No, thanks," she said over her shoulder. "I don't want to get raped in your car."

"I won't touch you."

"I know you won't." She opened the door. "You won't have the opportunity."

"I'm sorry," he said, pleading with her.

"I'm sorry too. I thought you were a gentleman." And with that she stomped out and slammed the door behind her.

At least he had the good sense not to go after her.

They had arranged to meet at Arizona at ten the next day, which was Sunday, but Fenly was unable to sleep past seven in the morning, so he went out, remembering that there was a church on Caballero de Gracia. When he got to the church he had to wait about twenty minutes for them to open the door. By then a few elderly women had gathered on the sidewalk, and he let them go in ahead of him.

Fenly didn't go to church regularly, and when he did he was driven by his memories of going to church with Camila. In fact, though he sought the presence of God in church, he was often more successful at finding the presence of Camila.

When the mass began there were about a dozen people in the church, and they were all at least twice his age. As he heard the familiar words in Spanish, he remembered going to mass at San Pedro in Yonkers with Camila, her mother, and one of her brothers—the other brother had decided to opt out of religion. The people attending were all Latino, mostly Puerto Ricans,

Dominicans, and Mexicans. There were only a few Colombians, and Camila's mother knew them all. After greeting the priest on the way out they always stopped and exchanged news of their home country, which was rarely good news.

"*Señor, ten piedad,*" the priest said.

"*Señor, ten piedad,*" Fenly responded. As usual he wondered if God was listening.

At the times during the mass when he had opportunities to say his own prayers, he said them for his mother, his sister, and all the people he cared about. At the end he added Raquel to the list, and finally Samira.

After communion he wasn't sure if he felt the presence of God within him, but he did feel the presence of Camila, whom he asked to intercede for him.

Leaving the church, he walked toward Montera and passed the building where the girls had their apartment. A guy in a suit came out the door, followed by a girl in boots. The guy had probably dressed for church and changed his mind.

He went to Arizona and sat at a table and asked the waiter to bring him a coffee and a roll. He left the table to buy a newspaper, and then he returned, finding the coffee and the roll on the table. He sipped the coffee, ate the roll, and read the paper while the street came to life around them. The cops who had been there all night were relieved by fresh cops, and a similar changing of the shift occurred with the girls.

Raquel arrived punctually at ten and joined him at the table. After ordering a coffee and a croissant she said: "It looks like our guy never came home."

"Or else he's been there all along."

"I don't think so, but if we don't spot him by noon today we'll go into his apartment. I have the key."

"Do we have a warrant?"

"We got it last night."

"I thought that nothing could be done here on a weekend."

"Anything can be done here on a weekend if people feel it's important enough."

"I wish they felt that way in Ecuador."

"I do too," Raquel said. "It would have been nice to hear from them before Monday."

"What name did he use to rent the apartment?"

"Michael Lathrop."

"Well, if he believes we don't know that name, then maybe he'll keep using it."

"That would give us one advantage."

"At this point we need one."

At noon, after talking with her police contact, Raquel got up and said: "Let's go."

They crossed the street and stopped at the entrance of the building. Acting as if she lived there, Raquel took out the key and opened the outer door.

He followed her into the lobby and to an elevator.

"I'm glad they have only one elevator," she said. "He can't come down in the other one while we're going up."

They waited for the elevator.

When the door opened a young couple got out and greeted them in passing.

Fenly and Raquel got into the elevator, and she pressed the button for the third floor. She was wearing a jacket, which she unzipped on the way up.

He noticed that she had a gun inside the jacket.

On the third floor they went to the B apartment, and she rang the bell. A few minutes later she rang the bell again, giving Daryl another chance to answer the door.

At that point she took out her gun and unlocked the door.

"Stay back," she told him.

He didn't like staying back while a woman went ahead of him, but she had the gun.

She moved carefully into the apartment, looking right and left. She went through every room that way, opening closets and checking every possible place where a person could hide. She finally said: "He's not here."

They went to a window in the living room that looked out onto Montera. From there you could see Arizona, and you could see Caballero de Gracia, where Najib had gone with Samira and Smith had gone with Lina. On the frame of the window was a mirror that gave you a view of the sidewalk below, where the girls were standing.

"Well, he doesn't have a camera," Fenly said.

"He might have a mobile one," Raquel said. "And he might have binoculars."

Fenly looked across the street, at the floor where Antonio and José were stationed. It was on the same level, and at night you could probably see right in.

"He could have figured out that we're watching the street," Raquel said. "With binoculars he could see our cameras."

"He could have, but I don't think he did. If he had, then he wouldn't have let us take his picture."

"Maybe he wanted us to take his picture."

"You mean to give us a chance to catch him?"

"Leandro says that mastermind criminals want to get caught so people will know how smart they are."

"If they were smart, they wouldn't be criminals."

They looked around, but they didn't find anything significant. There were just the things that any lone male would have in his apartment.

"It looks like he's still living here," she said as they stood in the bathroom. "He didn't take his toothbrush or razor."

"So where do you think he spent the night?"

"I don't know. Maybe at the home of a friend."

"Then he'll be coming back."

"Or going away."

Wearing gloves, they combed the apartment for an address book, a notebook, or a piece of paper that would give them a hint of where the guy had gone. But there was no trail, not even a phone to trace calls from.

Returning to the kitchen, they checked the garbage and found a plastic container from McDonald's.

"That tells us something," Raquel said.

"Yeah, it tells us that he likes McDonald's."

"So he's a typical American."

They left the apartment as they had found it, and they went back to Arizona, where they ordered *arroz con pollo* to share.

It was after two when they finished eating.

"Now what?" he asked since the guy still hadn't appeared.

"I have the feeling that he's not going to show," Raquel said, reaching for her cell phone.

"He might try to leave the country."

"I hope he does. We'll catch him at a border or at an airport. We have the bases covered."

"You're learning the terms."

She called Leandro and brought him up to date.

"What does he want us to do?" Fenly asked.

"He wants us to stay here. The guy could still come back to his apartment."

Around two-thirty Raquel suddenly raised her head as if she had noticed something.

"What is it?" he asked.

"Samira's not here."

"It's Sunday."

"She doesn't take off Sundays."

"Well, maybe she slept late."

"It wouldn't be like her. She's a hard worker."

"Do you know where she lives?"

"Yes," Raquel said, immediately getting up from the table. "We should go there."

He signaled to the waiter, who brought the check.

While he was paying, Raquel walked over and requisitioned a police car that was parked on the plaza.

They sat in back, with two cops in front, and they sped out of the city center to the outlying neighborhood where Samira lived. It reminded Fenly of the projects in New York, except that the buildings looked newer.

The four of them took the elevator to the floor where Samira lived, and Raquel asked the two cops to step to the side while she rang the bell, so that the sight of them wouldn't alarm Samira. She rang a few times and called to Samira.

But no one answered.

"She could be out," Fenly said.

"I don't think so," Raquel said tensely.

"I'll find the *portero* and get the key," one cop said.

"Maybe we should break down the door," the other cop said.

"I think we should," Raquel said. "I don't want to waste time looking for the *portero.*"

The cop who had suggested it broke down the door, using the heel of his foot.

Inside, they could see right away that something was amiss. A rug was tangled, a chair was toppled over, and shards of glass were scattered on the floor.

"I found her," one of the cops said from the bedroom.

"Oh, my God," Raquel said, hurrying in there.

Fenly followed her and saw Samira lying on the bed with a stocking around her neck. It was the same method that had been used to kill Lina.

Raquel tried to reach Samira, but a cop held her back, saying: "You can't touch her."

"I know that, damn it. I was a cop," Raquel shrieked.

Fenly went to her and took her into his arms while she sobbed uncontrollably. She buried her face against his chest as if she wanted to obliterate what she had just seen.

"Oh, God," she cried. "Why did You let this happen to her?"

NINE

WITHIN A HALF hour Leandro arrived at the murder scene along with an inspector. By then Raquel was under control, but just barely.

"I know how you feel," Leandro told her. "But you can't do anything for Samira. So go home and get some rest."

"I'm not going to rest until we catch this guy."

"I'm not going to rest either, but right now the best thing you can do for the team is to go home."

Raquel took a long, deep breath and exhaled, making a sound as if the air hurt her windpipe going out. "I just don't see why he had to kill her."

"I guess he wanted to cover his tracks," Leandro said.

"She wasn't involved in the operation. He should have gone after the guys who were, instead of her."

"He must have figured out that we're using them as bait."

"But if they're still alive to testify against him, then what's the point in killing her?"

"What's the point in killing anyone?"

Raquel looked up as if she were challenging God to answer that question, and then her face crumpled with pain, and her tears started flowing again.

"Come on," Fenly said, putting his hand on her shoulder.

She shook off his hand. "I can get home by myself."

"I know you can, but I'll go with you."

Leandro asked a cop to drive them to Malasaña.

Before leaving, Raquel went over to the bed and gazed at Samira hopelessly. Almost in a whisper, she said: "I'm sorry. I shouldn't have used you. God forgive me."

They rode in the back seat of the police car.

156

Raquel was surrounded by walls of grief that Fenly didn't try to penetrate. He had been there, and he understood what she was feeling.

She finally broke her silence by saying: "It's my fault what happened to her."

"It's not your fault."

"It is," she insisted. "If I hadn't used her to get information, the guy wouldn't have had any reason to kill her."

"Yes, he would have. She was going with Najib in the normal course of business. And since the guy was watching Najib, he must have seen her go with him."

"I guess he must have. But he must have also seen her go with the police."

"All the girls go with the police. So he wouldn't have cared about that if he hadn't seen her going with Najib."

"I guess he wouldn't have." She was silent for a while, gazing bleakly out the window. "But I still feel responsible."

"I do too," Fenly said. "I used her as much as you did."

She turned and looked at him as if she realized that they were in this thing together.

They stopped at the building where Raquel lived, and Fenly accompanied her to the entrance to make sure she got in safely. Then he joined the cop in the front seat.

As they drove through Malasaña the cop said: "You see all this damage? That's from Friday and Saturday nights."

He saw the garbage in the street, the broken windows, the bashed cars, and the fresh graffiti sprayed on walls. "What happened here?"

"Some kids from another neighborhood came here to party."

"It doesn't look like they had a party."

"I guess it's their idea of a party."

"Trashing a neighborhood?"

"I don't know what they were trying to prove," the cop said. "And they're from here, so we can't blame it on the immigrants."

"Then who can you blame it on?"

"Their parents. They don't give these kids any values."

"But the parents aren't entirely to blame. You can have good parents and still turn out bad."

The cop glanced at him. "Are you speaking from experience?"

"Yeah," he said. "I had a good parent."

"Well, you turned out good."

"I almost didn't. And I'm still working on it."

"Was your parent an immigrant?"

"Yeah. She was."

"I admire immigrants," the cop said. "They work hard, and they take care of their children. If I were the president of this country I'd let in more of them."

"Did you know Samira?"

"I knew who she was. And from what I saw of her, she was a good kid. It's too damned bad she had to do that kind of job."

"You make it sound like she didn't have a choice."

"She didn't have much of a choice."

"I guess she didn't," Fenly said, wishing there had been time to give her a choice.

The cop let him out at the metro station on Gran Vía and drove away. It was almost five, an hour on Sunday when he never knew what to do with himself, and he was even more at a loss than he was in New York at this hour. He was tired, but he knew that if he took a siesta then he would be awake all night. And he didn't feel like watching television. At the corner of Calle Tres Cruces he considered going into Zahara and having a coffee, but instead he walked down Tres Cruces. He stopped in front of his building and considered going in, but then he kept going. He passed the grocery store, which was closed, and he continued to the Plaza del Carmen, where he stopped and gazed at the statement on the wall of the building: "You cannot achieve peace through war. If you want peace, work for social justice."

He remembered the long discussions with Stephen, who had warned him about the futility of responding to terrorist attacks. Stephen had explained to him, as Leandro had, that the strategy of terrorists was to provoke governments into reacting in ways that would turn people against them. The more you reacted, the more you helped the terrorists achieve their goal. The only way to stop terrorism was to make a world where there was no reason for it. That sounds fine, he had told Stephen, but what are you going to do until we have that kind of world? Are you going to let the terrorists keep attacking us? Are you going to let them keep killing innocent people? But Stephen had said that in trying to stop the terrorists you're going to kill innocent people, as we're doing now in Iraq and Afghanistan. And how do you justify killing people for that purpose?

So far in this effort to stop the terrorists four people had been killed: a man accused of being involved in 11-M, a Romanian girl, a pimp, and Samira—four lives sacrificed in order to save an untold number of lives. But did that justify their sacrifice? Would their families accept that reason for their deaths? Would Samira's mother be glad to know that her daughter had died to save the lives of people in America? Would her mother survive without the money transfers?

Unable to deal with these questions, Fenly wandered across the plaza and down the street that led to the plaza on Mesonero Romanos. Before he got there he passed a restaurant called Ribs, which billed itself as "La Casa de Las Costillas." It looked like an American restaurant, and through the door he could see a long bar with people sitting at it, drinking.

He was drawn into the restaurant by its familiarity, by the possible comfort the place offered, and he was greeted by a pretty hostess in a cowgirl outfit who gave him a welcoming smile and asked him in English: "Are you here for dinner?"

"No, thanks," he told her. "I'm just going to sit at the bar."

"If you change your mind, we have a bar menu."

He thanked her and took a seat at the bar, wondering how she knew he was an American.

"What can I get you?" the bartender asked him in English. Like the hostess he had an accent, and he probably didn't know much English beyond the language you needed to take orders or explain menus, but like her the bartender knew an American when he saw one.

Noticing that they had Budweiser, Fenly ordered a bottle of it, though he really didn't like it. He would have preferred a Presidente, but he felt obliged to order a Bud because it was expected of him. And he forced himself to drink it.

When he finished it he ordered a *caña* of Mahou, the Spanish beer you saw everywhere, and he settled down for a long evening at the bar.

All night he berated himself for losing Camila before he even won her. He realized that he had made a wrong move, but after replaying the scene with her over and over in his mind he had to admit that he didn't know enough to have behaved differently. In all his life he had never encountered a girl who hadn't welcomed his advances.

He spent the weekend regretting what he had done but having no idea how to remedy it, so on Sunday evening he called Stephen and arranged to meet with him after work the next day in the hope that his mentor could enlighten him.

They met in Stephen's office in the community center.

"I have a problem," Fenly said.

"I know. Camila told me about it."

"What did she tell you?"

"I can't betray her confidence. But you can give me *your* version of what happened."

Without reservation he told Stephen what he had done and how Camila had reacted.

"What did you expect?" Stephen said. "Did you think she was going to have sex with you on your first date?"

"I don't know what I thought. I just did what I always do."

"And it always worked before?"

"It always did. But this girl's different."

"What do you mean?"

"I mean she's different," Fenly said, "and I have different feelings about her."

"Are you in love with her?"

"I guess I am. And I feel like I've lost her."

"Maybe you have. Without betraying her confidence I can tell you one thing Camila said to me—"

"What did she say?"

"She said I shouldn't have given you a good reference. She said I'd misled her. But that's all right. She has to learn that older people's judgments aren't infallible."

"Are you saying you were wrong about me?"

Stephen shook his head. "I'm not saying that. If she asked me again, I'd still give you a good reference. I'd just tell her to watch out for your fast hands."

"Thanks," Fenly said appreciatively. "Do you think I still have a chance with her?"

"The problem is, she thinks you don't respect her, and I can certainly understand why. You treated her like an object."

"I guess I did. So how can I change her mind about me?"

"Treat her with respect."

"I never had to do that with girls."

"They didn't care if you respected them?"

"I guess they didn't."

"Well, this one does," Stephen told him. "And I want you to respect her. She's one of my students, and I care about her. She hasn't had an easy life. At the age of twelve she saw her father get killed for a car. A few years ago she almost lost her mother. She works full time to help support her family, and she goes to college full time. She's an A student. And she's very religious. She goes to church every Sunday and two or three times a week in the morning before going to work. So grabbing her ass was the worst thing you could have done."

"I realize that now."

"Then maybe you can change her mind about you. But I warn you, it won't be easy."

The fact that Camila was religious gave him hope that she would forgive him if she believed that he repented what he had done. And he did repent it. He felt more contrition for it than he had felt for any of the bad things he had ever done.

To demonstrate his feeling he went to her floor the next day at five and stood at the entrance to her office, holding a yellow rose of friendship and waiting for her.

When she finally came out she was with another girl, a Latina, and they were talking in Spanish. She must have seen him, but she pretended not to. She just kept going to the elevator. As they got in the other girl asked: "Who's that guy?"

"No one," she said.

And the elevator door closed.

For two weeks he waited for her every day, replenishing the rose, but every day she came out with the other girl and ignored him. If she had been alone he could have approached her and appealed to her, but as long as she was with the other girl he could only stand there and hope that she would have mercy on him. And he realized that it wasn't an accident that she left work with another girl. It was a strategy to avoid talking with him.

So he stopped going to her floor for a week in the hope that she would lower her guard. It killed him not to see her for that long, but he stuck with the plan, and the following Monday he was rewarded. She came out alone.

She looked surprised to see him, evidently assuming that he had given up. And there was the merest hint in her eyes that she might be glad to see him after all, though he might have just projected it there because by now he was desperately in need of encouragement.

"Can we talk?" he asked her.

"We have nothing to talk about," she said, walking around him and heading toward the elevator.

"We have a lot to talk about. I love you."

"Maybe you do, but we have different ideas of love."

"How do you know unless you listen to me?"

"I don't want to know," she said, pressing the down button.

"I'm sorry for what I did."

"You should be."

"I'm begging you to forgive me."

"I don't feel like forgiving you."

He offered her the rose. "Would this help?"

She raised her hand as if she was going to bat the rose out of his hand, but then she looked at him with sudden sympathy. "You really *are* sorry, aren't you."

"I am. Please, please, please forgive me."

Gently, she took the rose from him. "All right. I forgive you."

"Could you have dinner with me tonight?"

"I can't tonight. I have a class."

"When does it start?"

"At seven. But I have to go home and change my clothes."

He tried not to imagine her doing that. "Well, when don't you have a class?"

"I don't have one on Wednesdays."

"Are you free this Wednesday?"

"I was planning to go out with the girls," she told him.

"The girls?" he asked, remembering their exchange on the use of this word.

She smiled as if she remembered it too. "It wouldn't sound right for me to say I was planning to go out with the women."

"Would it sound right for me to say that?"

"It would sound kind of silly."

"So if you're planning to go out with the girls on Wednesday, how about Friday?"

"Friday would be fine."

"How about going to the same restaurant and starting over?"

"That would be fine. I liked the restaurant."

On Monday he walked to the office in Chueca, arriving at nine. They hadn't set a time for a meeting, but he wanted to be there in case something happened.

Leandro was alone in his office.

"Is Raquel here?" Fenly asked him.

"She's on her way."

"Is she all right?"

"She sounded better when I talked with her, but she won't be all right until we catch this guy. And even then—" Leandro didn't have to finish the thought.

"Are there any reports?"

"Yeah, we got one from your agency. Are you ready?"

Fenly nodded, not knowing what to expect.

"His name is Daryl MacKenzie, and he's a former FBI agent."

"I don't believe it."

"Then look at the report," Leandro said, handing it to him.

The report said that Daryl was not only a former agent but also a former high-level official of the FBI. He had been missing since September 11, 2001 and presumed dead.

"I don't understand this," Fenly said.

"I don't either. I was hoping you could explain it."

"Well, he could be working undercover."

"I thought of that. But six years is a long time to be working undercover. And being dead is a pretty deep cover."

"It's as deep as you can get."

"And why would he be involved in money laundering?"

"I don't know. It could be a sting operation."

"I thought of that too. But who's being stung?"

"The drug people, or the people at the other end."

"But the FBI wouldn't do a sting operation in Spain."

"No. The CIA would have jurisdiction."

"Whatever he's doing," Leandro said after a pause, "I think he's doing it on his own, and the FBI knows nothing about it. They think he's dead."

"That's what they say," Fenly said, looking at the report.

"Are you suggesting that the FBI could be holding something back from us?"

"They could be, but I can't imagine why they would."

"The guy's been missing for six years, and now he's involved in a plot to attack America. It doesn't make sense."

"It must be significant that he's been missing since 9-11. If he was going underground, then maybe he wanted people to believe that he was killed in the attack."

"But why is he involved in this plot?"

"Raquel thinks he might want vengeance."

"Vengeance for what?" Leandro asked. "I understand what those guys want vengeance for—your invasion of Iraq. But what would this guy want vengeance for?"

"I don't know. But it might have something to do with 9-11."

"Your government invaded Iraq because of 9-11. But it doesn't make sense for an American to be involved in a plot to attack his own country because of 9-11."

"It doesn't make sense. But if he wants vengeance," Fenly reasoned, "then he has some grievance, and if we knew what that grievance is, then it *would* make sense."

Raquel arrived, looking as if she had gotten some rest, and there was a look of determination in her dark eyes.

Leandro brought her up to date on Daryl's background.

"I don't want to wait for him to appear," Raquel said when her boss had finished. "I want to find him."

"Where would we look? We don't have a clue."

"If the guy's not trying to leave the country, then he's hanging out somewhere."

"Where do Americans hang out?" Fenly asked.

"In Irish pubs," Leandro said.

"But he isn't Irish."

"From his name I thought he was."

"MacKenzie isn't an Irish name, it's a Scottish name."

"What's the difference?"

"The Irish are Catholic, and the Scottish are Presbyterian."

"How do you know about these differences?"

"In New York you grow up knowing about the differences between groups of people."

"This guy isn't hanging out in a pub," Raquel said.

"We're just brainstorming," Leandro said.

"Well, we're not getting anywhere."

After reflecting Fenly said: "We've been assuming he's still in Madrid. But maybe he's not. "

"He was here on Saturday night," Raquel reminded them.

"You mean assuming he killed Samira," Leandro said.

"We know it wasn't Smith because we had a tail on him, and it wasn't Najib because he had a relationship with her. So who else would have killed her?"

"No one I can think of," Leandro admitted. "The police say she was killed between three and four on Sunday morning."

"Daryl could have left Madrid right after that," Fenly said.

"If he did, he couldn't have gone by plane or train. There's nothing running at that hour."

"He could have gone by car," Raquel said.

"There isn't a car registered in his name, so he would have had to rent one, and the rental offices aren't open at that hour."

"He could have rented one before he killed her. He could have driven to her apartment and left Madrid after he killed her."

"Let's find out if he rented a car," Fenly said.

Leandro made a phone call and requested the information.

While they were waiting for a return call Raquel said: "I think we should look for this guy on the beaches. That's where most Americans go. I read that seventy percent of the Americans who visit Spain go to the beaches."

"They're missing the best things in Spain," Leandro said.

"It would make sense," Fenly said, "for him to go where a lot of other Americans go since he wouldn't stand out among them. So I agree with Raquel."

"If we look for this guy on the beaches," Leandro said, "we'll have to cover a large area."

"We can start with the beaches that are most popular with Americans," Raquel said. "Marbella and Torremolinos."

A half hour later they learned the make, color, and license number of a car rented on Saturday morning by a man named Michael Lathrop. So he was using the same name that he had used to rent the apartment.

Leandro sent this information, along with the sketch of Daryl, to police in all the beach towns from the Costa Brava to the Costa del Sol.

Around two in the afternoon, right after they sent out for sandwiches, the internal auditor of the bank in Ecuador reported back with information.

Fenly was surprised and happy to hear from him so soon.

"I'll send all this to you in an email," the auditor said, "but I thought you'd want to know right away."

"What did you find?"

"Those transfers from Spain were paid to a company. There were no instructions to pay individuals."

"I saw the instructions in the bank here."

"Well, they were replaced here by other instructions."

"Do you know who did it?"

"Yes. We know. It was the man who used to run our foreign transfer department. He's in jail now."

"That's good. So what can you tell me about the company that received the money?"

"It's a trading company based in Panama," the auditor said. "They deal in equipment for the oil industry. They've been doing business in our country for almost ten years."

"What kind of business?"

"Selling equipment to oil companies."

"What did they do with the money from Spain?"

"They used it to buy equipment from Russia."

"What kind of equipment?"

"Oil equipment," the auditor said. "They bought equipment from Russia before, but there was something different about the last transaction."

"There was? What?"

"The equipment was shipped to Mexico, not Ecuador."

"When was it shipped?"

"About three weeks ago."

"Can you tell me the name of the Russian company that sold the equipment?"

"It's in my email, along with all the other details."

"What's the name of the company that received the money?"

"I can't pronounce it, but it's in my email."

"Why can't you pronounce it?"

"Because it's French."

When he had finished talking with the auditor he checked his computer and found the email, which provided the details.

"Oil equipment?" Leandro said after hearing what he had learned from the auditor.

"Well, think about it. What might look like oil equipment packed in crates?"

"Missiles, projectiles. That sort of thing."

"Exactly. And they had it shipped to Mexico, from where it could be taken by truck to America."

"They'd have to go through customs."

"They could disguise the weapons as oil equipment. Or they could bribe a customs officer."

"You better alert your border control," Leandro said.

"I will," Fenly said. "But they may have already crossed the border. The equipment was shipped a month ago."

"Can you track the shipment?" Raquel asked.

"That may be difficult," Leandro said. "The Russians aren't likely to cooperate with us."

"I'll call my boss," Fenly said, "and tell him what we know about the shipment."

He went into another office and called his boss. He had been giving his boss daily updates, but this was the first time he had information about the shipment.

After hearing the update his boss still had a lot of questions, especially about the identity of Daryl MacKenzie. "This guy's been missing for six years. He was presumed dead. And now you tell me he's involved in a plot to attack his own country?"

"It looks that way."

"Why wasn't there any sign of him before?"

"He took another identity," Fenly explained. "He was going by the name of Michael Lathrop."

"Well, the higher-ups believe he's dead. They say you have a mistaken identity."

"I hope they're right. I mean, I don't like the idea of a former FBI agent being involved in something like this."

"So what are you recommending?"

"I'm recommending that we search every truck that comes across the Mexican border, and that we track down every truck that came across the border within the past three weeks."

"When was the equipment shipped from Russia?"

"About three weeks ago," Fenly said.

"Then we don't have to go back three weeks," his boss said. "It would have taken at least a week for a freighter to get from Russia to Mexico."

"I think we should go back three weeks just to make sure."

"All right. We'll do that. What are we looking for?"

"We're looking for weapons disguised as oil equipment."

"I'll get those things in motion. But you haven't convinced me that this is for real. And you haven't helped your case by bringing a dead man into it."

"He's not dead," Fenly maintained.

"You'll have to prove that."

He rejoined Leandro and Raquel, who had waited for him to return before they started eating their sandwiches.

"I understand," Leandro said, "that you do this sort of thing in New York."

"What sort of thing?" Fenly asked, chewing.

"You eat lunch at your desk."

"Sometimes we do. But we usually eat lunch while driving a car, with a sandwich in one hand and a cell phone in the other."

"How do you drive?"

"You steer with your knees."

"That's no way to live," Leandro said. "But they're trying to make us live that way. They're trying to make us have the same lunch hour as the Germans."

"How long do they take to eat lunch?"

"An hour or so. But if I had to eat their food, I wouldn't take that long."

"You don't like bratwursts and sauerkraut?"

"They can have it. I'll take Spanish food. And I'll take the time I want to eat it."

After they had finished eating, Raquel got up and told them: "I have to go somewhere."

"How long will you be gone?" Leandro asked as if he knew where she was going.

"I don't know. I've never gone to a Muslim funeral."

"Can I go with you?" Fenly asked.

"You can if you want to," Raquel said, not quite welcoming his offer, "but you don't have to."

"I want to."

"All right. Then let's go."

They took the metro to the neighborhood where Samira had lived. As they walked to her building Raquel got a headscarf out of her shoulder bag and covered her hair with it, tying it below her chin.

In the courtyard behind the building they found a group of people forming rows in front of the body of the girl, which lay on a table wrapped in white cloth. Her face was covered with a head wrap. A tall robed man in a white cap was standing by her shoulder, facing away from the people.

Raquel and Fenly joined the last row and waited for the service to begin.

The people who had gathered in the courtyard all seemed to know what to do, and the women all wore headscarves.

The robed man finally broke the silence by raising his hands and saying loudly: *"Allahu Akbar!"*

That was followed by what seemed to be a silent prayer.

With her head bowed, Raquel said her own prayer, just perceptibly moving her lips.

"Allahu Akbar!" the robed man said again. And that was followed by a series of other prayers, concluding with *"Assalamu alaikum wa rahmatullah,"* which the man said turning his head to the right and to the left.

Compared with a mass for the dead, it was a short service, though it might have been longer for someone more important than Samira.

Four men lifted the body and began to carry it away.

"Only men can go to the cemetery," Raquel said, "so I can't follow them."

As they watched the procession leave the courtyard Fenly put his arm around her.

After they had gone Raquel said what he had been feeling: "She was just a kid. She should have been in school."

"She should have been," he said, drawing her closer.

Raquel's cell phone started ringing as they emerged from the metro at Gran Vía.

It was Leandro, who had something to report.

From watching her face as she listened, Fenly figured out what it was, and he wasn't surprised when after finishing the conversation Raquel said: "We got the fucker."

"Where was he?"

"In Marbella. He was on the beach. The police tracked him from the hotel where he was staying. They're going to fly him back here."

Fenly started to give her a high five, and then he stopped, remembering that he was in Madrid, not in New York.

But she clapped her hand against his without hesitation.

"Where did you learn to do that?" he asked.

"From American movies," she told him. "That's what you do when you score, right?"

He laughed. "Right. That's what we do."

She raised her hand, inviting him to give her the sign again.

In jubilation they clapped their hands together, saying: "We got the fucker."

LATER THAT DAY they met Leandro at the police station on Montera, where Daryl had been taken for questioning. After a conference it was decided that Leandro should join the inspector in the interview room, so that he could participate. Raquel and Fenly watched through the one-way window.

Daryl, who was in good shape, was wearing a rugby shirt and designer jeans. With his healthy tan and his perfectly trimmed gray hair, he looked like an American executive on vacation about to play another round of serious golf. The only blemish in this picture was a scab on the left side of his chin, which could have been a scratch from a fingernail.

The inspector began the interview by asking: "Would you state your name, please?"

"Michael Lathrop," Daryl said.

"Do you have any other names?"

"No, that's my only name."

"Do you know a Daryl MacKenzie?" Leandro asked.

Daryl reacted faintly. "No. I never heard of him."

"Well, we have a sketch of a Daryl MacKenzie who looks exactly like you."

"A lot of men look like me."

"If you cooperate with us," the inspector said in a low key, "you could get off lightly. But if you don't, you could spend the rest of your life in jail."

"What for?"

"Money laundering."

"I don't know what you're talking about."

"We're talking about your operation that used prostitutes to pass money from a drug dealer to an exchange office. We have people who can identify you."

"A lot of people can identify me, but you can't prove that I broke any law."

"We have all the evidence we need, but we'll give you one last chance to cooperate."

Daryl shook his head. "I have nothing to say."

"Then we'll put you in a lineup," the inspector said, rising from his chair.

Leandro rose with him, and they left the room. A few minutes later two police officers came and took Daryl away.

The police had picked up Smith, Najib, and Moreno, who one at a time were shown a lineup and asked if they could identify the man they had dealt with. All of them identified Daryl without the slightest hesitation.

The questioning was then resumed.

"You've been identified," the inspector told Daryl, "as the man who arranged for Najib Khattabi to leave envelopes of cash under the bed in an apartment on Calle del Caballero de Gracia in the city of Madrid while going there with a prostitute. You've been identified as the man who arranged for John Smith to pick up the envelopes at that apartment and deliver them to an exchange office owned by Alberto Moreno. And you've been identified as the man who arranged with Alberto Moreno to receive these envelopes, deposit the money in his account, and have it transferred to Ecuador."

"What can I say? You know it all."

"We know enough to have you convicted and sent to jail, but we're hoping you can tell us more so that we can get the people who hired you."

"No one hired me. It was my operation."

"Then tell us what you did with the money."

"I sent it to Ecuador."

"Who received it?"

"A French trading company."

"Do you know what that company did with the money?"

"They used it to buy oil equipment."

"Oil equipment?"

"Yeah, oil equipment. They're in that business."

"So why did they need laundered money?"

"They're also in the drug business," Daryl explained. "They use the money they generate from drug sales to finance the purchase of oil equipment."

"From your experience is it usual for a company in the drug business to be involved in another business?"

"I wouldn't know."

"Well, you *should* know."

"Why should I know?"

"You worked for the FBI."

"No. I never worked for the FBI."

"We have people who can identify you as a former FBI agent. You could save yourself a lot of trouble by admitting it."

"All right," Daryl said after a long silence. "My name is Daryl MacKenzie, and I did work for the FBI—until I learned what our government did."

"What do you mean?"

"You know what I mean. Your government did the same thing after you were attacked."

"What did they do?"

"They used the attack for political purposes."

"I'd like to go back to the French company," Leandro said. "Were you involved in buying the oil equipment?"

"No. That was a separate operation."

"Then how do you know they bought oil equipment with the money you sent to Ecuador?"

"They were in the oil equipment business."

"They were also in the drug business, so they could have been in another business."

"What other business?"

"The arms business."

"I don't know anything about that."

"Do you know where they bought the equipment?"

"No. I assume they bought it in America."

"So your only role was to move the money from their drug business to their equipment business?"

"That was my only role," Daryl said unequivocally.

"What did you get out of it?"

"I got a commission."

"How much?"

"Fifteen percent. But I had to share it with those guys who identified me. So I netted five percent."

"How much money did you launder?"

"About five million euros."

"Over what period of time?"

"About three years."

"So you made about two hundred fifty thousand euros over three years," Leandro figured. "That doesn't sound like enough incentive for the risk you took."

"It gave me something to do in Spain."

"You like living in Spain?"

"Yeah. I love it here."

After the interview they met in a conference room in the police station to compare notes.

"I don't think he's being open with us," Fenly said.

"I don't think so either," Leandro said. "But he said one thing that was possibly revealing."

"What did he say?"

"He said he worked for the FBI until he learned what your government did. Now, that could fit Raquel's theory that he's doing this for vengeance. The way he talks, he has a grievance against your government."

"Why didn't you question him about the people he killed?" Raquel asked as if that was more important than her theory.

"We'll have time for that later," Leandro said. "Our top priority now is to find out more about the plot."

"Then in the meantime we could question Smith about Lina, and we could get a sample of Daryl's DNA to see if it matches what they found under Samira's fingernails."

"The police will do that. Our job is to stop this attack."

"Well, I don't want him to get away."

"Don't worry. We have him on the money laundering, so he won't get away."

"Unless they kill him," Fenly said.

"That gives me an idea," Leandro said. "If this guy's involved in the plot, then he knows what happened to the guy who first told us about it."

"You mean he knows that the guy was poisoned."

"Here's my idea. He eats some food that makes him sick, and he thinks they're trying to poison him, so he agrees to tell us everything if we agree to protect him."

"I thought we weren't going to torture people," Fenly said.

"We're not going to torture him. We're only going to make him think they're trying to kill him."

"One of my girlfriends," Raquel said, "got sick from milk that had been out of the refrigerator for a while."

"Did she drink it?"

"No. She put it in her coffee."

"Do you think this guy puts milk in his coffee?" Leandro asked.

"From his accent," Fenly said, "I'd say he's from the Midwest, and there they put milk, cream, or cheese in everything."

"Why do they do that?"

"They have a lot of cows there."

"You mean like in Asturias."

"I don't know. I've never been to Asturias."

"You should go there. It's beautiful."

It was after nine when they left the police station. Leandro headed home, and Raquel and Fenly went to the plaza on Mesonero Romanos, where they had drinks and *tapas*. They were both tired, so they left the plaza before eleven and headed home.

Back at his apartment, Fenly called his boss and told him they had caught Daryl, who had admitted being a former FBI agent. "We sent his fingerprints to the bureau, and they confirmed his identity. So Daryl MacKenzie is alive."

"All right. The man is alive," his boss said, "but that doesn't make him a reliable source."

"Who would you consider a reliable source?"

"I always considered you reliable, but now I'm beginning to have some doubts."

"Are you questioning your judgment about me?"

"I'm not, but other people are."

"What other people?"

"People at a high level who told me it was a waste of time to send you there."

"And what did you say in my defense?"

"What could I say? You gave me this story about a French company buying weapons from Russia and shipping them to Mexico. And the weapons turned out to be oil equipment."

"Where did you get that information?"

"From people at a high level."

"Where did they get it?"

"From the customs people. That shipment was checked when it entered Mexico, and it was checked again when it crossed our border. And it wasn't weapons, it was oil equipment."

"When did it cross our border?"

"Three days ago."

"Then the weapons are in our country now."

"There are no weapons."

"There *are* weapons. They were disguised as oil equipment."

"All right," his boss said, humoring him. "The weapons are in our country now. What do you want me to do about it?"

"I want you," Fenly said with urgency, "to find the truck that carried the weapons across the border."

"Where would we look for it?"

Fenly considered. "If it crossed the border three days ago, it's already in New York."

"If it's carrying weapons, it won't get into New York City. They check all trucks entering the city."

"It doesn't have to get into the city. They can hit the target with missiles launched from outside the city."

"Well, I can't order a search of the entire state for a truck that you believe is carrying missiles."

"If you wait until I know," Fenly said, "it could be too late. You have to act now on what I believe."

"I'll act when you have evidence," his boss told him. "When you have it, call me."

On Friday he took Camila to the same restaurant, where they ordered the same dishes as they had the first time.

When he reminded her that Stephen Wyatt had introduced him to this restaurant, she asked: "How did you meet him?"

He hesitated, sipping his wine. "I may as well tell you— I was a bad kid. I was in a gang."

"You were? What made you join a gang?"

"I wanted to be a member of something, and a gang was the only thing to join."

"You didn't have a church?"

"We had a church, but that was for girls." He caught himself. "I mean for women."

"You can say girls in that context."

"It wasn't cool for a guy to be an active member of the church. If you were, people might wonder what the priest was doing with you."

She grimaced at the implication.

"Anyway, I wanted to be a member of something, and it was cool to be a member of a gang."

"What did the gang do?"

"The usual things. It dealt drugs, extorted store owners, and mugged people."

"You did those things?"

"I told you I was a bad kid."

"So how did you meet Mr. Wyatt?"

"We mugged him."

"You did? I hope you didn't hurt him."

"We didn't touch him. There was something about him that held us back. He talked to us and gave us his money and invited us to come to the center."

"Did you go there?"

"Not right away. I went there after my friend got killed."

"A friend of yours got killed?"

"A rival gang shot him. I watched him die. I had his blood all over my jeans."

"Why did you go to Mr. Wyatt?"

"I needed someone to talk to," Fenly said, "and I couldn't think of anyone else."

"I'm interested in all this," she said after a moment, "because my brother joined a gang."

"They have gangs in Yonkers?"

"There's one in our neighborhood."

"How old is your brother?"

"He's sixteen. He was nine when they killed our father. He saw those people shoot him. So he should know better than to join a gang."

"If I'd seen people shoot my father, it would have made an impression on me."

"Mr. Wyatt talked with him, but it didn't help."

"If you want, I could talk with him."

"Would you?" she said hopefully. "Since you were in a gang, he might listen to you."

"Sure. What's his name?"

"Sergio. He was named after my father."

"It's hard for a guy not to have a father. You have your mother, but your brother has no one."

"Is that how you felt? Like you had no one?"

"Most of the time. And that's why Stephen made such a difference in my life."

"Well, maybe you can make a difference in my brother's life."

"I'll see what I can do," he told her.

After dinner he took her to his apartment. He moved two chairs over to the window so that they could sit there and look at the view. She was relaxed with him. She obviously trusted him not to try anything, and he had no intention of betraying her trust, though he wanted like hell to make love with her.

"What do you want to do with your life?" she asked him, gazing out the window.

"I want to make money while it lasts."

"While what lasts?"

"The boom in the economy."

"And then what?"

"I want to be like Stephen. I want to give back." He gazed out at the river, where he could see the lights of a tug towing a barge upstream. "What do *you* want to do with your life?"

"I want to get a college degree. I want to get a better job. And I want to make enough money so that I can help my mother and my brothers."

"I think we have similar goals."

"I think we do. But neither of us talked about getting married and having a family."

"I haven't thought about it," he admitted.

"I have," she told him, "but I have to achieve my other goals before I get married."

"How old are you?"

"I'm nineteen. You must have guessed I'm a virgin, and you should know I intend to remain one until I'm married."

"That's fine," he said, lying for the first time that evening.

"I want to save myself for my husband."

"What kind of guy do you want to marry?"

"You mean man."

"What kind of man?"

"A man like my father."

"What was he like?"

"He was a good man."

"Was he like Stephen Wyatt?"

"Yes. He was."

"So if I turn out like Stephen, will I have a chance?"

"You might," she said with a demure smile.

A week later, on a Saturday, he drove to her house in Yonkers, where she had invited him for dinner. He couldn't find a parking place on her street, so he left his car in a nearby lot that was almost empty, wondering if his car would still be there when he returned. In the neighborhood where he had grown up at least the hubcaps would be missing.

The houses on the street were detached, but they were small and there wasn't much space between them. Camila's house needed painting, and the narrow strip of yard needed tending. It looked as if her brother wasn't helping.

Camila met him at the door, wearing jeans and a simple top. She greeted him with a bright smile and let him in, saying: "Come and meet my mother."

He followed her through the house to the kitchen, where her mother was preparing dinner, wearing an apron. She was pure white, so Camila must have gotten her color and her Indian features from her father. Still, there was a resemblance between mother and daughter—they had the same proud demeanor.

"*Bienvenido,*" her mother said, wiping a hand on her apron and extending it. "*Un gran placer.*"

"*Igualmente,*" Fenly said, wondering if that was correct. From his experience with Colombians, he knew that they considered themselves the arbiters of correct Spanish in the Americas, and he was aware of his deficiencies, having learned the language from his mother and from the street. For the first time he wished he had studied it.

"I've heard a lot about you," her mother said, sizing him up.

"I hope it was good," Fenly said, playing the game.

"I heard you went to Princeton."

"Yeah," he said modestly.

"I wish Sergio wanted to go to college."

"He needs to go to a better high school," Camila said.

"He should go to Sacred Heart," her mother said.

"He won't go there. He says it's for girls."

"I felt that way when I was his age," Fenly said. "But thank God, someone woke me up."

"Then maybe you can understand my son," the mother said. "I can't, and my daughter can't."

"Where is he?"

"In the living room watching television."

"I'll take you there," Camila said.

He followed her into the living room, where a male version of her was lounging on the sofa, watching a rap video.

"Sergio? This is Fenly."

"Hi," the boy said without taking his eyes off the video.

"It's nice to meet you," Fenly said gamely.

"I'll leave you together," Camila said. "I need to go and help with dinner."

Fenly sat down in a chair and watched the video with Sergio. It wasn't even good rap. "You like this shit?"

Sergio shrugged.

"You think it's cool?"

"It's as cool as anything," Sergio said.

When the video ended Fenly asked: "Do you like cars?"

"I like some cars."

"Well, let's go and see my car. I think you'll like it."

Fenly got up and stood there waiting. Sergio finally raised himself from the sofa as if he were lifting a ton of dead weight.

After ducking his head into the kitchen to tell Camila where they were going, Fenly left the house with Sergio dragging along behind him.

As they walked toward the lot the boy asked: "Did you leave your car there?"

"Yeah. I did. Is there a problem?"

"It's not a good place to leave a car at night."

"You mean the guys you hang out with might trash it?"

"They don't trash cars."

"What do they do to them?"

"They steal them."

"You think that's cool?"

"It's as cool as anything," Sergio said again.

"Well, if anyone steals my car," Fenly told him, "I'll hold you personally responsible."

"What'll you do to me?"

"I'll beat the living shit out of you."

"My sister wouldn't let you."

"Yeah, she would. She gave me permission to do whatever I think is necessary."

Sergio didn't reply to that. He followed Fenly into the lot, and when he saw the car he finally showed a sign of life. "Is this your car? Where did you get the money to buy it?"

"I didn't get it from dealing drugs."

"Then how did you get it?"

"From working on Wall Street. I make more money in one week than a drug dealer makes in a year. I mean," Fenly added, "if he lasts a year."

Sergio stared at the car in wonder.

"You want to take a ride?"

"Sure. How fast does it go?"

"It goes a lot faster than the speed limit."

He unlocked the car with the remote, and they both got in. Before they were moving Sergio had turned on the radio and found a rap station.

"If you want to ride in my car," Fenly said, "you can't listen to that shit."

"What can I listen to?"

"Latina music."

"That's not cool."

"It's cool among winners."

Sergio found a *merengue* and left the dial there.

"So where can I show you how fast this car will go?"

"The Sprain Parkway."

"Tell me how to get there."

Following Sergio's directions, he drove to the parkway, and when he saw a long straightaway ahead of them he floored the accelerator.

At ninety the boy said: "Holy shit."

At a hundred and twenty he just held on, looking scared.

Not wanting to get stopped, and seeing a curve ahead of them, Fenly slowed down to eighty.

"That's awesome," Sergio said, almost in a whisper.

"It can go faster, but I don't want to get a ticket."

"You don't have to prove it. I believe you."

On the way back Fenly said: "Now, tell me about the high school you go to."

"It sucks," Sergio said.

"So why do you go there?"

"It's the school I was assigned to."

"But you could go to a better school."

"No, I couldn't. We don't have the money."

"The money can be found. It's not a problem."

"Well, I don't want to go where my sister went."

"Why not?" he asked, knowing the answer.

"Because it's for girls."

"So girls get all the good things in life," Fenly said, "and boys get all the shit?"

"I didn't say that."

"You didn't have to. I understand how you feel. I had an older sister who was perfect. She always made me feel like shit."

"That's how Camila makes me feel."

"But I finally realized, just in time, that she wasn't making me feel like shit. I was making myself feel like shit. So I couldn't blame her."

"What did you do?"

"I started taking responsibility for myself. And with the help of Mr. Wyatt I got into a better school."

"I don't want his help."

"Why not?"

"Because he helped Camila, and he helped my mother."

"You mean you want your own mentor?"

"If that's the word for it, yeah."

"Okay. Will you accept me as your mentor?"

"I'll think about it," Sergio said with his eyes on the road ahead of them. He had his sister's pride, and maybe he also had her brains.

When they left the car in the parking lot Sergio wrote a note on a piece of paper that Fenly found in the glove compartment, telling his gang not to mess with the car. At least it was a step in the right direction.

He was drinking coffee, watching the news on CNN, when Raquel called him and told him to meet her at the police station. He found her and Leandro there in a conference room.

"Daryl got sick this morning," Leandro said, "and he thinks they tried to poison him."

"Maybe they did," Fenly said.

"Yeah, maybe they did. Or maybe he put milk in his coffee that had been out of the refrigerator for a while. In any case he's ready to deal with us."

"Is he here?"

"He'll be here shortly."

"While we're waiting," Fenly said, "I'll give you an update. My boss says that the shipment from Russia was checked when it entered Mexico, and it was checked again when it crossed our border. And it was oil equipment."

"Where did he get that information?"

"From people at a high level."

Leandro snorted. "With all due respect to your people at a high level, I wouldn't believe what they say."

"I wouldn't either, but my boss has to believe what they say. He reports to them."

"I thought your country did away with hierarchies."

"To some extent we did in business, but not in government. And even in business we still have levels."

"So all that talk about flat organizations is a crock of shit?"

"It's like the talk about the world being flat."

"We proved it wasn't flat more than five hundred years ago."

"Well, now that's being questioned."

"What should be questioned," Leandro said disdainfully, "is that information from your people at a high level."

"My boss won't question it unless I can give him something to convince him."

"So let's hope that Daryl can give us something."

"Do we have a report on the DNA?" Raquel asked.

"We should have it by this afternoon."

Daryl looked pale when they brought him into the interview room. He had lost his perfect tan.

Leandro and the inspector interviewed him, observed by Raquel and Fenly.

"How are you feeling?" Leandro asked.

"I've felt better," Daryl said.

"Are you ready to tell us everything you know?"

"I am if I have your assurance that I'll be protected."

"Protected from what?" the inspector asked.

"From the people who tried to kill me."

"You have our assurance. But we can do a better job if you tell us who they are."

"They're terrorists," Daryl said.

"What kind of terrorists?"

"It doesn't matter what kind they are. They're all alike."

"Why do you say that?"

"They all want the same thing. They want to disrupt the status quo and change the world. At least that's what the leaders want. The followers don't have a clue."

"Can tell us about the leaders of this group?"

"I can give you descriptions of them."

"Can you give us their names?"

"I can give you the names they used in our dealings."

"That'll be helpful," Leandro said. "In our first interview you told us that the French company bought oil equipment with the laundered money."

"That was a cover."

"What did they buy?"

"Guided missiles."

"What kind of warheads?"

"Warheads capable of mass destruction."

"Did they say what their target was?"

"They only said it was in New York City. They talked about killing forty to fifty thousand people."

"Where did you meet with the leaders of this group?" the inspector asked.

Daryl told him all the places that he remembered, including his own apartment on Montera.

"You never went to where they lived?"

"They didn't want me to know where they lived."

"I'm troubled by something," Leandro said. "You now admit that you knew what they were planning to do with the laundered money. So why did you help them?"

"I want to change our government. The people in power betrayed our country," Daryl explained. "They knew in advance about the attack on 9-11 and they let it happen."

"Who let it happen?"

"The people running our government."

"Do you have any evidence of what you're claiming?"

"I have all the evidence you need."

"Where is it?"

"It's in a bank."

"Where?"

"In Madrid. If you go to my apartment and open the cover of the thermostat, you'll find the key to a safe deposit box."

"We'll look at your evidence," Leandro said, "and then we'll want to question you further."

"That's fine. Will you keep me here?"

"We'll keep you here until this evening. By then we'll have a safe place for you."

"All right. In the meantime I won't eat anything."

"Yeah, you should give your stomach a rest."

Before they left the police station Fenly called his boss at home and woke him up.

"This better be good," his boss said gruffly. "It's four in the morning."

"We have information that the shipment to Mexico wasn't oil equipment. It was guided missiles."

"What's your source?"

"Daryl MacKenzie."

"Fenly," his boss said paternally. "I agreed to keep an open mind, but there's a limit. Daryl MacKenzie isn't a reliable source of information. He has a screw loose."

"Where did you get that idea?"

"I got it from people at a high level. I got the whole story on Daryl MacKenzie. Are you ready for it? MacKenzie claimed they knew in advance about the attack on 9-11 and they let it happen. He said they wanted a terrorist attack so that they could use it for political purposes. And when no one paid any attention to him, MacKenzie lost it. He went berserk."

"So they say we shouldn't believe him now?"

"They say we shouldn't believe a word of what he says."

"Well, maybe they don't want us to believe him."

"They don't want us to waste our time."

"But they can't ignore him. Look what happened the last time they ignored him."

"They ignored him because he didn't have any information. He made up that story *after* the attack."

"Well, I don't think he made up *this* story. We have four dead people to corroborate it."

"That doesn't corroborate the story. Those people could have been killed for any reason." His boss paused, and then he asked: "Where are they holding him?"

"At a police station in Madrid."

"Are they going to charge him with anything?"

"They're going to charge him with money laundering," Fenly said, "and probably murder."

"So they're not going to release him."

"No. He's not going anywhere."

He and Raquel found the key where Daryl had said it was, and they went to the bank. After signing a paper they gained access to the safe deposit box. The only item inside the box was a flash drive, the kind you could put on a key chain.

They went from the bank to Fenly's apartment, where he copied the contents of the flash drive onto his hard drive and onto a DVD for backup.

They met Leandro at the office in Chueca, where they printed three copies of each file from the flash drive. The two main files were a memorandum written by Daryl and a journal he had kept over a period of two years ending on September 11, 2001.

Fenly started reading the memorandum, leaving Raquel and Leandro behind because of their lack of proficiency in English.

"Does this mean what I think it does?" Leandro asked.

After hearing Leandro's translation of the opening paragraph into Spanish, he said: "That's right."

"Mother of God."

ELEVEN

THE LAST BRIEFING from Daryl MacKenzie, director of a special counterterrorism unit of the FBI, was dated September 10, 2001. The briefing was marked as extremely urgent, and it read as follows:

Summary. Since early June of the current year we have received a steady flow of reports that al-Qaeda is planning a major attack on the US. We now have information that the attack is scheduled for September 11, and that its targets will be the World Trade Center, the Pentagon, and the Capitol. The method of attack will be to hijack airplanes and crash them into the targeted buildings. We therefore urgently recommend that all flights within, into, and out of the US be suspended immediately in order to ensure that security measures are in place that will prevent anyone from boarding a plane with any type of weapon.

Date of attack. Since early this summer we have been monitoring phone conversations between Khalid Sheikh Mohammed, a top operations planner for al-Qaeda, and Mohammed Atta, the presumed leader of the attack team. In a phone conversation yesterday they set the date of the attack for September 11.

Targets. Since spring 1995 we have received reports that the following buildings would be targeted in an attack: the CIA headquarters, the Pentagon, the Transamerica Tower, the Sears Tower, the World Trade Center, the John Hancock Tower, the Capitol, and the White House. Our most recent report indicates that the attack will be limited to the East Coast, and that the targets will be the World Trade Center, the Pentagon, and the Capitol.

<u>Method of attack</u>. Since 1995 we have received reports of terrorist plots to use airplanes as weapons against strategic targets. In 1999 we received a report from our colleagues in Britain of a plot to use commercial aircraft as flying bombs. In April 2000 we were told by a man who had been trained as a member of the attack team that they planned to hijack planes from JFK and fly them into buildings. In January 2001 we received a report from our colleagues in France that radical Islamists were planning to hijack planes and use them as weapons. In April 2001 we received a report from reliable sources in Afghanistan of a plot to hijack airplanes and crash them into buildings. The report said that members of al-Qaeda were already in the US being trained as pilots. In July 2001 an FBI agent in Phoenix reported that some Middle Eastern men were taking flight training lessons in Arizona, and that they had connections with al-Qaeda. In August 2001 FBI agents in Minneapolis reported their suspicions that Zacarias Moussaoui, who was arrested for immigration violation, was involved in a plot to hijack airplanes and attack buildings.

<u>Attack team</u>. We believe that the attack team will be led by Mohammed Atta (see attachment for his background). We have evidence that Atta was living in Brooklyn in early 2000 along with Marwan al-Shehhi, Khalid al-Mihdhar, and Nawaf al-Hazmi, who we believe were recruited for the attack team. We have information that links Atta with Sheikh Omar Abdel-Rahman, who organized the 1993 bombing of the World Trade Center. We know that Atta was living in Germany during 2001, and that he was being monitored there until he returned to the US in early June. We believe that other members of the attack team have entered the country since then, and that they are ready to launch an attack.

<u>Warnings</u>. For several years we have received warnings from colleagues in other countries, which turned out to be premature or false alarms. But since early this summer we have received a steady stream of more specific warnings from colleagues in Israel, Britain, Egypt, Afghanistan, Jordan, Morocco, and Russia. We should not ignore these specific warnings.

<u>Recommended action</u>. Effective immediately, suspend all flights within, into, and out of the US in order to ensure that security measures are in place that will prevent anyone from boarding a plane with any type of weapon.

The briefing was accompanied by documentation on each item. A journal gave a daily account of the FBI activities known to the writer for a period of two years leading up to the date of the attack. At that point it stopped.

"Why did they ignore him?" Raquel asked.

"According to my boss," Fenly said, "he made up that story after the attack."

"Do you think he did?"

"I don't know."

"If he did warn them before the attack," Leandro said, "and they ignored him, that could be his grievance."

"That could explain why he's involved in this plot," Raquel said, "but it doesn't explain why they ignored him."

"Maybe they wanted an attack."

"But why would they have wanted an attack?"

"So they could use it for political purposes. And they did use it for political purposes."

"If they wanted an attack," Fenly said, troubled, "then maybe they want another attack."

"For political purposes?" Raquel asked.

Leandro nodded. "Their war on terror has become unpopular, and they could use another attack to justify it. Governments do that kind of thing."

"We have to talk with him," Fenly said, "and find out more."

At that moment the phone rang, and Leandro answered it. He listened, nodding. "Thanks. You've done a great job."

"What was that about?" Raquel asked.

"You'll be happy to hear that the DNA sample from Daryl matches what they found under Samira's fingernails."

"It does? Then he killed Samira."

"Since he used the same method on the other girl, we can pin that on him. And maybe we can get him for the pimp."

"I don't care about the pimp."

"It was a human life," Leandro reminded her.

"I guess it was," Raquel said, chastened.

"Well, I don't want to mention this development until we've finished questioning him about his briefing. Do you agree?"

They both agreed.

An hour later Leandro and the inspector were in the interview room with Daryl, who looked better than he had that morning.

"We read your briefing," Leandro told him. "We'd like to ask you some questions about it."

"Fire away," Daryl said.

"Who saw it before the attack on 9-11?"

"My boss saw it, and his boss saw it, and his boss saw it."

"Did the president see it?"

"He should have seen it. If he didn't, then someone stopped him from seeing it."

"Who would have done that?"

"His advisors," Daryl said.

"But *why* would they have stopped him from seeing it?"

"To advance their interests."

"What do you mean?"

"There were two groups of people who influenced him. They still do. The oil people and the Christian Zionists."

"I know who the oil people are," Leandro said, "but who are the Christian Zionists?"

"They believe that Christ will come again only when the Jews have returned to their historic homeland, so they supported the creation of the state of Israel, and they supported the expansion of Israel. They want Israel to be the dominant power in the region. And then they can wait for the Second Coming, the Day of Judgment, the End of the World."

"The president was influenced by nuts like that?"

"He got their money, and he got their votes."

"But why would they have wanted an attack on America?"

"To give us a reason for going to war against Islam."

Leandro frowned. "So the Christian Zionists wanted an attack on America, and they influenced the president. Did the president want an attack on America?"

"I don't know, but he welcomed the reason for going to war, just as Roosevelt welcomed the reason for going to war when the Japanese attacked Pearl Harbor."

"Did he know in advance about the attack?"

"If you mean Roosevelt," Daryl said, "he knew in advance about the attack. It's common knowledge."

"I meant Bush," Leandro said.

"Well, I don't know if he saw my briefing. I only know that his advisors saw it, and they ignored it."

"You mean the Christian Zionists saw it."

"They saw it, and the oil people saw it."

"Why would the oil people have wanted an attack?"

"To give us a reason for invading Iraq. They wanted to gain control of a major oil-producing nation. They'd lost control of Venezuela, and they wanted to compensate for that."

Leandro considered. "So the invasion of Iraq wasn't about weapons of mass destruction?"

"No. But it wasn't only about oil. For once the two groups agreed on something. They agreed that we should invade Iraq but for different reasons."

"And they let the attack on 9-11 happen so that the president would have a reason for going to war?"

"They did," Daryl said definitely.

Leandro paused as if he were trying to deal with the enormity of what he had just heard, and then he asked: "Can you tell us more about the attack they're planning now?"

"I've told you everything I know."

"*Bueno*. I have one last question. Why did you help them?"

"I told you. I want to change our government."

"How would another attack do that?"

"The only success they can claim in their war on terror is that we haven't had a major attack on our homeland since 9-11. And I don't want them to be able to make that claim. I want to turn people against them."

"You're a typical terrorist," Leandro said. "You're willing to kill innocent people for your purpose."

"They're a typical government," Daryl said. "They're willing to kill innocent people for their purpose."

"That doesn't justify what you're doing."

"I don't have to justify it. But if you want a justification," Daryl continued, "killing forty to fifty thousand people now will save lives in the long run."

"It will? How?" Leandro asked doubtfully.

"By changing our government."

"It might not do that. It might only give your government a reason for expanding the war."

"Not if people know they could have stopped it."

"Are you saying they could stop this attack?"

"Yeah. If they wanted to, they could."

"But they don't have the kind of detailed information that you say they had for 9-11."

"They have enough information."

"You mean the information we gave them?"

"I mean the information *I* gave them."

For the first time Leandro lost his composure. "What? You gave your government information about this attack?"

"I did. And they're ignoring it."

"What information did you give them?"

"The same information I gave you. It's not the whole picture, but it's enough to stop the attack."

"If it *is* enough, then tell us how to use it."

"That's easy. Search the area within a hundred miles of New

York City. If you do that, you can stop the attack."

After thanking Daryl for his cooperation Leandro turned the questioning over to the inspector.

"Let's talk," the inspector said, "about the two girls and the pimp who were murdered."

"What about them?" Daryl asked.

"Your DNA matches what we found under the fingernails of the Moroccan girl who was murdered on Sunday. Did she give you that scratch on your chin?"

Confronted by the evidence, Daryl seemed to lose his will to deny what he had done. He seemed to want the relief that would come from making a confession. "Yeah. She did."

"Did you kill that girl?"

"Yeah. I killed her."

"How did you do it?"

"I strangled her with her stocking."

"Would you tell us why?"

"She saw me go into Caballero de Gracia the night the other girl was killed, and I was afraid that she would identify me."

"Did you kill the other girl?"

"Yeah. She saw Smith pick up the money, and I was afraid that she would report it to the police."

"What about her pimp?"

"I killed him too. The scumbag tried to blackmail me."

"Well, it's a good thing you like Spain," the inspector said. "You're going to spend the rest of your life here."

After they wound up the interview they walked to the plaza on Mesonero Romanos to get something to eat. It was after six, and none of them had eaten since breakfast.

They were drinking wine and eating an assortment of *tapas* when Leandro's phone rang.

From his expression Fenly could tell it was bad news.

"They killed Daryl," Leandro said, getting up.

"What? How?" Raquel asked.

"A sniper shot him while he was coming out of the police station. The shots came from a building across the street."

"Was anyone else hurt?"

"No. Whoever did it was an expert. He hit Daryl with three quick shots to the head."

"It sounds like a contract killing."

"That's what I was thinking."

"How did they know where Daryl was?" Fenly asked, having signaled the waiter to bring the check.

"They must have had a tail on him," Raquel said.

"So they were watching him all along?"

"They probably were," Leandro said. "They were probably waiting for a chance to get rid of him."

"They could have killed him in Marbella," Fenly pointed out. "It would have been easier."

"They could have. But they didn't have a pressing reason for killing him until we caught him."

Fenly remembered that his boss had asked where they were holding Daryl. He had given his boss the information, and his boss could have passed it on to people in the government who didn't want Daryl talking about 9-11. He couldn't believe that his boss had set in motion a plot to get rid of Daryl, but he couldn't dismiss the possibility.

They walked to Montera, where the street was cordoned off. The body was still lying on the pavement in front of the police station while technicians worked the crime scene.

They talked with the inspector who had interviewed Daryl.

"We think it came from the second floor of that building," the inspector said, pointing.

It wasn't the apartment where Daryl had lived.

"Let's go and see if Antonio has anything," Raquel said.

"That's a good idea," Leandro said.

The three of them went to the surveillance office.

"I was just going to call you," Antonio said when he opened the door and saw them.

"Do you have something?" Raquel asked.

"Yes. Come and see." Antonio led them to the table, where a series of pictures was arranged. They showed a window on the second floor of a building down the street with a rifle sticking out of it. The last one showed a puff of smoke.

"Can you enlarge them?" Leandro asked.

"We're doing that right now," Antonio told him.

They walked to the window and looked down the street toward the building where the shot had come from.

"It makes me think of Dallas," Leandro said. "I was just a kid then, but I still remember it."

"They never told us what really happened," Fenly said.

"There were conspiracy theories about that. And now we have a conspiracy theory about 9-11."

"Do you believe it?" Raquel asked.

"I don't know. We have one guy's story, but we have nothing to corroborate it."

"When they killed the guy who first told us about this plot, it corroborated his story."

"If they killed Daryl to stop him from talking about 9-11, it *would* corroborate his story. But if they killed him to stop him from telling us more about this plot, it wouldn't."

"Well, let's see what these pictures tell us."

José emerged from the other room with the enlarged pictures, which he handed to Antonio.

"Guess what?" Antonio said after examining them.

"What?" Leandro said.

"The sniper was an American."

"Let me see."

Antonio handed the pictures to Leandro, who examined them while Raquel and Fenly looked over his shoulder. The best ones showed the face of a man looking out the window before he raised the rifle and aimed it.

"You're right," Leandro said. "It was an American."

"You can see that in his face," Raquel said.

"How can you see that?" Fenly asked.

"From the look of innocence."

"Innocence in the face of a sniper?"

"Believe it or not," Leandro said, "you see a similar look of innocence in the face of a suicide bomber."

"Are you sure you have the right word for it?"

"I think we do," Raquel said. "It's the look of someone who doesn't know what the hell he's doing."

Fenly studied the pictures, beginning to understand what his colleagues meant. "So they hired an American to kill him?"

"It would make sense," Leandro said.

"It would be poetic justice," Raquel said.

They took copies of the pictures to the police, who by now had removed the body. The street was still cordoned off, so pedestrian traffic was clogging the side streets as it flowed both ways between Gran Vía and Puerta del Sol.

Since the investigation was in the hands of the police, Leandro suggested that they all go home and get some sleep and take a fresh look at the situation in the morning.

Fenly went back to his apartment, but he didn't go to bed. He sat in the living room, sipping brandy and wondering if Daryl had been killed to stop him from telling them more about the planned attack or to stop him from talking about 9-11.

They started having dinner on the weekday evening when Camila didn't have a class and again on Friday. Within a few months he was also having dinner at her house on Saturday, spending the night in Yonkers with his mother, and meeting Camila on Sunday for the mass in Spanish at San Pedro. Her mother and her brother Julio went to church while Sergio stayed home and watched television. But shortly after his ride with Fenly he quit the gang and started getting more serious about school. His decision to quit the gang was reinforced by the arrest of two of its members for stealing a car. By fall he had transferred to Sacred Heart and was doing well there, planning to go to college like his sister.

Camila graduated in May 2001. After the ceremony, which was held on the campus of St. Catherine, they left the crowd and strolled along the winding path at the edge of the bluff that overlooked the river. It was a beautiful afternoon, with cotton balls of cloud in the bright blue sky and silver ripples on the surface of the water, which darkened as you looked across into the shadow of the Palisades.

"You should be proud of yourself," he told her.

"I'm thankful," she said. "A lot of people helped me."

"So you've achieved one of your goals."

She nodded. "Yes. And now I have to make some money."

"Do you remember saying that you have to achieve your other goals before you get married?"

"Yes, I remember. I said that on our first date."

"It was actually on our second date."

"The first one didn't count."

"Do you still believe what you said then?"

She shook her head. "No, it was a stupid thing to say. You can be married and also make money. But I was only nineteen then. What did I know?"

"Do you remember what you said when I asked you what kind of man you wanted to marry?"

"Yes, I remember. I said I wanted to marry a good man."

"So have I turned out good enough?"

She turned and faced him with love in her eyes. "Are you asking me to marry you?"

"I guess I am."

She smiled. "You guess? Then I guess I will."

They set the date for October 7, and she spent the summer making preparations. The wedding was going to be at San Pedro, the reception was going to be at the Polish Center, and they were going to Cartagena for their honeymoon.

Toward the end of August his tooth started bothering him.

Of course they never found her remains, so they had a memorial service for her at San Pedro. He was staying with his mother in Yonkers since his building was off limits. In fact, he wasn't allowed to go back to his apartment for almost two months, and when he finally did he couldn't bear to look out the window. He sold his apartment for what he could get for it and moved to the Upper West Side, where he rented an apartment on a street off Columbus

Avenue. Meanwhile his company, which had lost all but ten of its employees, had relocated to midtown. He stayed with them long enough to help them get back on their feet, and then he left them and joined a special unit of the government that tracked the money being used to finance acts of terrorism. It gave him a purpose and a way of usefully applying his knowledge of financial systems.

At first he sought consolation wherever he saw a possibility of finding it, including rum but excluding women. His mother and his sister were helpful, but he turned most frequently to Stephen, meeting him after work at the center and going home with him for dinner. Stephen lived in a modest house in Sleepy Hollow with his wife Marya, a rose-cheeked blond with a lot of street smarts and a big heart. On these occasions Stephen cooked the comfort food that Fenly had been raised on, rice and beans and stewed meat with fried plantains, and they sat around the table talking and drinking Presidente.

On one of these occasions after Marya had excused herself and gone to bed, Stephen and Fenly stayed up talking.

"You won't get over it," Stephen told him. "You never will. But that doesn't mean your life is over, and it doesn't mean you'll never love again."

"How do you know?"

"My first wife was killed by terrorists."

"Oh, my God," Fenly said. "Where did it happen?"

"In Argentina. But it could have happened anywhere. From dealing with it I learned one thing that might be helpful to you."

He waited to hear it.

"Do you know the prayer of St. Francis?"

"I have it on a coffee mug that Camila gave me."

"Well, learn that prayer, and say it whenever you start to think about yourself. 'O Divine Master, grant that I may not so much seek to be consoled as to console, to be understood as to understand, to be loved as to love. For it is in giving that we receive.' It'll help you to think about other people."

He followed Stephen's suggestion, and it did help. He spent more time with Camila's mother who needed money as well as consolation, and with her brother Sergio, who was a senior now at Sacred Heart, and with her brother Julio, who missed his sister terribly. He resumed going to church with her family and having Sunday dinner with them.

And he drank coffee out of that mug every morning.

Fenly was awakened by his cell phone. He had dozed off in the living room holding the glass of brandy, some of which had spilled on his pants.

It was Raquel, and she sounded upset.

"What happened?" he asked her.

"They killed Leandro."

"What? Where are you?"

"I'm at home. The cops came here and told me about it."

He glanced at his watch: it was quarter after ten.

"They got him as he was walking from his car to the entrance of his house," Raquel said, choking on the words. "The cops think it was the same guy who killed Daryl."

"Then you're not safe."

"You're not either."

"We have to get out of here."

"Where would we go?"

"To America. We have to stop this attack."

"I know. But I wish we had more information."

"We may have enough. How many cops are there with you?"

"Four," she said, "with two cars."

"Well, have them take you to the airport. Find a way to leave your building so this guy doesn't have a shot at you."

"What about you?"

"Ask the cops to come and get me at my apartment."

"How will you get out of there?"

"The building must have a rear entrance. Tell them to stop a car in front and flash the lights to attract attention."

"Where will we meet?"

"At the Lufthansa ticket counter."

"Why there?"

"We're going to Frankfurt."

"I thought we were going to America."

"We are. But if we go from here to Frankfurt, they won't be able to track us so easily. And once we're there we can book the next flight to New York."

"*Bueno*. Be careful."

"You be careful too."

After quickly packing he was ready to go when he heard the buzzer from the entrance of the building. Through the intercom he asked who it was, and an unfamiliar voice said it was former colleagues of Raquel. At this point he wished he had arranged some kind of code with her, but it was too late. If the sniper got into the building, it would take him a while to blast through the door of the apartment, and during that time Fenly could call the police for help. There would be at least a dozen cops posted on Montera, only a few minutes away. So he took the risk of letting whoever was at the entrance into the building.

Watching the hallway through the peephole of the door, he saw two cops get out of the elevator. They got their bearings and headed toward him. They looked like cops, and they walked like cops in a dangerous situation, holding their guns in a ready position and glancing over their shoulders to make sure there was no one behind them.

When they stopped at the door one of them said in a low but clearly audible voice: "We heard from Ramón that you might need us."

He asked God to bless Raquel for thinking of a code that no one else, not even his boss, would know about, and he opened the door for the cops.

"Come on," the older one told him urgently.

There was no need for introductions.

He followed them to the freight elevator, which they took down to the main floor, and out the rear of the building into a courtyard. They came out on the street that ran parallel to Calle Tres Cruces, where an unmarked car was waiting.

At the invitation of the driver Fenly got into the front while the two cops got into the back, and they drove away.

"Is Raquel all right?" he asked the cops.

"She's on her way to the airport," the older cop said.

"We spotted the guy," the younger cop said. "He came to kill her, but when he saw us on her street he bolted. Our colleagues pursued him, but unfortunately he got away."

"He won't get far," the older cop said.

"If he has a car," Fenly said, "he could follow us."

"We have police cars behind us. They're going slow, and if he tried to pass them they could stop him."

"I assume they're watching for this guy at the airport."

"They put on extra security, and they're on high alert for him. They have his picture."

At the airport two bodyguards in plainclothes met him at the curb and then accompanied him to the Lufthansa ticket counter, where Raquel was waiting.

"*Gracias a Dios,*" she said upon seeing him.

Conscious of the bodyguards, he hugged her thankfully.

"I haven't bought a ticket yet," she told him. "The next flight to Frankfurt is at six tomorrow morning. It arrives at eight forty-five, and there's a flight to New York at ten. So we should be able to make that."

"If there isn't a delay," he said. "Let's buy the tickets and find a place to spend the night."

They reserved a suite at the Tryp Diana, which was next to the airport. They were driven to the hotel by the bodyguards in an unmarked car.

As they rode up in the elevator he said: "I hope you don't mind sharing a room."

"No, I don't mind," she said.

"I just think we should stay together."

The suite had all the amenities for the international business traveler, including a minibar and access to the Internet. They used the former and opened a bottle of red wine, which they drank sitting together on the sofa.

"Tell me what's happening," Raquel said.

"I wish I knew," Fenly said, trying to penetrate the mystery. "I mean, it's clear that someone wants to kill us, but I don't know why. Is it because we know about this plot? Or is it because we know what Daryl said in his briefing."

"We don't know much about the plot."

"But they may think we do."

"I can't believe they killed Leandro," Raquel said, beginning to cry. "He was a good man."

"He was," Fenly said, feeling the loss.

"His son and daughter are still in school."

"How old are they?"

"Sixteen and fourteen."

He put his arm around her, wanting to console her. Of course there was nothing he could say. He could only be there for her.

They set the alarm for four in the morning and tried to get some sleep. He took the sofa and let her have the bed. He finally dozed off, but his sleep was disturbed by images of a tower collapsing and a wave of debris rolling toward him.

TWELVE

STEPHEN WAS WAITING for them at the airport, standing among the drivers who held signs with the names of the people they were meeting. Since Fenly and Raquel had only carry-on luggage, they went directly with him to the parking lot and got into his car. At Stephen's insistence Raquel sat in front while Fenly sat in back.

As they left the airport he began to explain their predicament to Stephen, not having gone into details when he had called from Frankfurt and asked Stephen to meet them at the airport.

Stephen listened without interrupting.

Raquel made a few clarifications, but otherwise she let Fenly tell the story.

At the end Stephen asked: "Who do you think killed Daryl?"

"We don't know," Fenly said. "We have two theories. One is that the terrorists killed him to stop him from telling us more about this plot, and the other is that our government killed him to stop him from talking about 9-11."

"The other is a conspiracy theory."

"I know it is, but it could be true. When they found out that he wasn't dead, they could have been worried. And they could have known where Daryl was."

"Who could have told them?"

"My boss could have told them."

"You think your boss is part of a conspiracy?"

"He could be. Or he could have just been doing his job. He could have told them where Daryl was in the normal course of business."

"Yeah. He could have."

"Whichever theory is correct," Fenly concluded, "they killed Leandro for the same reason they killed Daryl. And they want to kill us for the same reason."

"At least for now," Stephen said, "it doesn't matter which theory is correct. What matters is keeping you both alive and stopping this attack. Does your boss know where you are?"

"No. You're the only one who knows."

"I assume you have the information that Daryl gave you."

"I have the flash drive in my pocket, and I backed it up on my computer as well as on a DVD. I think we should put the drive into a safe deposit box."

"I'll take care of that today," Stephen said. He then turned to Raquel and asked: "What about your family? Won't they be worried about you?"

"I don't have a family," Raquel said.

"You have a family with us," Stephen said.

It was early afternoon, so they didn't run into much traffic going to Westchester, and they arrived at Stephen's house in Sleepy Hollow within forty minutes of the time they had left the airport. Fenly was familiar with the house, which had been built almost two hundred years ago as a farmhouse on land that had belonged to Frederick Philipse, the lord of a domain extending from the Bronx into Putnam County who had sided with the British in the War of Independence and had consequently lost everything. The house, no longer on a farm, was on a street of a village that had a growing Latino population. The house wasn't large, but it met the needs of Stephen and Marya, who each had an office on the second floor where they did the paperwork for their community activities.

Marya greeted them at the door, and she hugged Raquel as if she were a daughter coming home. After more than twenty years of working with Latinos in the Bronx community center, Marya had become fluent in Spanish, and she took over where Stephen left off. She graciously showed Raquel to the guestroom, where they remained while Stephen and Fenly talked in the kitchen, sitting at the table and drinking Presidente. It didn't take long for

Stephen to start telling Fenly about a boy he had met on the streets of the Bronx, who hadn't tried to mug him but had told him to go and fuck himself for no apparent reason. The boy was now playing basketball at the center and helping younger kids learn to play the game. It sounded like an invitation for Fenly to come and work with Stephen, and in his present situation Fenly was open to the idea.

"And guess what," Stephen said. "We have a baseball team."

"You do? That's great. Where do they play?"

"At a nearby park."

"How are they doing?"

"Better than the Yankees."

"I haven't been following them," Fenly said. "Their games aren't televised in Spain."

"They've lost five straight. They were swept by Boston last weekend, and then they were swept by Tampa Bay. They play Toronto tonight at home. And then they play Boston again this weekend. They need to get their act together. With all that talent they should be leading the division."

"What about the talent on your team?"

"We could use more, but we have this Dominican kid who I think could be a great pitcher."

"Where's he from?"

"Where else? San Pedro de Macorís. His family came here when he was twelve."

"So he's a real Dominican."

"Unlike you and Alex Rodriguez." Stephen was referring to the fact that Fenly and the Yankee star were born in America, though they were labeled as Dominicans.

"Well, I agree with his decision not to play on the Dominican team in the World Baseball Classic last year."

"A lot of Dominicans criticized him for not playing on their team, but he was right. He was making a statement that he's an American, not a Dominican."

"I wonder if the time will ever come when we won't have to make those statements."

"You may always have to, but your children won't have to."

"I can't imagine having children," Fenly said. With the death of Camila he had lost the ability to imagine having children. As far as he could see, he would spend his life helping the children of other people as Stephen and Marya did.

"I understand," Stephen said. "But don't rule anything out."

At that moment the women appeared, looking as if they had made a decision.

Stephen went out to take the flash drive to the bank, and then he returned with some more bottles of Presidente, which he had bought at a local bodega.

The four of them sat in the kitchen while Stephen cooked a *paella*. When it was ready the men switched to white wine, which the women were already drinking. They ate the *paella* in the kitchen helping themselves from the round pan in the center of the table. They avoided the subject of terrorism, but it hovered over them like a ghost of the old farmhouse.

Around ten Raquel admitted that she couldn't keep her eyes open any longer, which wasn't surprising—in Spain it was four in the morning now. So Marya took her upstairs to bed while Fenly helped Stephen clean up the kitchen.

"What's your plan for tomorrow?" Stephen asked.

"Before I can make a plan," Fenly said, "I need to learn more about guided missiles."

"We have a wireless network in the house, so you can get into the Internet."

"Is your network secure?"

"Of course it is. We don't want the neighbors to know our business."

"Are your neighbors nosy?"

"Most of them aren't, but a yuppie couple moved in across the street. You know, with Audis and designer bikes and cross-country skis."

"Cross-country skis? Do you get enough snow for them?"

"No. But they look good on the front porch."

"Who's going to notice them?"

"No one. But they want people to notice them. When they heard there were Colombians next door they thought that meant alumni of Columbia University."

"Well, isn't upward mobility what our country's about?"

"Yes. But in my mind upward mobility means enabling people to meet their material needs so they can address their spiritual needs. Instead, we're creating more and more material needs, which aren't essential, and we're ignoring spiritual needs."

"The churches aren't ignoring them."

"But every other institution is. Our society is based on division of labor. Education is the job of the schools, the economy is the job of businesses, health is the job of the medical system, and spiritual development is the job of the churches. People's lives are fragmented."

"I guess they are. But how would you deal with that problem?"

"I'd empower the family," Stephen said. "And I'd get the other institutions to work together helping the family."

"You mean the nongovernmental institutions."

"Right. We can't rely on the government."

"I know you have a policy of never trusting the government," Fenly said, "and now I understand why. We can't even trust them to protect us, and that's their primary responsibility."

"It's our responsibility. And when we make a better world, we won't need them to protect us."

"Yeah. I know. In the meantime I need the password to get into your network."

"*Sancocho*," Stephen said.

Sancocho was a typical Dominican dish, a stew that included beef, chicken, pork, plantains, yucca, yams, potatoes, peppers, garlic, and sour oranges. His mother still made it once or twice a month. "Do you know how to make one?"

"I got the recipe from your mother."

"Then why don't you make one for Raquel."

"You want to introduce her to Dominican food?"

"I just thought it would be something different for her."

Stephen looked at him closely but didn't pursue the matter. "Do you need anything else to work with?"

"I need a map of New York and the states around it."

"I have a good one in my car. I'll get it for you."

By the time Stephen returned with the map Fenly had logged on to the Internet and was typing the keywords.

He stayed up most of the night learning about guided missiles. From an enormous amount of information he concluded that the terrorists were most likely to use surface-to-surface cruise missiles, whose low trajectory would make them harder to detect. Among the missiles made in Russia the most likely type had a maximum range of one hundred seventy-five miles with the capability of delivering a four-hundred-forty-pound warhead if launched from land.

He studied the map to determine the most likely launching area. By the time he fell asleep on the sofa he had drawn some conclusions, which he planned to present to the others so that they could challenge him. There wasn't enough time to be wrong about the launching area.

Sitting with them at the kitchen table the next morning, he reviewed his research and described the type of missile he believed the terrorists would use.

"How would they guide it?" Stephen asked.

"With an inertial navigation system," Fenly said, having learned the terms. "The missile has a computer and sensing devices on board. Its position, its speed, and its direction can be detected and modified without external references."

"You mean without radar or satellite."

"Yeah. It's a self-contained guidance system."

"I wish my car had one of those."

They laughed nervously.

"These missiles," Fenly said, "have a maximum range of one hundred seventy-five miles, so they could be anywhere within that distance of New York City, though I think they'll be as close as possible to the city."

"Why do you think that?" Marya asked.

"The closer they are, the less time they'll be in the air, and the less time there'll be to detect them."

"Daryl told us to search the area within a hundred miles of New York City," Raquel said.

"He did," Fenly said. "But we can rule out much of that area. The missiles can't be on Long Island or anywhere east of the Hudson River since you have to cross a bridge to get there, and we have pretty tight security on the bridges."

"We can also rule out New Jersey," Stephen said, "since it's so densely populated."

"Which leaves Pennsylvania and upstate New York."

"That's still a big area."

"But if you go west in Pennsylvania beyond the densely populated areas you run into mountains, and if you go west of the Hudson River you also run into mountains. Which narrows the likely area since you wouldn't want to send cruise missiles through the mountains."

"You could send them over the mountains."

"You could. But that would increase the likelihood of their being detected."

"Where does that leave us?"

"In a relatively small area northwest of New Paltz, southwest of Kingston, south of the Catskills, and northeast of the Shawangunk Mountains."

"Shong-gum," Stephen said. "At least that's how the locals pronounce it."

"Is that an English word?" Raquel asked uneasily.

"I think it's a Dutch word."

"It's a sparsely populated area," Fenly continued, "so you could do almost anything there without being noticed."

"They used to make moonshine in that area," Stephen said.

"How far is it from New York City?" Raquel asked.

"About eighty miles," Fenly said. "So the target is well within the range of the missiles. They're far enough away from the target to be in a sparsely populated area but near enough so they won't be in the air for very long."

"How fast do they fly?"

"They're supersonic."

"So there won't be much time to detect them," Stephen said.

"That's why we have to find them before they're launched."

"You keep saying missiles, but where did you get the idea there was more than one missile?"

"From Daryl," Fenly said. "He talked about missiles."

"He did," Raquel said. "He used the plural."

"Well, let's hope they're not in different areas."

"Yeah, that would complicate things."

After a silence Stephen said: "We need a plane to search the area and take pictures."

"Do you know anyone who has a plane?"

"I know a guy who could help us. Let's see if I can reach him." Stephen got up and went to the phone.

"Could you explain how the missiles work?" Marya asked. "I'm not good at science."

"Whatever I know," Fenly said, "I learned last night."

"It's more than I know," Raquel said.

He explained to them how the missiles worked, drawing from his research on them.

"We can get a plane," Stephen said, returning from the phone. "It's a plane they use for doing surveys. It has a camera and everything. The guy has to get a clearance to fly over the area, but he doesn't expect to have a problem. He can take one passenger, so Fenly should go with him."

"When does he expect to get the clearance?"

"Within a few hours. He'll let us know as soon as he gets it."

"How far away is the airport?"

"Only fifteen minutes. He keeps his plane at the airport in White Plains."

"Does he have maps of the area?"

"Yeah. He's done surveys there before."

A little more than an hour later the guy called and said he had clearance, so Stephen drove Fenly to the airport, leaving the women together in the house.

The pilot, whose name was Kyle, was in his thirties, and he talked like the pilots Fenly had heard over the intercom while traveling in commercial planes, with a low-key voice that would reassure you even if you saw a fire in an engine. He didn't say much before they took off, and he said even less while they were flying. The engine made too much noise for them to hear each other anyway.

Kyle had a map in a holder by the dashboard, and responding to a gesture Fenly pointed to the area he wanted to cover. It didn't take them long to get there, and while Fenly gazed down at the countryside, looking for objects that could be missiles, Kyle methodically took pictures, going back and forth over the area as if he were plowing a field.

After they had landed Kyle drove him to an office, where he copied the pictures to a DVD. He had just finished doing that when Stephen arrived to take Fenly back to his house. They arranged with Kyle to keep searching the area until they found what they were looking for. Of course they hadn't told Kyle what they were looking for, and Kyle hadn't asked. He seemed happy flying his plane and taking pictures.

Stephen printed the pictures on a machine in his office so that they could all look at them, and they spent the rest of the day sitting at the kitchen table, examining the pictures. They passed the pictures around from Raquel to Stephen to Marya to Fenly, so that all four of them could examine every picture.

They set aside the pictures that showed suspicious-looking items, but after examining them again they agreed that these items couldn't be missiles.

They took a break to eat dinner and to watch the first few innings of a game that the Yankees ultimately lost to Toronto. A new pitcher named Phil Hughes looked promising, but the Yankees never got their offense going.

"I'd rather look at pictures," Stephen said, "than watch them play like that."

"I don't understand baseball," Raquel said.

"I'll explain it to you when this whole thing is over."

"You should take her to a game," Marya said.

Around eleven they stopped working, and they decided that the next day they should search an area they hadn't covered, a little further north and west. This area overlapped the area they had covered the first day by about thirty percent.

But they found nothing the next day, and they were further discouraged by a game that the Yankees lost to Boston. Andy Pettitte didn't make it through five innings, and the team had its seventh straight loss. About fifty-five thousand people, mostly Yankee fans, were in the stadium watching the game and expressing their feelings.

The next day they had the pilot cover an area to the south and east, again overlapping the areas they had covered the first two days. But again they found nothing, and they stopped to watch the Yankees beat Boston, with Kei Igawa pitching a shut-out after taking over from the injured Jeff Karstens.

When he retired three straight hitters, Stephen said: "That's the way to do it. One, two, three."

Raquel stared at him. "What did you say?"

"I said one, two, three. You want me to explain?"

"No. I want to look at the pictures again," Raquel said, jumping up. She went to the table where they had been working. She put her hand on a pile and asked: "Were these pictures taken on the first day?"

"Yeah." By then Fenly had gotten up to join her.

"And were these taken on the second day?"

"Yeah. Why are you asking?"

"I think I might have noticed something." She shuffled through the pile from the first day and found a picture, then did the same with the piles from the second and third day. She arranged the three pictures on the table from left to right, saying: "One, two, three."

By then the others were looking over her shoulder at the pictures. In the first picture was something that looked like a sewer pipe, and in the picture from the second day there was another pipe of the same length, and in the picture from the third day there was another pipe of the same length. And all three were oriented in the same direction.

"Those could be the missiles," Raquel said.

"Where is this?" Fenly asked, looking for the map.

Stephen got it and laid it on the table.

With the map and the data on the pictures they were able to determine the exact location.

"How long will it take us to drive there?" Fenly asked.

"About two hours," Stephen said. "It's a Saturday night, so there won't be much traffic on the thruway."

"Then let's go."

"Are we all going?"

"We're all going," Marya said.

"Then pack what you need to spend the night there."

Along with their overnight bags they took a camera and a pair of binoculars that Stephen said his mother had used for bird watching.

As they headed south toward the Tappan Zee Bridge they encountered very little traffic. It was after ten, and everything in Tarrytown looked closed.

"Where are all the people?" Raquel asked.

"They're home in bed," Stephen said.

"In Madrid they'd be going out now. It would never be this dead on a Saturday night."

"This isn't much of a party town."

They crossed the bridge and headed north on the thruway.

"We won't be able to see anything tonight," Stephen said. "So when we get near the area we should look for a motel."

"That's fine," Fenly said. "I just want to be there when the sun comes up."

"I think we should contact the police before we go there."

"And have the police go there with us?"

"Why not?" Stephen asked. "If we're wrong, we'll only make fools of ourselves."

"I don't mind making a fool of myself," Raquel said.

"Then we'll stop at the nearest police station," Fenly said.

They left the thruway at New Paltz, where they found a motel that had two rooms available. It had taken a while for an old man to answer the door since it was almost one in the morning and he had undoubtedly been asleep.

They paid the man in advance, explaining that they had to get up early in the morning, and Stephen asked him where the nearest police station was, saying they needed help in finding a girl who had run away and may have been spotted in the area.

"That was a good story," Fenly said as they stopped in the corridor outside their rooms.

"I don't know where they come from," Stephen said.

"What time do we have to get up?" Marya asked.

"I think the sun rises at six," Fenly said.

"It does," Stephen said. "A few of us are up to see it rise."

"Well, I'm not a morning person like you."

"So we should meet no later than five," Fenly said.

"We need time to get the police," Stephen reminded him.

"Then make it four-thirty."

"Will the police be up at that hour?" Marya asked.

"They're up all night," Stephen said, "though there won't be many of them up at that hour."

"We don't need many of them," Fenly said.

"Let's hope we don't."

Raquel and Fenly went into their room. It had a regular double bed and no sofa.

"I'll sleep on the floor," he told her.

"Why?" she teased him. "Are you afraid of me?"

"No. I thought you'd be more comfortable not sharing a bed with a man."

"I don't mind sharing a bed with you. We're partners."

"Okay. Which side do you want?"

"I'll take the side near the bathroom. I might have to get up in the middle of the night."

"We could leave a light on."

"I couldn't sleep with a light on."

"You really expect to sleep tonight?"

"At this point I don't know what I expect." Her tone of levity had suddenly vanished. "I just want to get through the night."

"I understand," he said, remembering that in the past week she had lost her mentor and a girl she really cared about.

They stayed on their respective sides of the bed, and they did sleep, though not very well.

The next morning Fenly made coffee with the apparatus in the room while Raquel took a shower. The coffee was awful, but it helped to wake them up.

They left the motel before five. They followed the directions they had gotten from the old man the night before, and they easily found the police station. They decided that only Raquel and Fenly should go into the station since they both had identification as security agents.

There were three cops inside the station. Two of them, who had evidently just come on duty, were sitting in the reception area drinking coffee. The other was sitting behind a counter, looking as if he had been there all night and was more than ready to be relieved.

"Good morning," Fenly said, approaching the counter. "My name is Fenly Aquino. I'm a special agent for the Department of Homeland Security."

The cop behind the counter squinted at him. "Can I see some identification?"

"Sure." He handed his ID card to the cop.

The cop examined the card and then asked: "What are you doing in this neck of the woods?"

"We're here on an urgent matter. My colleague is a member of a Spanish counterterrorism team."

Visibly impressed, the cop asked Raquel: "You came here all the way from Spain?"

"Yes." She reached into her shoulder bag and produced her ID card, which she offered to the cop.

He waved his hand as if it wasn't necessary for him to check it. "How can I help you?"

"Well, it's a long, complicated story," Fenly said, "but the bottom line is, we believe that terrorists are planning to launch missiles aimed at New York City from a position about fifteen miles north of here."

The cop's jaw dropped.

The other two cops, who must have overheard Fenly, rose to their feet and came over.

"Did you hear that?" the cop behind the counter asked.

"I heard it," the first cop said. "It sounds like a plot from a movie, but you don't look like you're from Hollywood."

"I'm from the Bronx," Fenly said.

"My wife is from there," the second cop said.

"Can you give us a location?" the first cop asked.

"Here," Raquel said, taking the pictures out of her bag. She laid them on the counter.

"It looks like sewer pipes," the second cop said.

"It does," the first cop agreed. "But I don't know of any project in that area."

"You better check it out," the cop behind the counter said.

The two cops who had been drinking coffee left their cups for him to dispose of, and they headed out. The first cop opened the door and gallantly held it for Raquel as if to demonstrate that upstate cops weren't country bumpkins.

"Follow us," he said. "We know the way."

In Stephen's car they followed the cop car along a local road and then onto another local road. After going up a long hill the cop car slowed and pulled over.

The road had woods on both sides so you couldn't see anything but trees.

"It's over there," the first cop said, pointing through the woods. "There's a road that goes into that area, but if you're right I think it would be better to surprise them."

The cops each got a rifle from their car and led the way.

They moved slowly through the woods, being careful not to make any noise. Above them two birds were exchanging salvos, probably over territory.

The first cop stopped them before they reached the edge of the woods. From there they could see out into a clearing where three missiles, pulled out of the sewer pipes and pointing in the same direction, were in position for launching.

"Jesus Christ," the second cop whispered.

"You're definitely not from Hollywood," the first cop said.

Stephen handed the binoculars to Fenly, who used them to survey the scene. He counted three men who looked like they would have been profiled in Madrid.

"How many are there?" the first cop asked.

"I count three, but there could be more."

"We have to assume they're armed."

"Yeah, though they're not carrying weapons."

"They must be technicians," Stephen said. "They don't need thugs for this operation."

"Then maybe we can take them," the second cop said.

"Maybe we can," the first cop said, "but before we try, I'll call for backup."

They waited while he quietly used his radio to call the station.

"How do you want to do this?" the second cop asked him.

"I want to have them all in sight," the first cop said, "so that we can kill them before any of them can run for cover."

"Do you want to give them a chance to surrender?" Stephen asked before they raised their rifles.

"Did they give those people in the World Trade Center a chance to surrender?"

"No, but we put a higher value on human life."

"We do," the first cop agreed. "We put a higher value on the lives of the people these fuckers want to kill."

Stephen, who seemed to accept that, said nothing further.

The opportunity came when the three men walked together to the missile on the right and inspected it, and then walked to the next one."

"It looks like a final check," Fenly said.

"When they're between that missile and the last one," the first cop said to the second cop, "we'll fire at them. You take the guy on the right, and I'll take the guy on the left. If we get them, we can both get the guy in the middle."

The cops raised their rifles.

The three men spent what seemed like a long time inspecting the missile, but they finally started walking toward the last one.

"Fire," the first cop said.

They fired, and two of the men dropped to the ground. They fired again, and the third man dropped. They waited to see if anyone else appeared, and then they advanced into the clearing.

The missiles, like horses at a starting gate, looked ready for launching.

Two of the men were dead, and the third one was seriously wounded. To make sure that he couldn't pull anything, the first cop rolled him over and cuffed him.

Drawing on his background in engineering, Fenly found the cable from the missiles to the power supply and unplugged it.

"Will that stop them?" the first cop asked.

"I don't know. I hope so."

"Should we push them over just to make sure?"

"That won't make them explode, will it?" the second cop said.

"They're programmed to explode," Fenly said. "They won't explode on impact."

"Then let's push them over."

It wasn't easy, but with all six of them working together they pushed the missiles over so that they were all lying on the ground.

"They can't take off from that position," the first cop said with satisfaction.

At that point their backup arrived, and they waited at what they hoped was a safe distance for the army specialists, who arrived in a helicopter, responding to their call.

The specialists, two geeks in uniform, approached the missiles with the confidence of experienced veterinarians dealing with dangerous animals. They opened a missile and used their diagnostic instruments, discussing what they found in their own language. It took them only a few minutes to cancel the guidance program and disarm the missile. Within about twenty minutes they had dealt with all three missiles.

One of the specialists came over to them and said: "Guess what they were aimed at."

"The Empire State Building?" the second cop said.

"No. Yankee Stadium. They were programmed to hit the target during the Red Sox game."

"With fifty-five thousand people there?"

The first cop turned to the wounded terrorist and started to reach for his revolver as if he were going to put the man out of his misery, but he stopped and shook his head in disgust.

They walked back through the woods to Stephen's car, stunned by what had almost happened. They got into the car and sat there in silence for a long time.

"I think we should go home now," Marya said.

"Raquel and I can't go home," Fenly said.

"Why not? They have no reason to kill you now."

"The terrorists don't, but the other people do."

"You mean," Stephen said, "the people in our government who don't want you to talk about 9-11."

"I don't know if these people exist, but if they do we have to deal with them. We don't want to spend the rest of our lives hiding from them."

"Especially if they don't exist," Marya said.

"There's only one way to deal with them," Stephen said, "and that's to go public with the information you got from Daryl."

"I know," Fenly said. "But I don't know if we're ready to do that. Are you, Raquel?"

"No, I'm not ready. Too much has happened."

"We have to think about it," Fenly said.

"I have an idea," Stephen said after a moment. "I have a friend, a good friend, who has a cabin in the Adirondacks. If he's not using it, you could go there."

"You'd be safe there," Marya said. "It's in the boondocks."

"I like that idea," Fenly said.

"I do too," Raquel said.

"I'll call him now," Stephen said, taking out his cell phone.

The cabin was available for as long as they wanted it. Since they were already halfway there, they decided that Fenly and Raquel should go directly there. It would not only be more convenient, but it would also be less risky.

Stephen insisted that they take his car, which couldn't be traced to them. They just had to leave Stephen and Marya at a rental car office in New Paltz and then get back on the thruway, heading north. It would take them only about two hours to get to the cabin.

Stephen, who had stayed more than once at the cabin, gave him directions and told him where to find the key. He also gave him five hundred dollars in cash, which he withdrew from a cash machine in New Paltz, so Fenly wouldn't leave a trail by using his credit card to buy food and other necessary supplies.

They parted in New Paltz with long *abrazos*.

The cabin was on a dirt road, about eight miles from the nearest town and out of sight from the nearest neighbors. It was built of logs, with a bedroom and a common room that served as a living room and a kitchen. It had electricity and indoor plumbing as well as a wood stove for heating. It even had a ceiling fan.

Along the way they had stopped at a supermarket, where they had bought enough food and supplies to last a week, and after entering the cabin the first thing they did was to put these items away in the cupboard and in the small refrigerator.

Then, exhausted, they lay down on the bed and slept.

It was late afternoon when Fenly awoke. He sat up and looked at Raquel, who was still asleep, lying on her side with one hand under the pillow. From working with her and seeing her in action he had gradually developed a feeling toward her that now he realized was love.

He got up without waking her and wandered out the back door and onto a flagstone patio. From there he could see a long green valley, with mountains in the distance. The light of the sun, which was low in the sky, was streaming through the clouds like a benediction. He stood there for a long time, wishing they could stay in this cabin forever.

The light was turning a rose color when he felt Raquel's hand on his shoulder. He covered it with his hand, and said: "I feel like we're in paradise."

"I do too," she said softly.

When the sun had set they went back into the cabin, fleeing mosquitoes, and discussed what to have for dinner. They had bought a whole chicken, and Raquel made *pollo chilindrón,* in which the chicken was cooked slowly in sweet red peppers. The chicken was accompanied by white rice and green beans, which were cooked in olive oil.

"This is better than anything I had in Spain," he told her after tasting it. "And I had some really great meals there."

"I don't get to cook very often. I have no one to cook for."

"You don't cook for yourself?"

"I do, but I don't enjoy it. I think cooking is something you do for other people."

"If we get out of this alive, will you still work in security?"

"Oh, I don't know. In that job you're dealing only with the symptoms. In vice at least you can help people."

"So will you go back to your job in vice?"

"I might. Or I might become a social worker." She stared across the table. "I had a moment of satisfaction from catching the guy who killed Samira, but it didn't last. And I don't want that kind of satisfaction. I want the kind of satisfaction I would have had from getting Samira off the street."

"I understand. You want to deal with the cause."

"I want to work for a better world, where children don't have to sell their bodies."

"I do too. I could work with Stephen helping immigrants in the Bronx."

"We have immigrants in Spain that you could help."

"I don't have a permit to work in Spain."

"Dominicans can get permits."

"I'm not a Dominican."

"You could pass for one."

Encouraged, he said: "I probably could. But there's another way I could get a permit."

"What's that?"

"I could marry you."

"Is that a proposal?" she asked, smiling.

"Yes," he said. "I love you, I respect you, and I want to spend my life with you."

She turned serious. "I feel the same way about you."

"Is that an acceptance?"

"Yes," she said with light in her eyes.

They stayed at the cabin for two weeks, prolonging their sojourn in paradise, and then they decided that it was time for them to face the world.

Before calling Stephen he asked her: "Are you sure you want to go public with that information?"

"It's the only way we'll ever be free."

"They could kill us."

"I know. But I don't want to spend the rest of my life being afraid of them, whoever they are. It's what terrorists try to do to us, and I'm not going to let them do that to me."

"I'm not either."

"So let's go ahead," Raquel said. "If they don't kill us, then we can move on and put them behind us."

The next day Stephen and Marya arrived at the cabin. Stephen had brought Fenly's computer, which had all the information on it, and he had arranged a press conference for the next day at a hotel in Lake Placid.

Marya had thoughtfully brought some clothes for Raquel, who had been washing her underwear in the sink.

Fenly wrote a speech and rehearsed it with them, taking their suggestions to improve it. He realized that it was the presentation of his life, and it had to be good.

"That's fine," Raquel said after hearing it translated. "But we need to tell them why we're doing this."

"What should we tell them?"

"We should tell them what my brother wrote on that wall at the Plaza del Carmen—that you cannot achieve peace through war. If you want peace, work for social justice."

"She's right," Stephen said. "We can't achieve peace through a war on terror."

Fenly agreed. He rewrote the beginning of his presentation, and then he read it to them again.

"You have it now," Raquel said, nodding.

There wasn't room for Stephen and Marya to sleep in the cabin, so they spent the night at a motel and returned the next morning. Then, in two cars, they drove to Lake Placid.

There was tight security for the hotel, but they entered it through the kitchen to avoid taking any chances. The members of the press in the meeting room had all been screened before they were admitted, and there were police guarding the doors.

He stood with Raquel on a platform, hoping that after they revealed the information they wouldn't need security since there would no longer be a reason to kill them.

A few minutes later he got the signal from the cameraman to begin his presentation.

"We're here," Fenly said, "to present evidence that people at a high level in our government knew in advance about the attack on 9-11, and they let it happen."

There were cries of shock and disbelief from the members of the press, many of whom rose from their chairs as if they were going to leave the room.

A seasoned journalist, who remained sitting in the front row, gave Fenly a skeptical look, and he imagined the headlines of the man's story: "Agent Claims Conspiracy."

He glanced at Raquel, who stood there ready to take a bullet with him. She nodded, encouraging him to continue.

"Two weeks ago," he informed them, "the woman you see standing beside me and other members of a Spanish team, with the help of police in Ulster County, stopped a terrorist attack that would have killed about fifty-five thousand people at Yankee Stadium. Two members of the team were killed on this mission. You owe them the courtesy of listening to me."

He paused, surveying his audience. They looked as if they were still debating whether to leave.

"Almost six years ago a band of terrorists attacked the World Trade Center. Many of you lost colleagues, friends, and family members in that attack. I lost more than a hundred colleagues, and I lost the woman I was going to marry. I wanted to get back at the people who did that. I wanted to catch them and make them pay for what they had done. And I wanted to stop them from attacking us again. So I joined our homeland security force, and I supported our war on terror. But after I saw what we were doing in Iraq and Afghanistan, I realized that a war on terror isn't the way to achieve peace." He paused again, preparing to affirm what he had learned from Stephen and Leandro and Raquel and her brother. "You cannot achieve peace through war. If you want peace, work for social justice."

The members of the press who had risen from their chairs began to sit down. They began to listen. They began to take notes. And they began to nod in agreement.

BOOK CLUB GUIDE TO

Infamy

Tom Milton

An introduction to *Infamy*

Fenly Aquino, who works in America's homeland security, arrives in Madrid to help a Spanish security team stop a terrorist attack. He is assigned to work with Raquel López, a former cop, who meets him at a prearranged place and identifies him through a code. Though they both speak Spanish, they have different accents and different cultures since Fenly was born and raised in the Bronx by a mother who came from the Dominican Republic, whereas Raquel was born and raised in Madrid. In their first serious conversation Fenly reveals that he lost his fiancée in the terrorist attack on the World Trade Center, and he learns that Raquel lost her brother in the terrorist attack on commuter trains in Madrid, so they have a common motive that enables them to bridge their differences and become partners.

The Spanish team heard about the current plot from a man on trial for the attack on the commuter trains who would like to exchange his information for leniency. The man claims that the plot involves the use of laundered money to buy weapons that will be directed at a target in New York City, but he doesn't know what the target will be, what kind of weapons will be used, where they will be bought, or how they will be deployed. Since Fenly is an expert on methods used by terrorists to finance their operations, his function on the team is to pick up the trail of the money being laundered and follow it to the weapons and stop the weapons from being deployed.

The leader of the Spanish team is Leandro Ezkarra, a veteran security agent who from years of experience in dealing with Basque terrorists understands that the goal of terrorists is to provoke a government into responding in ways that will make it lose moral authority, so he stands by his principles and refuses to resort to torture to get more information from the man on trial. Leandro arranges an interview with the man, who gives them a few more details about the plot: the money will go to a French company which will buy the weapons, the weapons will produce a spectacular explosion, and the terrorists are hoping to kill forty to fifty thousand people.

Leandro has doubts about the man's story, and so does Fenly's boss, who wants some evidence to corroborate it. They feel they have such evidence after their informant is killed by poison in his food, presumably to stop him from talking, but Fenly's boss is still not convinced, and with the man's death they have lost their only source of information.

At this point they turn to a surveillance system that was put in place to monitor the heavy volume of people walking back and forth on Calle de la Montera between Gran Vía, a major thoroughfare, and Puerta del Sol, the center of the city. On the third floor of a building overlooking Montera are members of the team who operate equipment to capture, catalog, and analyze images that might reveal suspicious patterns of behavior.

Across the street from the surveillance office, standing on Montera, is a line of prostitutes who are mostly immigrants and whose clients are mostly foreigners, including the people the team is monitoring with its cameras. Among the prostitutes is a Moroccan girl who cooperates with Raquel because her sister was killed in the attack on the commuter trains. Her name is Samira, and she becomes a key participant in the team's efforts to pick up the trail of money.

As they work together Raquel introduces Fenly to Madrid and its underworld of drug dealers, prostitutes, pimps, and money runners. According to their informant they have only two weeks to stop the attack, so time is running out on them as they desperately try to unravel the plot.

A conversation with Tom Milton

Your first three novels all had action in them, but this one is a real thriller. What made you decide to write a thriller?

I thought a thriller might be a good vehicle for exploring the themes that I explored in my previous novels—the themes of war and peace and love and redemption.

As Fenly walks around the neighborhood where he's living in Madrid, he sees a mural with the statement: "You cannot achieve peace through war. If you want peace, work for social justice." That sounds like the theme of your first novel, No Way to Peace.

It is. They both question the idea of a "war on terror."

In All the Flowers *the students apply the principles of the just war doctrine to the Vietnam War, and they find that it's not a just war. Did you want your readers to apply those principles to our war on terror?*

I want my readers to understand that even though the events in that novel happened years ago, the same principles apply to our wars in Iraq and Afghanistan.

Let's talk about the events in Infamy. *The main event, which has already happened when the story begins, is the terrorist attack on the World Trade Center. We learn that Fenly lost his fiancée in 9-11, and that as a result he gave up a lucrative career to work for homeland security so that he could stop another attack.*

It's important to understand that when we meet Fenly his only purpose in life is to stop another terrorist attack.

His partner, Raquel, has a similar purpose since she lost her brother in the bombings of the Madrid commuter trains, which the Spanish call 11-M because it happened on March 11.

Raquel has a personal mission that goes beyond stopping the attack. She's a former cop who worked in vice trying to protect and help prostitutes. She has a feeling for the girls, who are virtually all immigrants with an average age of about fifteen. And she has a special feeling for a Moroccan girl who lost her sister in the attack on 11-M.

By involving the girls in the money laundering the story connects Raquel's purpose of stopping the attack and her personal mission. It gives her an inner conflict that intensifies as she and Fenly pursue the terrorists.

Yes, there's a conflict between her mission to protect the girls and the necessity of using them to stop the attack. By using the girls for this purpose she's exposing them to danger, which goes against her mission to protect them.

As in your previous novels, the female protagonist is the moral compass and the male narrator is guided by her.

Through empathy he begins to share her feeling for the girls and her responsibility for using them. And through his eyes we begin to see how the girls are used—by their pimps, their clients, the terrorists, and the counter-terrorists.

In flashbacks we learn that he grew up in the Bronx with a single mother and a perfect older sister. To achieve his own identity he became a "badass" member of a gang and got into trouble.

He was dealing with the experience of being abandoned by his father when he was two. Raquel lost her mother when she was five, so they both grew up without a role model of the same gender. It's something they have in common besides losing a loved one in a terrorist attack.

A major event of Fenly's life was his meeting Camila in the elevator of the World Trade Center and falling in love with her.

Camila challenged his ideas about women, which had come from his imagined father, and Fenly had to change those ideas in order to win her.

You wrote so movingly about how he lost Camila in 9-11. Did you lose a loved one in the attack?

I knew people who lost parents, spouses, and children. When it happened I was at a location where I could see the towers collapse. I'll never forget it.

The title of this novel comes from the speech that Franklin Delano Roosevelt made after the Japanese attack on Pearl Harbor. Do you think the two attacks were comparable?

The attacks were both infamous. And they were both used by our government to get us into a war.

Do you think the two wars were comparable?

Based on the principles of the just war doctrine, I believe that World War II might have been a just war but our invasion of Iraq was definitely not a just war, even though our government tried to justify it.

Like The Admiral's Daughter *and* All the Flowers, *this novel has a conspiracy theory. According to that theory, our government knew in advance about the attack on 9-11 and let it happen. Do you believe that?*

It's possible. Our government had a lot of warnings. But whether or not they knew in advance about the attack, they used it for a political purpose, and they got us into an unjust war the casualties of which are immeasurable.

Discussion questions

1. We learn early in the story that Fenly and Raquel both lost a loved one in a terrorist attack. How do they deal with that loss?

2. Both Fenly and Raquel grow up without a parent of their own gender as a role model. How did they deal that experience?

3. How are their mentors similar and different?

4. How is Fenly affected by the unexpected return of his father?

5. What does Fenly learn from falling in love with Camila?

6. What inner conflict does Raquel reveal in her words and actions?

7. What role does Leandro play in the story?

8. What role does Samira play?

9. How does the author use the characters of Antonio and José?

10. How does the method used by the terrorists to launder money relate to the theme of the novel?

11. What do you think of Daryl? Do you believe his claim?

12. What role does the mural at the Plaza del Carmen play in the story? Do you agree with its message?

13. Why did the author call this novel *Infamy?*

14. How might the ideas expressed by characters in this novel apply to situations in the world today?

No Way to Peace
Tom Milton

Nepperhan Press, LLC
Paperback $12.95
ISBN 978-0-9794579-0-6

"The setting is superb. The characters are clearly defined. This book makes an excellent book club choice, with pertinent questions in the back. We rated this novel five hearts." — *Heartland Reviews*

"This novel represents to me achievement of a high order and it's to be wished that more such elegantly fashioned novels by this author will soon be forthcoming so that in time we can be treated to an extensive body of work of this fine literary talent." —David A. Sawyer

A novel about the courage of five women in Argentina's war of terror during the 1970s. Their lives are observed by an American banker who has stayed in Buenos Aires after most foreigners have been evacuated. He meets a young woman, a refugee from another country who is living in Argentina under a false identity, and they fall in love. They try to build a life together but are drawn into the war between the guerrillas and the military. The dilemmas they face are like the ones we face in today's global war of terror.

You can purchase this novel, which includes a book club guide, at any bookstore including online or directly from the publisher with free shipping at www.nepperhan.com.

The Admiral's Daughter
Tom Milton

Nepperhan Press, LLC
Paperback, $12.95
ISBN 978-0-9794579-1-3

"This novel has all the elements of a Greek tragedy—a great man who falls from grace, a family drama that pits father against daughter, and retribution for ancestral sin—while at the same time it's a moving story of love and redemption."
—Eileen Lanahan, author of *An Act of Love*

"A well-told story of an important time in our history which we only gradually are leaving behind." —Robert W. Towler

Kristy McKay, a young woman from Mississippi living in New York in the early 1960s, is trying to expiate the original sin of slavery on which her family fortune was built. She is active in the civil rights movement in conflict with her father, a retired admiral who is a white supremacist. She suspects that he is behind the violence against civil rights activists in Mississippi, and unable to live with the possibility that her father is having people killed, she needs to learn the truth so that she can finally free herself from a legacy of guilt and hatred.

You can purchase this novel, which includes a book club guide, at any bookstore including online or directly from the publisher with free shipping at www.nepperhan.com.

All the Flowers
Tom Milton

Nepperhan Press, LLC
Paperback, $12.95
ISBN 978-0-9794579-3-7

Featured in *Publishers Weekly*.

"A story of the growing loss of innocence through the years of the Vietnam War, a fascinating read all the way through." — *The Midwest Book Review*

"One of my favorite parts was explaining the just war doctrine, something I think should be mandatory reading for every member of the U.N. as well as everyone in our State and Defense departments." —Anita V. Davis

A love story set in the late 1960s about a young singer, Teri Ryan, and a piano player, Andre Malinowski. Teri and her brother Tim are close fraternal twins who haven't sorted out their gender identities. Teri is a tomboy, and Tim is a sensitive boy who falls short of their father's expectations. Tim believes he can prove his manhood by dropping out of college and enlisting in the army, and Teri tries to stop him since she is afraid that he will be sent to Vietnam. When she falls in love with Andre she begins to find her gender identity, but she struggles to maintain her spiritual identity when her faith is tested by events.

You can purchase this novel, which includes a book club guide, at any bookstore including online or directly from the publisher with free shipping at www.nepperhan.com.

Always Say Hello to Life
James M. McMahon

Nepperhan Press, LLC
Paperback, $12.95
ISBN 978-0-9794579-6-8

The most influential relationship we will ever have is with mother. In this book the author shows you how to stay awake in this relationship, to celebrate the love, and to leave the troubled parts behind.

"McMahon offers a path to emotional and spiritual health that encourages and empowers each of us to care about ourselves and each other and to become our personal best. They will find a path to freedom, joy, and peace." —Barbara Benjamin, author of *Face to Face*

"In person and in his writings Dr. Jim McMahon is a real, genuine person, respectful of the ideas of others and very funny. He touches one's heart by richly and lovingly sharing his psychological observations and insights thus providing a freedom path back to one's true self." —Michael A. Garcia, Ph.D., Psychologist and Psychoanalyst

You can purchase this book at any bookstore including online or directly from the publisher with free shipping at www.nepperhan.com.

Face to Face
Barbara Benjamin

Nepperhan Press, LLC
Paperback, $12.95
ISBN 978-0-9794579-4-4

"If you want to have a moving mystical experience, pray these poems. If you want to have just plain fun, browse through these remarkable poems on a bright sunny day, and then meditate on them on a melancholy rainy day. You will never tire of reading this book." —Joseph F. Girzone, author of *Joshua*

"Reading Barbara Benjamin's poetry is like reading Walt Whitman's Leaves of Grass or the mathematical source code of the Absolute Infinity. Only silence can describe its magnificence." —Orest Bedrij, author of *Celebrate Your Divinity*

"In Face to Face Barbara Benjamin sings an involvement with life and inner spirit that is breathtaking. Deceptively clear and straightforward, she touches the deepest in us and around us in every poem." —James M. McMahon, Ph.D., author of *Radical Self-Acceptance: The spiritual birth of the human person*

You can purchase this book at any bookstore including online or directly from the publisher with free shipping at www.nepperhan.com.